FOLLOWING EVAN

ELIDA MAY

© Elida May 2015

The Right of Elida May to be identified as the Author of this work has been asserted by herin accordance with the Copyright, Designs and Patents Act 1988.

All Rights Reserved. No part of this book may be printed, reproduced or utilized in any form or by any electronic, mechanical or other means, now known or hereafter invented, including photocopying and recording, or in any information storage retrieval system, without permission in writing from the publishers.

A catalogue record for this book is available from the British Library

ISBN: NUMBER 978-1530428618

Edited and Typeset by Wrate's Editing Services, London
(www.wrateseditingservices.co.uk)

Acknowledgements

Thank you to my mum for being my best friend, and for giving me a lifetime of love and support. Much love and thanks to all my friends who have supported me through writing this book. I'd especially like to thank my dear friend Sabawoon for providing encouragement, advice and inspiration. A big hug and thank you to my special friend John for his continued guidance and assistance. A huge thank you to my editor Danielle Wrate for her patience, and for helping me to turn my unlikely dream into a reality.

To my son, Elidon, the light of my life

1

Wiping the silver frame, Laura stared sadly at a picture of her and Matt skiing in the mountains. Her mind was lost in a white chill: empty, unconnected and exhausted. Too weary to feel, to think, to escape even into the usual comforting fantasy she had built for herself. This is what her world had shrunk down to.

She moved slowly and listlessly to the window without disturbing the stillness that had been her armour for three interminable years, 37 months, more than a thousand tired days and unrefreshing nights. She had seen the old pear tree at the end of the garden lose its fruits, the last of which were still rotting on the grass. Now the wind was taking its leaves and rain dripped from its branches.

This window was her eye to the world; its gentle quietness demanded nothing and spoke to her in language she could understand, especially during these winter evenings. The grey sky, the falling darkness, the approaching night…this was as much as she could cope with.

***

Holding her hand to her chest, she walked silently into her bedroom and buried herself in the empty bed. The room was stale and dark; the window shut, the heavy curtains drawn. The light was not welcome inside. The clock beside her bed had long since stopped. Time no longer mattered and her sleeping pills now lay where she used to put her jewellery before going to sleep.

Looking at the ceiling, she waited for sleep to come but her jumbled thoughts and feelings gave her no rest. There was no escape into the oblivion she craved which, in any case, would only last a few precious hours. She knew that the struggle for sleep would be fought again and again, tonight like every other one…

***

Reluctantly sliding her legs out of the bed, Laura pushed herself to stand up. This was the first battle of her day. The night hadn't brought any refreshment. Sleep had come, but not from anywhere pleasant. A heavy chemical blanket had smothered her consciousness, but had failed to conquer the dreams that had demonised her night.

Her first heavy step took her to the kettle.

Coffee.

Why do kettles have to be so bloody loud?

She reached for her morning mug and the coffee jar. Her hand trembled. The steam from the cup was the promise and the first gulp of the dark liquid was a reunion with her companion through the darkness.

Lightly stimulated, her eyes wakened as an unexpected knock alerted one of her other senses. Startled, she wrapped her dressing gown tightly around her and went to the door. Four years ago, when Matt had bought it for her as a Christmas present, they had both loved its sensuality. But now it was as ragged as she was.

She opened the door to be confronted by a fern tree. A freckle-faced boy with blonde hair peered at her from behind it. He thrust a small white envelope towards her.

"It came with the order," he explained.

"What order?" Laura asked, tearing open the envelope.

"Pay the boy and start decorating!" read the note inside.

Laura grinned at Carla's familiar tone. Stepping aside to let the boy enter, she shook her head and muttered: "I don't do Christmas."

"Where do you want me to put it?"

"Oh, right by the window."

After the boy had left, Laura stood in front of her tree. She smelled its resin, felt the chill that clung to it from outside and spotted the loose pines on the carpet that had already fallen from its branches. Why do I need this in my life? What is there for me to celebrate?

The ringing of the phone arrived like a rude poke in her ear, and she let it go straight to answer machine.

"I'm Laura, I'm not at home…so you know what to do!"

"Come on, girl, pick up, or don't because I'm coming over tomorrow anyway to take you out. I don't want any excuses. Five pm sharp!"

Carla was the only one of her friends who had defied Laura when she had stopped receiving visitors. Their pity, sympathy and inability to know her pain was too much for her to bear; their lives were continuing but hers had died, and she really didn't feel that there was any way back for her.

When she had thrown that handful of earth onto the coffin and heard its soft thud, her own existence, with its emotions, appetites and hopes, had stopped. Since then, isolation and pain were all that was left for her.

Only Carla continued to kick at the door she had locked in order to keep out the rest of the world. Carla visited her frequently, wiping away her tears, checking that she was taking her prescription medication and forcing her to have a bath and wash her hair.

Carla had kept her spare house keys ever since that day, three years earlier, when she'd used force to open the door and found Laura unconscious following an overdose. She continued to keep a close eye on her friend, adamant that such a terrible occurrence wasn't going to happen again.

Back then, a panicked Carla had shaken the thin body of the once vibrant Laura. Her lips were cracked, her eyelids were swollen and her tears and dribbles were dry on the pillow. "Come on, kid, you're not killing yourself today," she said. "I am not ready to let you die yet."

Laura's head was swimming. She was dizzy and sick, but her stomach was too empty for her to vomit.

"You have no right to do this," she lashed out. "Who told you that you could do this? Do you think you are God? Just leave me alone!"

"Come on, girl," Carla reasoned. "You can decide on a lot of things but not this, and don't imagine I will leave you like this. No way, no damn way!"

"I want to die, leave me…I can't go on any more…I can't," came Laura's heartbreaking reply.

Hot tears burned Carla's eyes before they rolled down her face. "Why my baby, why?"

***

What a mess Laura's life had become. Her little baby, a son, so longed for and so loved, was gone. The only ultrasound picture she had was already faded from constant handling. This precious person, with tiny fingers and toes, was all that she had wanted for her future. She had longed to be a mum for as far back as she could remember. She had even been looking forward to the labour.

Then one morning, still reeling from loss, she noticed he wasn't moving and the ordinary events of a tragedy unfolded. She called the hospital, took a cab, met the consultant, got undressed, put on a gown, took the anaesthetic, felt the nausea…

Then home, alone.

The place she had loved was now suffocating.

Getting into bed was like climbing into her coffin, and every event of that awful day was a screw on its lid.

No wonder she had wanted to end it all.

"I know it's not fair, it's horrible," Carla had said after finding her in such a bad way, following the overdose. "You just cry. Hell, even I am crying!"

Carla held Laura's almost weightless body until her tears finally stopped. "Don't you worry, kid," she said. "I'm going to be here. Death isn't getting any more out of us, not this week."

Laura's guts felt as if they were being ripped apart as everything she had and hoped for fled from her wreck of a body.

Exhausted and completely empty she sank her wet face into her pillows, drew her knees up to her empty belly and slowly drifted off to sleep. Carla tenderly pulled up her covers and lay down next to her, cuddling her back and gently stroking her head until her breathing calmed and the shaking stopped. Then she quietly reached for the bedside phone and rang for a doctor, explaining what had happened and asking for someone to come quickly.

A young Indian doctor helped Carla to sit Laura up. She examined her and made a swift assessment.

"We will have to get you to hospital," she said.

"No bloody way," came Laura's vehement response.

"Well, at least let me take some blood samples to make sure you haven't done yourself any permanent damage."

Laura let her arm be stretched out and didn't even flinch as the needle penetrated her vein.

"How are we going to make sure that you are going to be all right?" asked the doctor. "I can't leave you here on your own like this. I could actually get you detained in hospital for a short time, even if you don't want to go."

"I'm not very busy at work just now," Carla interjected. "I could easily take a week off to stay here with her."

After a lot of further discussions and instructions, the doctor left, promising to send a community psychiatric nurse daily to check on Laura's progress.

For a full week, Carla stayed with Laura, pouring life slowly back into her: bathing, dressing and feeding her, and giving her the correct medication. At first she could hardly speak or stand up. Sleep was her only escape, but even then she cried and fought, not knowing whether she wanted to live or die. Carla's stubbornness shielded the small flame that was her life. This flame wasn't enough for light or warmth or nourishment, it was merely sufficient to keep death away.

It wasn't really life.

But, as time wore on, Laura slowly and very reluctantly began to do the things that living people do. At first, just sitting up in bed was a huge effort. Gravity seemed so much more powerful than before. Carla even had to help her get to the toilet. Drinking was painful. Her tummy rebelled over cold fluids and she was only just able to tolerate warm milk. It was over a week before she could swallow any solid food. When she could eat, buttery brioche with strawberry jam was all she wanted. Even getting warm was almost impossible; her hands and feet stayed pale and cold for weeks.

But Carla and James, the Mauritian nurse, managed to pull her back into some semblance of life. After Carla returned to work she visited her every night to keep her guard against death, staying with Laura for weeks.

Thankfully, the medication Laura had taken hadn't caused any permanent damage and slowly, as the weeks stretched into months, she began showing signs of recovery. She gradually built up her days into a pattern of doing; washing, dressing and feeding herself. She was progressing, but these tasks were all achieved without thought or feeling. Her breakfast always consisted of the same thing: coffee in the same KitKat Easter egg mug, toast with strawberry jam, always made with the same knife. Lunch was either a tin of spaghetti hoops or soup, or, if she could be bothered to make it, some cheese on toast. Most days she didn't feel like eating much in the evenings. Her stomach felt like a tightly clenched fist, but when she eventually felt hungry she would snack on skimmed milk and shortbread biscuits. Before retiring to bed every night she put the same set of dishes in the same position in the dishwasher, and whenever she became aware of their presence she would gather socks, knickers and bedding together and stuff them into the washer dryer. The only interruptions in her routine were Carla's Wednesday and Sunday visits and her twice-daily phone calls from her doctor's office to remind her to take her meds.

Radio Four, with its porridge of human sound, was the aural wallpaper of her days and she kept it on right through from the Today programme to the melodious anaesthetic of the Shipping Forecast. But the words never penetrated her thoughts; instead they formed a fence around her mind.

In bed at night she could feel the weight of her body on the mattress. It was too firm for her on her own, and the queen-sized duvet seemed to drown her. Her hands and feet hardly ever got warm and even a hot water bottle clenched between her ankles only comforted her feet. Her hands were permanently cold and yet moist. More than anything else, she missed having somebody to lean against. Her sleeping pills would eventually press her down into a kind of empty sleep, but it would still take her about two hours to quieten the thoughts and noises of her mind until the darkness took over.

Those nightly three hours, maybe half an hour more if she was lucky, formed her only mental rest. It wasn't enough for repair, let alone for refreshment, and all too quickly her slumber was cruelly invaded by frights, accusations and terrors without names. These would start to push into her resting mind like uninvited weeds poisoning her peace and bringing her too soon into her daily struggle with the wounds that had so nearly killed her…

2

Laura appreciated everything that Carla had done for her, and she was no doubt better than she was, but her friend's latest gift left her puzzled.

"What the hell do I need a Christmas tree for?" She asked out loud, talking to the walls of her empty house.

The sound of a passing police siren from a distant street immediately jolted her back to the worst moment of her life, when her baby was still alive inside her.

She had opened her front door to find two young police women standing there; they had come to rip her world to pieces, explaining that Matt, her darling husband of 14 years, the father of her three month foetus, was lying lifeless and shattered in the local mortuary after being involved in a horrific motorway pileup.

Laura heard the women's gentle and compassionate words, but she simply wasn't able to absorb them, and when she eventually realised what they meant she lost control of her body. Her head seemed to explode and, though she couldn't hear it herself, a noise, something between a groan and a scream, erupted from deep inside. Although she didn't know it then her baby, along with all her future, died.

She vomited and fell unconscious on the hall carpet. Her home would forevermore be a place that evoked dread. Similarly, sirens and dark blue uniforms would always cause her to shiver.

***

As the noise of the sirens faded, Laura turned to the mirror and glanced at her reflection. The ornately-framed glass had been her statement piece when she and Matt had designed the house. They never went out before checking it first. What an image they had presented to the world. Whether dressed in his business suit or weekend chinos, Matt always looked smart. Laura loved him best when he came home from his weekly football match, all freshly showered with his hair still damp and combed back with a scent of shampoo.

Matt's smart nature extended to his choice of wife. In fact, she was his best-ever acquisition. When they met she was newly graduated with a master's degree in art history and interior design. Energy and humour fizzed out of her petite but determined body. They were such an inspiration for each other. Laura used her vibrancy and skill to transform the run-down, three-storey Edwardian terrace they'd bought into to a modern, chic and comfortable family home. She'd picked a warm, earthy cream colour to paint the walls with, and the house oozed that 'wow factor' from the moment the door was opened to reveal the hallway. Modern was cleverly mixed with traditional, and every last detail had been thought of and created by Laura. Everything had to be in the right place. Her soul was one of an artist's and she felt privileged to accept the compliments of friends at the many parties she threw. Everything was infused with love and passion.

"You are the muse of the house," Matt used to say to her.

Laura loved her work and it provided her with much wealth.

"Why did I come in here?" Laura asked herself. She had found herself in her office, a room she rarely visited any more. She quickly rolled down the blind; the light and sound of the outside were not welcome. Lord Lane neither faced or backed on to any busy roads, so it was usually quieter and more in harmony with Laura's inner state.

She traced her steps back again, her arms crossed around her, and stopped in the middle of the living room. Her movements were as directionless as her thoughts. Her gaze rested once again on the tree.

"What now?" she asked it. "What can I do with you?"

This uninvited thing had come to a place where time – past, present and future - was frozen. There was no border between them.

She circled the tree and remembered the one they'd had when she was a little girl. It had been decorated in the same way for years and it had been her job, before bedtime, to hang each new delivery of Christmas cards on it. As time went on, and space on the tree became limited, her dad would lift her up so she could reach the highest branches. By Christmas morning it would be covered with dozens of colourful, glittering cards.

Now Laura had just three precious cards, all carefully saved, which had been sent from her parents in previous years. In each of them it said, "love you", but now the tradition had been broken. Laura's mum and dad followed each other to the grave, suffering fatal heart attacks within the space of a year. Along with her memories, Laura had other reminders of her parents. She had her father's green eyes and the beautiful smile and quiet nature of her mother.

Without thinking much, she left the living room and padded into the hallway, where she sank her hands into the mountains of envelopes which had been dumped on the side table and left untouched for weeks, maybe months. There were no Christmas cards; she was all but forgotten, nameless except for bills and a listing on the electoral roll. She had been erased from any kind of living and joyful event.

"No wait," she muttered. "There is one."

One of the letters was heavier than the others. It contained a card. Tearing it open she looked inside.

"Merry Christmas from Virgin Atlantic."

It was almost a relief. She closed it and threw it back on to the large pile.

When she'd received the first lot of greeting cards following Matt and her unborn baby's deaths they had made her feel angry.

"Laura, I wish you…" they'd read.

"What can they wish for me?" she'd thought. "Am I supposed to be happy about this?"

She could still hear the voice of her priest saying: "May our dear Lord bless his eternal soul and take it into his keeping."

"But what about my soul?" Laura had felt like screaming.

She wasn't inclined to accept the deaths of her husband and son. How could she even begin to think that they were never coming back?

She didn't want to see anyone. Her friends' good intentions only irritated her.

"Just leave me alone, all of you," she'd said when they came to pay their respects at her husband's grave. Inside she was thinking: They can't teach me how to live my life. What kind of life is left for me anyway? All I have left is my grief.

Laura turned her back on the mountain of uninteresting letters and went to drink the coffee she had made earlier. She found that it had gone cold.

3

"So?" Carla smiled sarcastically when she saw that Laura was slumped in her chair by the window.

"So what?"

"What are you still doing over there?"

"Where else should I be?"

"In front of the mirror, of course. Do you think I came here for nothing?"

Carla chucked her handbag onto the cream sofa, zigzagging her gaze from her friend to the tree next to her. Glittering in gold and red, it seemed to be smiling. Carla was relieved - at least Laura had decorated it. This was the first time in three years that she had made any kind of effort to mark the holiday.

Was she starting to live again?

"Come on, we don't have all night," she said and dashed into the kitchen. Her short, dumpy body moved quickly as she reached for a glass from the cupboard and poured herself juice from the fridge.

Then she was back in the living room.

"What are you still doing there?" she chided.

Laura was sat in the same place, staring at the tree. Having avoided it all day, she voiced what was on her mind.

"Why did you come to disturb me?" she asked. "Wasn't I OK the way I was? What bloody business is it of yours anyway? Who gave you the right to push in?"

Her face was full of resentment as she shot a defiant look in Carla's direction. "I really don't feel like going out tonight," she said, this time more softly.

"I didn't ask how you felt," Carla replied. "I asked you why you aren't ready yet. Do you think that I will go out alone? No damn way!"

"I can't," protested Laura, turning to face her friend. Her big eyes were wide open as she shook her head. "I'm not ready to go anywhere."

Taking a gentle grip of her arms and looking her straight in the eye, Carla continued with her encouragement.

"Come on, darling, you need to wake up. What kind of life is it when you are stuck inside all the time? Sometimes I think that you don't even know whether it is morning or night. Isn't it about time you started to come back to the world?"

"What for? What am I supposed to be doing? What do you want from me?"

Laura's words were sticking in her throat and tears started to roll down her face.

"I just want you to live. I need my old friend back. Your happiness matters to me."

"You must not worry about me. I will be fine."

"Don't tell me that. I want you to be better now. It's about time!"

"My time has gone."

"I'm not taking you out to a tarts and vicars ball," said Carla. "It's only a dinner, idiot."

Despite herself, Laura grinned. She just had to give in. Sometimes it was easier than keeping the fight going.

"Come on, let's find some glad rags for you," Carla said, clapping her hands and pulling Laura up the stairs and into her bedroom. She went through Laura's wardrobe and grabbed a black coat with a big collar and shiny black buttons and a red wine coloured woollen dress that used to be one of Laura's favourites. As Carla busied herself choosing the outfit, Laura leant against the doorframe. She watched Carla as she threw the clothes onto the bed.

"You get yourself organised," Carla instructed, "and I will wait in my car. I need to call my man and tell him not to wait up because I am taking you out!"

Alone again, Laura turned to the mirror.

She barely recognised herself and didn't much like the bits she did. Her face was tired, her eyes were dull and her hair bore the effects of weeks of neglect. Her beauty had gone. Putting on the dress gave her a glimpse of how she used to look.

Next, she rummaged through the drawers for some makeup, but it had all been thrown in the bin long ago. Even her underwear drawer proved a challenge. Beige, cotton or silky dark blue? Without making a choice, she reached inside it and grabbed the first thing she touched. Once satisfied that she was as presentable as possible, she went to join Carla.

She didn't ask where they were going, but soon enough she saw a sign for Greenwich. She immediately knew where Carla was taking her: Corte, her favourite restaurant by the river.

She felt disarmed from the moment she stepped inside, and guilty for enjoying this moment outside of her comfort zone. She immediately turned her gaze to the floor.

"Why is everyone staring?" her inner voice inquired.

Strangers surrounded her, talking and laughing. The sound of a mobile rang out from somewhere, barely noticed by anyone but Laura. It was now such an unusual sound to her.

"Why did I come here?" She muttered under her breath. "I shouldn't have."

"Oh, there we are," Carla said, taking her seat. She seemed very satisfied with her achievement. She had released her friend from her self-imposed cage and intended to keep it that way.

Their table was by the window, facing the terrace by the river. The flowers in the big square pots were still blooming. Despite the arrival of winter, it still wasn't cold.

Laura swayed uncomfortably, everything was moving so fast today. Beside them sat an older couple. The lady still looked beautiful and the old man was resting his hand on top of hers. Laura glanced at them for a moment - they seemed so content. She spotted a young boy passing by the window, absorbed in sending a text. From another direction she caught the sound of champagne glasses clinking. At the table in the corner a young girl sat alone, anxiously looking out for her companion and constantly checking her watch.

But nobody was looking at Laura. Everyone was so busy with their own worlds. Was she invisible to them all? She lifted her eyes up. The light of the antique crystal chandelier shone on her face.

"Now I have to find a boyfriend for you," Carla said.

"What?"

"Or do you want to do that yourself?" Carla's eyebrows shot up.

"Wow...wows!" Laura couldn't hold it in any more and exploded with laughter.

The waiter, who was tall, thin and blonde, no more than a boy, arrived to take their order. He had to wait until they had calmed down.

"Warm seafood salad with fried king prawns and baked bananas with chocolate for dessert," Carla said. "Oh, and white wine."

"And the same for me, too," Laura said, gazing out of the window.

Outside on the pavement the young boy was still texting. Laura remembered that she had a mobile too. It was lost somewhere in one of her drawers. The waiter poured their wine.

Had her life been like this before?

"Cheers, my friend," Carla smiled.

"Cheers."

"I am serious, Laura."

"What about?"

"About you, and you know it. It's time for you to start living again."

"I will not enter into something that I won't be able to handle," Laura replied. She took a sip of wine then lowered her eyes, trying to hide the feelings inside.

"Just open the door," Carla said. She leant over the table and scooped Laura's hand into her own.

"You think it's easy to close one door, open the other and leave behind everyone and everything you loved?" Laura protested.

"Yes, you leave them behind. You're alive, damn it, move on." Carla stared intensely into Laura's eyes and gripped her hand tighter. This was just one of her many attempts to get her friend to start living again.

"I just can't," Laura protested. "I look at myself and feel like I'm a hundred years old."

"Try to see yourself as others see you. You are a very beautiful woman. Don't waste yourself." Carla paused to raise her glass. "Now," she added, "enough of this bullshit and cheers to your new life."

As they clinked glasses, Laura smiled and wondered whether she would ever fit back into the messy and noisy life outside her house again. There was no doubt in her mind that she had become an outsider.

"What do you think about working again?" Carla asked.

Laura looked at her calmly, but didn't answer.

"Larry is looking for a new designer for his company," Carla continued. "How do you feel about that?"

"I don't…" Laura shrugged.

"It would be very good for you. Larry mentioned it to me the other day."

"But..." Laura started before trailing off. She knew that Larry, Carla's husband, would jump at the chance to take her on, but her thoughts weren't fluid or easily expressed.

"Just think about it, okay?"

Laura was touched by Carla's concern. She was a very good friend.

When they stepped out of the restaurant the night was ruled by the River Thames. Laura stayed watching it while Carla went to get her car. Boats floated away and disappeared into the dark and the chilly air penetrated her skin. On the way back home the traffic was heavy and the asphalt on the road was shiny from a light splattering of fresh rain. Laura turned her attention to the bright city streets, feeling like a kid at Disneyland. Her face muscles were tender from smiling and laughing and she was hungry to take in her surroundings, which felt brand new. She took a deep breath before turning her attention back to Carla.

"How are the boys?" she asked.

Carla shook her head and compressed her lips. "It feels as if they are slipping out of my hands."

"Why is that?"

"Luka is always playing football and is gearing up for secondary school, and Tom is now sixteen and has a girlfriend."

"Wow, congratulations," Laura said.

"Oh, don't," Carla replied with a hint of admonishment. "At some point you discover that they've become strangers and you are left completely baffled. As long as they are little and you hold them in your arms, everything is just fine. But when their wings start to grow, you don't have peace of mind any more."

"You will always be behind them."

"If they will let me," Carla replied. "I don't want them to make the same mistakes I did."

"But you have Larry!"

"He is my soul mate but you know how difficult it was for us, me being pregnant and graduating at the same time."

"You can't say that your marriage was a mistake."

"No, I am happy we did it. Sometimes I think that if we didn't do it at that time then maybe we wouldn't be together now and life would be very different. Who knows? But I like the way we are. In fact, I love every minute of it, even when we argue. Some things are just meant to be."

"I assume Larry knows what the boys are up to?" Laura asked.

"Yeah, he does, he is the softy of the house, but that is why I love him."

They had reached Laura's house. She stepped out of the car and raised her big collar to protect herself from the tiny droplets of rain.

"Do you want to pop in for a coffee?" she asked.

"I'd better not, my boys would kill me," Carla replied. "They must be hungry and I am sure they are already prowling around the kitchen."

"I bet they are!" Laura replied. She waved, took out her keys and then disappeared into the solitude of her house. Once inside, she leant against the closed door and remained there for a few seconds, listening to her own breath. Here she was again, all alone. But tonight she felt a little bit different. She realised how much she had been missing the thing that she had been deliberately running away from: the open air.

She meandered through the house, picturing the boy with the phone, the sad girl waiting, the old couple, the tall waiter...

How weird.

Why was she remembering these strangers in such detail?

Something had changed. The murky area of her brain had been disturbed. For the first time in years she was thinking about something that had no connection with her house and her memories. She felt tired so she dragged herself to her bedroom, slipped on her pyjamas and climbed into bed.

4

THE following day, Laura stayed in bed until noon. She looked around, resting her gaze on the cream suede curtains that covered the windows. Bright light penetrated the room from around their edges. Suddenly, she felt the need for some space and air and decided to go for a walk. She dressed in a faux fur hooded jacket, the colour of eggshell, a knitted beret and some black leather knee-high riding boots. By the time she left the house it had started to rain, but the drops on her face felt good. A car whizzed past her through a puddle, and water splashed her legs, but she didn't care. She was ready to walk for hours. She felt as if she was following her feet, such was her lack of direction. Eventually, she stopped in front of an internet café on the corner of Kings Road. She was already two miles away from home. Stepping inside, she shook out her arms in an attempt to get dry before sitting down. The café was bright, tidy and divided into two separate spaces, one for tables and the other for computers. In front of her, a tall boy with short black hair, skin the colour of dark honey and a stubbly face, was serving from behind a glass counter filled with croissants, cupcakes, apple and jam tarts, sandwiches and fruit salads in clear plastic bowls that were beautifully presented on a tray edged with magnolia flowers.

"Do you want to use the internet?" asked the boy.

"No, I'll just have a latte, please," Laura replied.

She went to sit down at a table by the window. "Why would he think I needed the internet?" she mumbled to herself.

She reached for a copy of *Closer* magazine that had been left behind by a previous customer and began flicking through the pages without any interest. She stopped at the page with the horoscopes on it. She'd never been too serious about this kind of stuff, but read what it said for her sign, Sagittarius, anyway.

"Venus rising will help you manage your resources, and an idea you get from the TV or newspapers could bring a new interest into your life and spur you to do some investigating. Your future is clear."

Laura shook her head and smiled. She had no intention of relying on astrological calculations and pushed the magazine away.

"What new interest in my life?" she thought. "A man?"

A shiver ran down her spine at the thought of having someone new in her life. Even if the stars were willing to give her a second chance, she would never be ready to give her heart to someone else. Just then, a number 78 bus, which had come to a stop outside the café, caught her eye. A movie poster emblazoned across it read, "The stars of your life."

"It's just a coincidence," Laura said to herself.

After a few seconds pause, she gave a rueful smile. She seemed to be catching every small detail of her surroundings.

An old man wearing a brown hat meandered to the table next to her, but seemed unwilling to take a seat.

"Do you mind if I sit next to you, my dear?" he asked Laura. "You see, it's my lucky table, I never plonk my bottom anywhere else."

"Be my guest," Laura replied.

The man was in his late 70s. He had a large forehead, a long, aristocratic nose, small grey eyes and a nice smile.

"On such a boring wet day I really need a nice coffee and a chat," he said to Laura. "In my day we spent our time playing chess, not like them…" He pointed to the other side of the room where three young girls were staring at their computer screens.

Laura smiled in agreement. Her computer screen was always switched off. Her PC was only an object for buying things online from time to time. It was much easier than going out shopping, which she'd lost interest in long ago.

"Even cats and dogs have their own websites nowadays," the man continued, before catching the attention of the young man behind the counter and ordering his usual.

Laura turned her thoughts in on herself. She speculated how long had it been since she'd had a conversation with anyone outside her small little universe. It was as if she was relearning how to chat.

Her coffee arrived, along with the old man's tea and a couple of croissants, which obviously made up his usual.

"I used to drink coffee every day but my heart and blood pressure don't like it anymore," he said, stirring his steaming beverage. Then he rolled his eyes, cleared his throat and leant forward.

"You see, everyone is acting so weird," he said. "They're using these little things in front of their faces anytime and anywhere. I have two little nieces and they're no different."

"They should keep you busy!" Laura smiled, taking a sip of her coffee.

"Oh, they don't have time for me," the man said. "Day and night they are busy with those contraptions...." He paused to imitate the pushing of buttons. "They even take them when they want to go to the...well, you know."

Laura laughed. She knew exactly what he was trying to say.

The man turned his attention to the magazine that Laura had discarded moments earlier.

"Horoscope?" he asked.

"Yes."

"Hmmm…do you believe in fate and destiny?"

Laura shrugged. If fate existed, then it had certainly given her a slap in the face. She'd been cursed rather than blessed by it.

"Do you want to join me, my dear?" asked the man, offering her one of his croissants.

"No thank you," Laura replied. "I've had enough of my latte."

"As I was saying, destiny is something I believe in strongly. A long time ago I went to a wooden caravan in the woods. It was set well away from the road and I was obviously a bit reluctant to go there."

Laura fixed her gaze on the wrinkles around the man's mouth. *What was coming next from the old devil?*

She was like a kid who can't wait for the beginning of a fairy tale.

"My friend Nikko took me there. I guess I was unbearable after I broke up with my girl, Sonia…"

The old man stopped for a few seconds, breathing deeply as he gathered distant time in his thoughts. "I didn't want to do anything or go anywhere, my heart was broken. I remember that day. It was awful weather, lots of snow. It was very dark, too. I passed horses tied to a tree on the way in, walking over branches that covered the wet, snowy ground. I could smell chimney smoke and there were three wooden steps up to the door. It was quite warm inside, but small. Just six foot wide, narrow and muggy. Something was cooking and from the smell I decided that it was rabbit and potatoes. The walls of the caravan were painted red and green, and the place was crammed with pots, guns and axes.

"A gipsy woman was sitting cross-legged on the bench. She had big blue eyes and jet-black, curly hair partly covered with a gaudy scarf. She was wearing an embroidered blouse that was showing too much of her large breasts and a big golden coin was glued to her brow. Her hands were embellished with twisted flowers and leaves that snaked from her palms up to her elbows.

"I was intrigued, even hypnotized by her. Pulling my hand towards her breasts, she ran one of her long-nailed fingers over my palms. Then she looked me straight in the eye without wavering and said, 'Tonight you will find the love of your life.'

"I jumped up in disbelief. 'Tonight?' I said. 'No way.'

"'Yes, tonight,' the gypsy replied. 'And you will be tied to her for the rest of your life!'

"I was stunned, paid the woman with a ten shilling note and quickly made my way back home. But that night, I tell you, just two hours later…"

The old man's tone lifted. Laura was staring at him by this point, utterly captivated.

"…I had a call from my boss telling me that I had to do an emergency delivery. The streets were icy and slippery and the van could hardly hold on to the road. As I was driving, a very big lorry skidded and slammed into me. When I came round I was in hospital with three broken ribs and a shattered left leg. I was in a lot of pain, but saw that a lovely nurse was injecting a painkiller through my drip. I sank back to sleep knowing that I had seen my future and that everything was going to be alright.

"We were engaged before I got out of the hospital and I married my Marja three months later. It's been 50 years now."

Laura shook her head with astonishment. "50 years," she repeated.

The man's phone vibrated in his pocket. "My old lady is checking up on me," he chuckled, clutching the table to give him the leverage to stand up.

"I am going now," he said. "It's very nice to talk to young, attractive people, you know? There is nothing that lifts your mood as surely as a beautiful woman. It makes me feel young again."

Laura smiled while thinking, "The old man doesn't know that I feel a hundred years old and not at all beautiful."

She watched him walk away, feeling a rush of admiration for this happy old man. He had such high spirits, refused to

accept the weight of the years on his shoulders. She suddenly wondered how had he had filled all those years.

Finishing her latte, she stepped out of the café and straight into a puddle.

"Phew, what a life," she thought. "Some people's lives are completely full but mine is like this puddle. My foot goes in and out of it without ever leaving a trace."

***

When Laura arrived back home, the thrust of the shutting door behind her felt like a powerful slap on the back. Her throat felt tight. Being inside just didn't feel the same any more. She looked around the house like she was seeing it for the first time. She felt strange, pulled away.

"Just what is happening to me?" she wondered. "Is it the horoscope I read? What am I doing?"

It felt as if something had erupted inside her, something she had no control over.

Perturbed, she stopped in the middle of the living room.

"This is not me," she said to herself. "I am somebody else in my body."

She felt guilty but didn't know why. Was she somehow betraying the memories that had kept her hidden inside these walls? All these years she had been nursing ghosts and living like a dead person herself.

Her knees buckled and she fell to the floor. Clenching her stomach, she pulled her head to her chest. Her mind was shooting off in different directions and she had no control over any of her thoughts. A deep voice inside her body was shouting, "get up, Laura, get up". She lifted her head and slowly got back on her feet, feeling worn out by such a simple movement.

Her cloudy head was in turmoil and she felt a sudden urge for a glass of wine.

Quickly slipping off her wet clothes and dropping them on the floor, she went into the kitchen wearing only her underwear and poured herself a glass of sparkling white wine. Then she climbed the stairs up to her bedroom.

She lay down carefully on the bed, while still clutching the glass in her hand, and closed her eyes. She felt that her life was changing…something inside was boiling very powerfully and she couldn't stop it. Her mind and her heart were not working in conjunction with each other. Her heart had a different plan…

Opening her eyes, she took a big gulp of wine and placed it on the bedside table. Her gaze went to the window. She'd carelessly left part of it uncovered. The sky was heavy, loaded with dark grey clouds. She tried to give meaning to their forms and shapes, work out what they resembled, but she felt tired and unable to think any more. Her eyelids grew heavy, and it wasn't long before she fell into a deep sleep.

5

For Laura, the day before Christmas Eve started unusually. She kept picturing the faces and the movements of people, but she had no idea who they were. It was only as she started performing her everyday rituals that a familiar form returned to the day. As usual, she filled the little wooden houses in her garden with food for the birds and squirrels; her only welcome guests. The clouds had shifted and the morning sky was clear.

"My little friends, it's Christmas for you as well," she said, looking towards the birch tree, inviting them over.

She stayed outside for a while, breathing in the cold air before returning to the warmth of her large kitchen. The ceiling spotlights were still on and spectacularly reflected off the marble floor and worktop.

Laura sat on a high stool next to the ottoman, grabbed hold of her notebook and jotted down a list of groceries and toiletries. She completed her boring online order once a month, which meant she didn't have to bother going out shopping.

Pulling on some white slippers, she went into her study, switched on her computer and waited for the screen to light up.

"It's Christmas," her inner voice reminded her.

She remembered how it used to be. She'd loved the shopping, had spent hours choosing the right presents for everyone, jumping from one brand to another, hauling bags around the different shops.

"God, do miss that time," Laura mumbled.

She started to type the name of her supermarket into a search engine when something made her hesitate.

"Maybe I can do some of this myself," she thought suddenly.

Without giving herself any time to dwell, she switched off the computer, strode out of the office and got ready to go out. She put on some brown cowboy boots and a terracotta-coloured coat with a white wool collar, before draping her handbag over her shoulder.

Just before reaching for the front door, she glanced in the big mirror. Her reflection sent her a few years back in time and made her smile. She'd worn this outfit to meet Matt at the airport following a trip to Australia.

"You look like you're coming from the ranch, my cowgirl," he'd grinned, pressing his lips on her neck.

"And you are very welcome in my ranch, city boy," she'd shot back.

"And I am ready to make myself very dirty in your ranch, my darling…"

Not all her memories made her cry any more.

Laura closed the door behind her and stopped to inhale the wet air deep into her lungs. The fresh, outside smell was so good.

Reaching into her pocket she found a long forgotten Vaseline stick. Pursing her lips into a tight, forced smile, she smothered them to protect against the cold breeze.

The supermarket was just a ten-minute walk from her home, but before she got there she stopped outside the butcher's shop.

"Will he still remember me?" she wondered. "What was his name? Andy? Yes, it was Andy."

The butcher, a shiny-headed bald man with a pink face and grey blue eyes had always served her with a broad smile. But as she crossed the threshold of the shop, the screaming sound of his big machete against hard wood stopped her in her tracks. An awful sadness churned inside her stomach. She wasn't ready for this. Turning around, she ran quickly from the disturbing echo of the knife.

The supermarket was crowded. Everyone was in a hurry to

finish off their Christmas shopping. Laura picked up a trolley and headed for one of the aisles. As she did so, her attention was caught by a big festive display showing Santa with his sleigh. A split second later there was an almighty crash. Laura looked from the display to her trolley - it had made contact with another woman's, spilling some of its contents, which had been piled up high, all over the floor.

"So sorry," Laura said to the woman, who was already doubled over and picking up her shopping. As she straightened up, she looked directly at Laura.

"Oh my God, is that really you?"

Laura stared back at the woman. Her almond-shaped eyes, straight, jet-black hair and thin red lips definitely looked familiar, but it took her a while to put a name to the face.

"Wow, Stacey, how are you doing? It's been so long."

"Yes, must be ten years I think."

Stacey and Laura had been best friends as kids. They'd grown up in the same neighbourhood until Stacey's parents had sold their house and moved to another town. They'd both liked the same music, told each other their secrets, and even had a crush on the same guy.

"I've been in the States all this time…California," Stacey explained. "Ben had a contract with a telecoms company over there."

"Ben? Who's that?" Laura asked.

"My husband, and I have two daughters, too…twins."

"So far so good for you," Laura replied warmly. "Double excitement!"

"Twins run in my husband's family," Stacey said. "He's a twin himself. I often say to him that he spends more time with his brother than he does with me."

Laura chuckled. "Hope you enjoyed the Californian sun," she said.

"I did, but I missed the London clouds."

A few seconds of silence passed between them. They were both painfully aware of the subject that had to be addressed.

Stacey swallowed before speaking. "I heard what happened to you," she said. "I'm so sorry. How are you keeping?"

"Things didn't turn out so good for me," Laura mused. "In fact, life kicked me very hard."

"I am sure you'll get past this," Stacey soothed. "You'll find your way again."

"It's not easy," Laura admitted.

"I remember you as a courageous girl. You found a way out of my basement, remember? You climbed out of that tiny window when we were hiding from my brother."

Yes, Laura could recall that little incident. They'd found themselves locked in down there. The window had been stuck and she remembered struggling to use some tools she'd found, how big and clunky they'd felt in her tiny hands.

"Once upon a time, eh," she said, before adding, "things are a bit more complicated now".

She decided to quickly change the subject and asked Stacey about her work.

"I now work from home," Stacey said. "It means I have more time for my girls."

"What doing?"

"Customer satisfaction surveys for a bank," replied Stacey. "But we'll be moving to Cape Town soon. Ben has accepted another contract. I certainly have enough experience of packing up our worldly possessions."

"How wonderful," Laura replied.

In her mind she pictured Stacey's two girls playing beside her as she worked at her desk.

The encounter left her feeling light years away from the normal life she'd once had. When she remembered fragments of her old existence, it felt like she was picturing someone else's life, as she had done Stacey's.

She paid for her groceries and left the supermarket, her arms already aching from the weight of carrying so many plastic bags. Outside, she felt her nose turn cold while her body stayed warm. She felt the sharp leaves of a tree brush her coat and turned her gaze to see that it was being carried under the arm of a fellow pedestrian. He seemed intent on overtaking her and his large feet were making big strides forward.

"Last minute preparation," Laura thought to herself. "How late to be buying a tree."

She imagined what would happen when he arrived home. There were bound to be kids waiting for him. She pictured them gathering around him, holding up the decorations they'd picked out ready to hang. She saw his wife watching from a distance, heard their laughter. The vision was too painful. Laura took a deep breath and shook her head, as if trying to shake off the images of other people's happy lives.

***

The morning had begun with a thin veil of frost coating all the roofs, cars and grass on Laura's road. But by the time she arrived home the clouds had rolled away and the sun had taken over, melting it all away. After putting her shopping away, she stood for a while at the window wondering what she could do next to keep occupied. She thought about her big walk-in closet upstairs, the one situated between the bedroom and guestroom, and decided to give it a tidy. Inside the small space, her gaze immediately fell on a wooden box on one of the shelves. She pulled it down and sat crossed-legged on the floor before opening it. Lying on top of the box's contents was a CD of her favourite song, *Here Without You,* by a band called 3 Doors Down.

"A hundred days have made me older…" she instinctively started to sing.

Listening to the song always made her feel so emotional. Sometimes, it even made her cry. Putting the CD back in the box, she reached for a card on which was depicted a bird in glitter. It was clutching a pair of baby's shoes in its beak. She knew what the words said inside without even opening the card.

Thanks for choosing to be a mum for my kid...

Matt had presented her with the card on what had been the happiest day of her life. Falling pregnant hadn't been easy, and after various tests they'd resorted to IVF.

Laura felt the steady thud of her heart quicken, and her eyes welled with tears. A weak sob rose up through her chest. She dropped the card back in the box and then closed it. The pain was part anger. Everything she loved was in that box. "But what about me?" she cried. "Where am I?"

She knew it was time to accept that her husband and child were dead, gone, but how? She felt too weak to get up. Loneliness was eating away at her. She was so broken that her own body felt hollow. Burying her head between her knees she stayed like that until her muscles began to stiffen. Eventually she pulled herself up and shuffled through to the bathroom while taking slow, deep breaths. She looked in the mirror. Patches of dried tears resembled scribbles on her face. Turning on the cold tap, she scooped her hands under the flowing water and splashed her face with it.

"Okay, that's it, I'm done," she said impassively to her reflection. "I will cry no more."

Stepping back, she slipped out of her clothes and examined her naked body, seeing it a new way. She looked so innocent, so untouchable by a pleasure that she had denied herself for so long. A craving was reaching out to her from inside her body. She brought her hand up to her breasts, circled one of her nipples with a fingertip, and felt a jolt of electricity shoot through her. Then she slid her hand down to her tapered, trim waist and towards her long thighs. It felt as if her body was waking up from a long coma. She closed her eyes, enjoying the sensation of heat beneath her skin. In her mind's eye she saw a twirl of flaming colours…

Abruptly, she opened her eyes and bit her lip, feeling slightly guilty. This had been unknown territory for so long. Grabbing a thick white bath towel, she wrapped it tightly around her bust and ran to her bedroom to change.

6

"No," Laura said, her voice on the phone sounded strong, unwavering. "I have my reasons to be alone."

"Don't be silly," Carla said. "It's Christmas Eve!"

But Laura wanted to be with her memories, the ones of past joy and present sorrow.

"Do you want me to come over?" Carla persisted.

"What? Do you want to babysit me?"

"I would prefer a man to be doing that."

As usual, Laura found herself giving in. "All right, I'll pop round for a little while."

"Good. Oh, and there's something I almost forgot. Go and check outside your front door, there'll be something there for you. Take your time and look at it very carefully."

Intrigued, Laura bid farewell to Carla and hurried to the door. On the outside mat she found a big brown envelope. Tearing it open, her eyes widened with surprise. On a number of folded A3 sheets was an architectural plan.

She recalled her conversation with Carla a few days earlier.

"Very clever of you, Larry," she grinned. He must have popped round earlier that day. Laura hadn't seen Larry since Matt's funeral. In fact, the last design project she'd meant to work on was still in the drawer. Following her double loss, she hadn't been able to bring herself to touch it. She and Matt had been too much of a team.

But now, looking through these new plans, she found it surprisingly easy to slip back into work mode. She recalled the last major project she'd work on with Matt for their company,

Sparks Enterprises. They'd spent weeks in front of the computer constructing 3D plans of how the final layout would look, going over the details of the surface finishes, lighting, fabrics, as well as the ceiling and wall colours. For Laura, work had never been about the money. Being creative and working with her beloved husband were all that mattered to her. She decided to take the plans to her study, where so many projects had been worked on in times gone by.

After Laura had given up on her career and decided to close the studio, her assistant Anthony, a slightly built boy with a soft voice, had turned up at the house with a box full of things that he hadn't known what to do with. On top of some folders was Matt's grey felt hat. He'd worn it on chilly days and Laura had loved to tease him about it.

"Where can I leave this?" Anthony had asked, his voice shaking.

Laura had pointed to her office and followed him in there, watching as he placed the box on one of the shelves. Now her life seemed to be nothing but closed boxes, all filled with shattered plans and dreams.

"Laura, I am so sorry," Anthony had said. "I can't even find the words to say what I feel…I'm not even crying for Matt today. I am crying for you."

Anthony had hugged his boss tightly, his tears moistening her cardigan. Then, with a deep sigh, he turned away and left. Laura watched him walk through the front garden, his head downcast, and release the catch on the metal gate. She waved at him, holding on to the knot inside her throat, her chest nearly ready to explode. She knew she would never see him again.

***

Placing the plans on her desk, Laura sat down in front of her computer. Behind her, the light from a large window illuminated the room. To her left was an enormous bookcase crammed with volumes of design books and planning papers. The other side of the wall was decorated with personal photographs, which she had chosen and framed in satin wood frames of different shapes and sizes. The images showed some of the most precious moments of her business and married life.

She remembered hanging them up. She'd cordoned off the room using official police tape, which read, 'do not enter'. She wouldn't let Matt inside until she'd finished.

"Please, darling, I just have to use the computer," he'd pleaded.

"No trespassing or you may find yourself in a court of law and serving a lot of time at Her Majesty's Pleasure."

"I'm happy to serve a life sentence in your prison, sweetie," Matt had replied.

She'd gone to him then and let him hold her in his arms, their bodies melting into a pool of desire.

And here she was now looking at a new project, though her passion seemed to be gone. Shutting down her computer she left the study, not wishing to stay in there a moment longer than she had to.

***

Laura rattled the heavy tiger-shaped knocker on Carla's front door twice before her friend's familiar shape appeared behind its frosted glass. As she opened the door she was blasted by a cold draught, which ruffled her curly hair.

"Come on in," she said, shuddering. "It must be freezing out there."

Laura smiled and wiped the soles of her long black boots on the doormat before stepping into the hallway. She unpeeled the soft woollen shawl that she'd layered over her black coat before handing both items to Carla, who was holding out her arms, ready and waiting to hang them up.

Laura looked elegant in a black, cone-shaped skirt and a light green silk shirt with a thin collar and tiny, diamond-shaped crystal buttons. As she headed inside, Carla followed, admiring her appearance as always. Laura looked good in everything.

***

Laura walked into Carla's living room and the first thing she noticed was the striking canvas print of a sunset, which had been expertly placed behind a cream coloured leather sofa. By the side of it, two floor lamps enhanced the natural glow of the picture. Carla's two boys were in the room, but they were so busy squabbling over a smartphone that they were oblivious to Laura's entrance.

"I told you not to touch it," said Tom, the older one.

"Oh yeah…and is that because of your stupid girlfriend, because she sends you messages all the time?" Luka taunted.

"It's mine so don't go near it, understand?" Tom replied.

Luka crossed his arms over his body, as if hugging himself. He stroked his bare feet over the soft, cherry-coloured carpet and looked as if he was about to cry.

Carla clapped her hands to gain the boys' attention.

"Come on, get over it," she ordered.

"But mum, it's my phone. I don't want Luka to mess it up."

"Why has he got everything?" Luka whined.

Tom poked his little brother before meeting Laura's gaze. He immediately stood up and stretched out his hand in a very grown up manner. Laura smiled, ignored his hand and kissed him instead, causing him to blush. She noticed how he had transformed from a lovely boy into an incredibly handsome young man.

"Wow, look at you," she said brushing his face with the back of her fingers and feeling the beginnings of a stubble.

Tom blushed again and stepped away, so Laura turned her attention to his brother. Luka's straight black hair slightly covered his moistened eyes and he was embarrassed in case Laura had heard him arguing with his brother. Laura crouched down to his level and stroked his hair.

"Oh, look at you," she said. "Come on, I need a hug."

She pressed her cheek against his and asked: "Did you miss me?"

"Yes, I missed you lots, Aunt Laura," Luka replied.

It had been such a long time since Laura had been called aunt, and the word caught her quite by surprise. She was touched that Luka had remembered. Being an only child meant she'd never imagined herself having any nephews or nieces.

"What are you going to call the baby?" Laura remembered Luka asking three years earlier, when she and Matt had thrown a party to celebrate their happy news. Once upon a time, Laura had loved throwing parties…

"We still need to think about that," Laura had replied. "But what do you think the name should be?"

"I want him to be called Corey," Luka announced.

"Okay, I will keep that in mind if I have a baby boy."

"But he is a boy, Aunt Laura," Luka had replied determinedly.

Just then, Tom's phone beeped, pulling Laura back to the present. He grinned at his mother's best friend before rushing up to his bedroom. Meanwhile, Luka turned on the TV and started browsing the channels.

"I can smell cake," Laura announced.

"There's a chocolate one in the oven," Carla confirmed. "Let me check up on Larry, see what he's doing."

Carla headed for the kitchen with Laura trailing behind.

Larry, the chef of the house, was at the sink scrubbing the glass bowl he'd used to stir the cake mixture in. He loved to cook and eat, which meant that Carla never had to get her hands dirty in the kitchen.

Larry turned around to face Laura. She hasn't seen him since Matt's death and she couldn't help smiling at the sight of him with his elbows lifted up and his hands dripping with soapy water. Larry was a big man with a big heart. He quickly wiped his wet hands and gave her a big hug.

"Let's have a welcoming glass of wine," he said, pointing at a bottle of red on the ottoman.

Laura glanced around Carla and Larry's big kitchen, which she'd designed for them herself. The walls were surrounded with creamy wooden cupboards and the sink was in front of a huge window with plants entwined around the frame. Nothing about the room had changed.

Laura positioned herself on one of the high stools by the kitchen island as Carla poured the wine. The pendant lights above her head made the wine sparkle and Laura was struck with an irresistible urge to take a big gulp.

"Join us, Larry," said Carla, beckoning her husband to come over.

Larry lifted a glass and turned towards his guest. "Welcome back into our home," he said. "We missed you."

Laura was touched and felt a pang of guilt for keeping her distance from these wonderful people. But at the same time she knew that her empty, dull life wouldn't fit into theirs. The contrast was too great.

"You ladies chat away," said Larry when he'd finished his toast. "I need to take some time over my recipe. It's one of my own inventions!"

"Oh, I am blessed to have you, you know that don't you, darling?" Carla said.

"I do, my pumpkin," Larry replied, calling his wife by his pet name for her.

Carla picked up her and Laura's glasses and led her friend to the dining room, which was connected to the kitchen via a big archway.

"I'm so glad you came, Laura," she said warmly.

"I hadn't realised how much I'd missed you," replied Laura, still feeling guilty for not seeing Larry and the boys for so long.

"Tom and Luka missed you too," Carla said. "But they felt uneasy about asking any questions."

"I don't want you all to worry about me," Laura protested.

"Don't be ridiculous, besides, they see you as their Aunt Laura, and there is nothing I can do about that."

Laura felt her eyes moisten. She took a deep breath and quickly managed a smile. She felt her heart was so small compared to Carla's, like a bird's. How could she have rejected the love and warmth of these people? She realised that she had never lost her love for them.

Larry called them all to the table for dinner. The dining table was decorated with a cream organza runner, embroidered with red grapes and trimmed with thick, gold stitches. Larry had already laid out the food on square porcelain plates: stuffed veal rolls with salad accompanied by Chardonnay in crystal glasses. The presentation deserved so many stars.

Laura breathed in the warm steam coming from the plates and then took her first bite.

"Hmmmm,' she exclaimed. "There are so many flavours going on here, and it's incredibly moreish."

"That reaction is what makes cooking so worthwhile," Larry replied, clearly delighted.

Laura couldn't remember the last time she'd cooked a proper meal thanks to frozen food and her microwave. But this was more than a tasty dish, it was a social gathering around the table. Oh God, she had missed that so much.

The boys were still not themselves, though, and were refusing to talk to each other.

"Come on," pleaded their mother. "Call a ceasefire or you will both be grounded."

Tom didn't pay much attention to his mum's words. He was tapping his fingers rapidly on the screen of his phone as if the people talking and eating around him didn't exist.

"This Facebook is taking up all of his time," Carla remarked.

As if to prove her point, Tom didn't lift his face from the screen.

"Do you have a Facebook page, Aunt Laura?" Luka asked.

"Me? Oh no," Laura replied. Then she remembered that she had signed up to it years earlier. She'd had so much fun posting up pictures and exchanging messages with her friends. The profile photo she'd chosen was snapped on holiday with Matt in Scotland. She was dressed for the cold and carrying a rucksack on her back. The memory alone made her feel as if fresh spring air was pumping into her lungs.

"Why don't you set up a page?" Luka pressed.

Laura frowned in response, she didn't know what to say.

"Luka!" Carla interjected. "If you've finished your dinner then go and get yourself ready for bed. Put your pyjamas on and brush your teeth. And no computers, okay? I'll be coming to check on you."

"But mum," Luka whined.

"No, I've made up my mind," said Carla. "Now come and give me a kiss, my sweet."

When he had left the room, Carla turned her attention back to Laura.

"Actually, it's not a bad idea," she said.

"What isn't?"

"Starting a Facebook page."

"No way. I can't do that."

"Why not? You don't have to go out and meet people. You can just talk, it will stop you feeling so alone."

Carla scooped up Laura's hand. "Who knows, maybe, you'll end up 'liking' someone on there. Life is too short, my darling, to spend it without love."

Laura couldn't talk. She inhaled some air deep into her lungs. Every time she dug deep and tried to conjure an image of someone she could love, she found only confusion. If she didn't move on soon was she in danger of losing herself? Larry's words interrupted her chain of thought.

"Did you get chance to take a look at the plans for the new project?"

"Oh, Larry, you don't need to look out for me," Laura replied.

"Actually, they asked for you."

"Who on earth would do that?" Laura wondered out loud. She was no longer known, part of anything.

"They wanted the same designer who transformed the Tapey house," Larry explained. "This was no favour."

With that he pushed himself back in his chair and clapped his hands on the table.

"So, what do you think?"

Laura looked away for a moment as she gathered her thoughts.

She was aware of Carla and Larry staring at her, waiting to hear what she would say. She felt exposed, as if she was standing in a field with strong winds coming at her from all sides.

"I will see," she said finally.

"Welcome back to the world," Carla cried, raising her glass. "To great opportunities."

***

By the time Laura left Carla and Larry's house the rain and the wind had become one, sweeping over the rooftops as if washing away the dirt and grime of the day. On her way home, she started to imagine working on the project. She recalled the plans and mentally chose colours, surface finishes, lighting, fabrics, and thought about exterior landscaping. That plain brown envelope had brought with it an explosion of ideas and Laura decided that the offer was too good to refuse. She called Larry as soon as she got home.

7

THE following day brought with it a mild breeze, a hint of spring still trapped in its winter cage. Laura hadn't slept, had spent all night chasing thoughts that seemed to be running away from her. She went to the park, sauntering along with no real purpose, as if trapped in a labyrinth of mirrored walls. The naked trees surrounding her were singing the quiet symphony of the sleeping winter.

She stopped at a little kiosk to order coffee and from there she could see the top of a large office block. She was due to meet the architect there at 11am.

"Nice morning to be in the park," said the kiosk man, his fat belly was wrapped in an apron and he sported a moustache.

But Laura didn't want to be drawn into a conversation. She thanked him for the coffee and carried on walking.

"I'm not here for the nice morning," she thought to herself. "The sky could be falling in for all the difference it would make to how I feel."

A couple of joggers ran past her, their breathing laboured. Meanwhile, Laura felt as unsteady as a toddler, and was worried she might trip at any moment. An old lady with a dog walked past and smiled. She held Laura's gaze as if waiting for an exchange, maybe a compliment about her dog, but Laura was lost in her thoughts about the project. Scooping the paper cup with both hands she took a final sip of coffee.

"Time's up," she said out loud, though the words were directed only at herself.

As she approached the office block on the other side of the

park, she undid the top button of her coat and breathed air deep into her lungs. An imposing glass door formed the entrance to the building.

"What am I doing?" Laura sighed. "Will I be able to handle it?"

Her doubts had an almost physical effect on her, preventing her from moving forward. When she eventually managed to step inside the building she had to summon up yet more courage in order to take the elevator up to the 18th floor.

Pulling her shoulders back as the lift doors opened, she finally felt ready to present herself as Laura, the interior designer.

Behind the reception desk a young woman with short blonde hair looked up from the paper she was reading.

"Hello madam," she said. "What can I do for you?"

"I have an appointment to see John Stratham," Laura replied.

"Okay, I will let him know you are here," the receptionist replied, gesturing to a seating area.

Laura peeled off her coat and scarf. The light green dress she was wearing underneath showed off her body's beautiful shape. Positioning herself on the leather sofa, which was the colour of sand, she admired the sky blue walls. Then she picked up a magazine from a pile on the side table by the sofa, but she didn't get chance to open it. The receptionist had come over to show her to John Stratham's office.

His door was slightly open so Laura pushed it gently and stepped inside, instantly feeling the weight of responsibility on her shoulders.

The luxury office had a floor to ceiling window and was flooded with natural light. John Stratham was on the phone, seated behind an enormous desk. In his mid 60s, he was wearing a tailored dark grey suit and a blue and yellow striped shirt. Laura was struck by how handsome he was.

Pulling the phone away from his ear, he stood up and reached for Laura's hand.

"I appreciate you coming here," he said pleasantly.

Laura smiled, feeling her cheeks turn red as she took a seat in front of him. She decided from his accent that her new employer was from Wales.

"I think the plans for the project have already reached you?" John continued.

"Yes, they did," Laura replied, thinking to herself how Larry had done a good job of ensuring that. "But I want you to know that it's been quite a long time since I've been involved with a project. And, to tell you the truth, I wasn't even sure about coming here today."

"But you did and I'm glad," John said warmly. "And I'm sure you're going to do a very good job."

Laura had to stop herself from asking how he knew that. Instead she lowered her eyes and smiled, living up to her reputation as a charming woman with an impeccable track record for design work. She was on the horse now, and she felt ready to ride it.

A collage of photos inside a brown leather frame on John's desk caught her eye.

"You have a beautiful family," Laura said, looking at the smiling faces of two young girls and an older woman, whom she presumed was John's wife.

"My daughters are much older now than they are in those pictures," John explained. "The birds have flown the nest now."

He pointed to one of the girls. "This is Megan, she's in Australia," he explained, "and her sister is Elian, she's in New York.

"Now instead of their presence I wait for a message from them to pop up on my computer screen."

John's mind was far away now and Laura noticed the melancholy hidden inside of him. She felt bad for starting this conversation, which was obviously very painful for him.

"You will allow me to be your companion today and introduce you to everyone on the project," John said, changing the subject. "I'll drive you to the house. Are you ready?"

"Yes," Laura replied. "And that's very kind of you."

"The only thing is, we have a deadline."

"When for?"

"Six weeks...oh, and before we leave, don't forget to sign some papers, the secretary will have them ready for you."

"Yes, I'm aware of those," Laura replied. "I've already read through them."

"Are you happy with the figures?"

"More than happy."

"You will have all the assistance you need. And leave your mobile number with my secretary."

"Sure," Laura replied, but his request had caught her by surprise. Her mobile was hidden away somewhere in one of her drawers, unused for years. As the secretary waited, her pen poised to catch the number, Laura's memory failed her. Luckily she had a brainwave and checked her handbag for an old business card. She found one and immediately read out the number.

Leaving the office with John by her side, she felt immensely relieved and much calmer. They rode the lift in silence, and when the doors opened on the ground floor they were confronted with a mountain of pizza boxes. In his haste, a delivery boy nearly crashed into them.

John touched Laura gently on the shoulder, letting her pass in front of him. He seemed like a good man and Laura knew instinctively that she was going to get along with him.

The pair headed to Fulham, West London, where the mansion Laura was going to work on was situated.

This was a multi-million pound project, and Laura felt overwhelmed as she looked around the massive residence. It was quite a lot of house to do. The property was surrounded by a big landscaped area, and each of the en-suite bedrooms had a huge balcony overlooking it. Standing in one of the bedrooms, Laura pictured looking out onto waterfalls, carefully placed ornamental stones, dimmed lighting.

"Should be a magical view from here," she said.

"It's all yours now," John replied.

As Laura explained how long it would take her to get the initial plans ready, John's phone buzzed in his pocket.

"Just give me minute, my darling," he said to the caller. "I'll call you back."

Then he turned to Laura. "Sorry, dear. I can't avoid this call."

A group of workmen were standing nearby. They were chatting, laughing and enjoying their break. John called out to one of them, a man called Oscar.

Breaking away from the group, Oscar strode towards them, his hands deep inside the pockets of his paint-spattered jeans. He slowed down when he clapped eyes on Laura, shooting a hungry look her way and flashing a smile that made her feel uneasy. She couldn't help but notice Oscar's physique; his sleeveless t-shirt showed off his toned biceps and tanned skin.

"Please show Laura around," John said.

"It will be my pleasure," Oscar grinned, his expression like that of a wolf eyeing a sheep.

Despite herself, Laura felt highly flattered by the attention. Her gaze drifted down from Oscar's masculine, unshaven face, down to his sweaty t-shirt, which clung to his muscular chest, then further down still to his six-pack...

Her faced reddened. Sexual, clandestine thoughts forced their way to the forefront of her mind uninvited.

"Nah, it's not for me!" she told herself, biting her lower lip and moving her gaze to the floor in order to hide her emotions. She couldn't believe that she was indulging in a sexual fantasy after all those years.

"I'm the head of the decorating team," Oscar explained.

"I'm the designer," replied Laura.

"We have quite a ride to take together," Oscar laughed.

"Yeah, seems like we do."

"Well, I'm ready and waiting to take orders, miss."

Despite trying to look serious, Oscar couldn't hide his comedic expression. He proceeded to show Laura around the vast property, and by the time they returned to the master bedroom, John had finished his conversation, his eyes sparkling with amusement.

"Maybe one of his daughters called him," Laura mused.

"Sorry again," John said.

"It's okay, don't mention it," Laura replied. "Would it be possible for me to meet with the owners of the house? I'd like to see what art work they'll be selecting to put on display."

"Very clever idea," John said.

Laura realised that part of her old self was back. This project was going to be a success.

Driving back from the house, it was John who broke the silence between them.

"It was my wife on the phone," he explained. "She's not herself at the moment."

Laura didn't quite understand what he was talking about. What did he mean by 'not herself'?

"I miss her," said John, his voice trembling. "I don't want to lose a single moment when she comes back."

"Where is she?"

"Home...she is home, but she has dementia. She come and goes."

Laura felt an instant jolt of pain. She didn't know what to say, and when she did try to speak her words froze in her mouth.

When they got to Knightsbridge, Laura asked to be let out.

"I want to take a look around," she explained.

"Do you want me to wait for you?" John asked, ever the gentleman.

"I'll be fine," Laura assured him. "I'm not in a hurry. When I'm done I'll jump on the Tube."

"Okay then. Have a good time. Shopping is a woman's territory. My wife used to shop in Knightsbridge a lot."

When Laura had got out of the car, John leaned over to speak to her. She ducked her head down to the window in order to be back at his level. "Yes?" she asked.

"I am really happy that we are going to be working together."

Laura nodded, smiled and then waved her goodbye. After John had pulled away she watched his car until it disappeared into the heavy traffic. Thinking of the weird situation he was facing every day, she realised that she understood it completely. She was, after all, all too familiar with pain.

8

KNIGHTSBRIDGE. The best shops in Europe, maybe even the world.

"Hmmmm...I smell shopping," Laura thought to herself.

The hunt began.

Looking at various window displays, a long buried sensation rose to the surface: the pleasure of shopping.

She remembered all the times she'd spent matching her jewellery and accessories, worrying about her appearance, making sure that her hair and nails were perfect.

This all gave her confidence, and the result? Few men could resist her. But these days her image was boring.

She headed first for the lingerie department and picked up a black and red silk bra.

"A good choice," volunteered the sales assistant, startling Laura slightly. She blushed. Forgotten sensations had started to move her and she felt almost naked.

Did she really want to forget what was in her hand? Could she oppose her hormones and sexual nature?

"What size do you wear?" the sales girl continued.

But how could she begin to know her bra size? Her body was much thinner since the last time she had bought underwear, which was years ago. Laura felt embarrassed over not knowing such an important detail.

"Don't worry, follow me," the sales assistant said. "I will measure you."

Laura smiled. She felt good, alive - something new was starting…

Once measured, Laura and the assistant headed out onto the shop floor to pick up the correct size. As she paid for her purchases, Laura noticed how the store was busier now, people were coming at her from all directions and cameras flashed above her head.

"What on earth is happening here?" a young boy asked.

Laura turned to him and shrugged.

"Oh my God, it's Cheryl!" A woman behind her gasped. Then she pushed Laura to the side, eager to join the rest of the crowd.

"Who?" said the boy, who had messy hair almost hidden beneath a ridiculous hat. He started pressing the screen of his phone, which, going by the curses that came from his mouth, was running out of battery life.

Laura shook her head and wondered, "What is wrong with these people?" She had never idolised celebrities.

She left the shop to get away from the madness and crossed the road to a cosy and cool bistro, where she ordered a cappuccino and a chicken sandwich.

She watched the melee through the window until the 'goddess' was whisked away, presumably to her next celebrity event.

On the way home, Laura stopped at another department store and bought some new perfume and makeup, replacing the cosmetics that had long since expired and been thrown out.

***

By the end of the day, Laura felt exhausted. Back at home, she went up to the bathroom, closed her eyes and splashed cold water over her face. The vision of a man with a toned chest and biceps to die for invaded her thoughts. Laura immediately opened her eyes. "This is ridiculous," she thought. But her desire was one step ahead of her and she couldn't control it. She quickly dried her face, hung her towel and, she hoped, her sinful thoughts on the hook.

That night, Laura lay in bed and ran her fingers over the silky underwear she had bought that day. It felt so good, and she quickly, as if uncontrollably, removed the garments. Then she rolled her body over the soft faux bed cover and, one by one, gently cupped her breasts in her hands. She slid her fingers down to her tummy, then to between her legs; she had not touched her flower down there for so long. A strong current moved through her as she let the night take over, throwing herself deep under the waves of her sensuality. Her hands were moving intensely now and blood was firing through her veins. Every pore of her body felt thirsty…she was cutting the cord with her past in this one beautiful and erotic act. It felt exciting, mysterious, and Laura loved it. She realised that some part of her had been craving this kind of pleasure all along, only she hadn't had the courage to admit it. Now her fear had evaporated. Laura was finally beginning to challenge herself again.

***

The following morning she woke up feeling different, warmer. Her muscles felt more relaxed. She sat up in bed and stretched out her arms, her gaze falling down to her breasts. She was still naked. She placed a finger on a nipple and circled it, smiling. Closing her eyes she breathed deeply, savouring just a hint of the sexual relish she'd enjoyed the night before. Still naked, she padded to the bathroom to take a quick shower. Then she wrapped a large towel around her torso and went to the kitchen. It was chilly but her body was still steaming from the warmth of the shower. She heated a glass of milk in the microwave, set it on a tray with a vanilla cream filled croissant and headed to her office. Her mind was in work mode and she plugged in her scanner and printer, figuring that she'd need to use them. Sitting at her computer, she gripped the edge of the desk with her hands and took a deep breath. Once upon a time, she had spent hours here for work and leisure. It seemed like ages ago.

"Ready to relate again?" She asked her computer as she logged on.

Her first email was from John, congratulating her again for joining the project. It made Laura feel highly privileged.

As her fingers moved across the keyboard, her green eyes sparkled, becoming hungrier and more alive.

This little box, with its infinite 'brain' and its magnetic power, was pulling her in, welcoming her back.

"I have a lot to catch up on," she admitted to herself.

Everything that had been frozen in time, hidden or swiped away from her mind, had to be restored. Her mind was like a dry sponge, thirsty to soak up knowledge without caring where it came from. Laura lost herself for almost three hours, and by the time she got up her joints had stiffened. She let the big towel slip away as she walked from her office stark naked. She felt free from the weight she had been carrying for so many years.

9

WHEN Laura knocked on her neighbour Martin's door, she could tell from his expression that he was more than a little surprised to see her. She didn't go out much these days, even to her own back garden. He sometimes did her gardening, without her asking to him to, and he knew it was appreciated.

"I can't start my car," Laura said. "Can you help?"

"It's probably the battery," replied Martin, knowing how long it had been since she'd driven.

Next to Martin's feet was Mimo. The white, curly-haired dog was spinning around, following his tail. He looked so adorable in his red collar and Laura reached down to pet him.

"Hey, boy, how are you? It's so good to see you."

From the depths of the hallway, she heard a familiar voice. "What a pleasant surprise!" exclaimed Sylvia, Martin's wife. "Come on inside, Laura, I'll put the kettle on."

"Oh, thanks, but I don't have time, I have something to do."

Time? What was she talking about? The one thing that Laura had was time. She'd barely been out in three years.

"Oh," Sylvia replied, sounding baffled and a little disappointed. Laura felt bad for refusing.

"Okay, just for a quick tea, then," she said, dropping her car keys into Martin's hands. "The garage door is open," she said, following Sylvia and Mimo into the kitchen.

Sylvia put the kettle on before turning to Laura with a smile.

"It's good to see you, Laura, you look good, and even Mimo is happy to see you."

"Thanks, it's good to see you too," Laura replied, lowering

her eyes. Again, she felt guilty for being so near to Martin and Sylvia while refusing to let them take part in her grief. She realised that she had shrunk herself into a cage of her own creation.

"I've started to work again," she said.

"That's really good news. I am so happy for you."

By the time she had finished her tea, Martin had got her car started. Laura realised how much she had missed the excitement of driving.

***

Laura was due to meet the Hamptons, the owners of the mansion she was working on, for the first time. She got herself organised and prepared a folder with everything she needed to present to them, before realising that she had two and a half hours to kill before their meeting. It was time to take some action over her appearance. She needed a decent look. She put on a blue cashmere coat, pulled on some elegant black boots, packed a small makeup bag and parked outside the first hairdressers she could find. Luckily, they had a spare appointment. Two hours later, Laura looked at herself from various angles in the shop's large mirror.

"Wow! I can't believe this is me!" she said.

It had been a full 360-degree transformation. Her dull hair was now shiny, and it had been cut and coloured in the latest style. It brought out the colour in her face – her ghostly look had vanished.

The hairdresser seemed even more pleased than Laura was.

"You look beautiful," she said.

"Thank you," Laura replied, still smiling at her image in the mirror.

Mission complete, she slipped on her coat and thanked the hairdresser profusely. She felt more confident and her steps out on the street were lighter. She was ready to go out and challenge the world.

The meeting with the Hamptons at their new house went better than Laura had hoped. The couple were younger than she'd expected. He owned an insurance company and she was a modern, stylish redhead with her own career. Presenting her ideas to them, Laura had felt confident. They'd shown her a folder containing copies of the pictures they wanted to display in the house. They were contemporary black and white ones, which showcased their personality. Laura shared their taste, which would make her job so much easier.

After they had left, Laura felt happy and proud of herself. She went to have a quick chat with Oscar about the developments. He looked at her intently as she talked, breathing in her scent. Of course, he was hoping for more than a work conversation and sensing this, Laura almost felt sorry for him. He wanted something that he'd never be able to have. Even so, she couldn't pretend that she hadn't given into some outrageous thoughts about him, imagining his muscled body next to hers, the pleasure he could give her. Letting her imagination run wild like this had made her feel more animated than she had done in years. Yet she still wasn't comfortable with her feelings. She was determined not to mislead Oscar and give him false hopes.

Keeping their conversation strictly professional, she wrote him a list of things that needed doing.

"It's good to work with you," she said to him. "And I mean just work."

"Yes, I understand," Oscar replied, lowering his head in disappointment.

***

Before driving away, Laura texted Carla and the two women arranged to meet up. The traffic was heavy, but thanks to GPS she was able to use secondary roads, which made her journey much faster. She parked up and started walking to the café where they'd agreed to meet.

A warm breeze caressed her face and she felt protected by the armour of her newfound confidence. Just then, as if the universe wanted to bring her down a peg or two, she found herself stumbling.

"Miss, are you okay?" asked a bald-headed man with a round face. He put down the bags he was carrying and gripped her arms.

As Laura looked up, he exclaimed, "Wow, what a pretty lady!"

Laura regained her balance and carried on, spotting Carla seated outside the café. As she strode towards her friend, she felt her newly styled hair brush against her shoulders.

"Oh my God, you look stunning," Carla cried. "What have you done? Wow, your hair! You bad girl. What is it that I don't know yet?"

"It's nothing," Laura replied, her green eyes so pure an innocent. "What can it be? Just a little fun is all."

"Oh, come on. You look so different, so alive. I am so happy to see you like this again." She let out a deep sigh of satisfaction. "Men are going to love this new look. No one will be able to resist you!"

"Wow, do you think so?" asked Laura, raising an eyebrow.

"Yeah, one look is enough to make any man horny. Darling, trust me on that."

"Silly you!" Laura said, laughing. When the waitress arrived she ordered a croissant and a sparkling water.

"It's time for you to be a little silly, girl, don't you think so? You could have any man you want, and you have the right to have some fun."

"I don't want to," Laura replied. "I don't want to be tied to anyone."

Her gaze dropped down to her glass, where the bubbles of her sparkling water were wrestling with each other.

"You could do some flirting online," Carla urged. "It won't do you any harm."

But Laura still didn't feel ready to welcome another man into her life, her heart was wounded enough. The new hair, makeup and lingerie had only succeeded in helping her feel a little more alive. Her scars still hadn't healed.

"Just give it a shot," Carla went on. "I am sure a nice man is out there waiting for you."

She rummaged around in her handbag and pulled out a shimmering purple box about the size of a wallet. She pushed it in Laura's direction.

"What is that?" Laura asked, her eyes widening.

"It's something for you, to help with your new image…a manicure kit."

Laura grinned, feeling her emotions soar. She loved her friend enormously.

"I'm getting a promotion," Carla said before Laura had the chance to say thank you. "I can't believe they are promoting a big fat chicken like me, can you believe that?"

"Of course I can. You deserve it, and you are a beautiful fat chicken."

The pair spent the rest of their time gossiping. Laura didn't even know half the people that Carla was talking about, but it didn't matter one bit.

As she got up to leave, Carla wished her a good weekend.

"Weekend?" she said, repeating the word. She realised that now the days on her calendar had names. Saturday and Sunday were once again different from the rest of the week. But what was she going to do?

Back at home, she unbuttoned her coat and threw it on the sofa. There was something that needed doing which she'd been putting off for a very long time…

She went upstairs and changed into tracksuit bottoms and the first t-shirt she came across in the drawer. Then she dashed into the kitchen, pulled out a box of cleaning materials from the cupboard under the sink, and put on some rubber gloves.

With that, the scrubbing, polishing and rearranging of her things began.

After tackling nearly every corner of the house, she went to the one room that she hadn't set foot in for nearly three years. Taking a deep breath, she gripped the handle and pushed the door open. Tins of paint sat untouched in the corner, along with a roll of wallpaper decorated with yellow ducks. This was the room she had been preparing for the baby's arrival. In another corner of the room, a cot, still in its box, rested against the wall. She swallowed hard to get rid of the knots that had formed in her throat and fought back tears as she piled everything together, ready to be taken away.

Job done, she sunk into the sofa and let her head fall back, feeling her eyes grow heavy. A cool breeze from the open window brushed against her exposed décolletage, a pleasant sensation on her otherwise clammy skin. She pushed her hand beneath the waistband of her tracksuit bottoms and reached into her knickers. Pushing her feet against the floor she rubbed her body against the sofa, her breathing quickening, a moan rising from deep inside her. She bit her lower lip as she moved, her mouth dry, her hot liquid wetting her fingers, before she finally let herself cry out.

As her breathing returned to normal, Laura opened her eyes. Darkness had fallen outside and raindrops splashed the windowsill by the open window. Laura's cheeks were burning and her clothes were in disarray. She stood up slowly, walking through the living room without turning on the light. She needed to stay in the dark.

10

Laura gazed at the sign. 'Fox Hill,' it read. The usual morning ritual of her weekend years ago involved walking amid the trees there. Now she was back, leaving footprints in the soft virgin soil, which was still wet from the previous night's rain. She reached the top of the hill and rested against the trunk of a tree. Taking a deep breath, she surveyed her surroundings from this vantage point. She could see the riding school she'd joined as a kid and remembered the incident that had ended her time there. After falling off a pony and coming home with cuts on her knees and elbows, her mum decided to stop her attending.

"But mum, please," Laura had begged.

"No. Today there are scratches, tomorrow there may be broken bones. My decision is final."

Laura turned her head, trying to spot the roof of her parents' old house. It was a beautiful building, but she hadn't been back there since they had died. Matt had made all arrangements with the estate agents when it came to selling it.

Looking down from the hill, under the shadow of the trees, everything seemed brighter. Laura smiled as she remembered her parents taking tea in the garden, their speakers moved to the window so they could hear their music. She once found them dancing barefoot on the grass and couldn't stop laughing. Her dad was doing some pretty ridiculous movements. They were happy moments.

She lifted up her hands and grasped her shoulders, taking air deep into her lungs. A sunray cut through the woods and shone into her eyes, forcing her to close them. As she enjoyed this welcome peace, she heard soft steps and sensed someone stop in front of her. She kept her eyes closed as they gripped her arms and squeezed hard. A man's touch. She could feel his warm breath on her temple as her face was pushed against his heavily built chest. His skin was steaming hot and she could hear the beat of his heart as his hands pressed gently against her back.

"It feels so good," she whispered, feeling intoxicated.

Then she opened her eyes. She found herself facing the cool bark of the tree and looked around. Only woods.

"Oh," she said. "I was lost in fantasy."

She banged her forehead against the tree, scratching the hard surface of the bark until she felt physical pain.

A cuddle, just a warm cuddle, that's all her body needed.

She started walking slowly downhill before quickening her pace to a run. Tears pooled in her eyes, blurring her surroundings. She ran until she was too breathless to go on.

Taking a deep breath, she wiped her eyes and her view became clear. She'd become a small part of this silent, naked forest. Walking home, she felt confused. Her body and heart were craving something different from her mind. The pain and grief of the past couldn't hold her anymore. Her trapped desire wanted to cut loose.

***

Back at home, she gave into the promise her computer held. She started typing; it was time to find a friend or two.

"I'm not sure if I can do this," she mumbled. "But I'm only giving it a go. I just want someone to talk to, not someone to be involved with."

She was determined that the touching, kissing and hugs would remain in her imagination.

She found a dating site and logged on to the section where you had to fill in your profile.

"Who am I?" She asked, saying her thoughts out loud. "I barely know myself any more."

She rested her elbows on the desk and put her chin in her hands while she stared at the blank screen.

"What to do?" she said, sighing. But it was now or never. "Okay, then. Let's do it."

Name: Laura
Age: 41
Profession: interior designer
Hobbies: no comment

She couldn't think of anything she did to pass the time any more, apart from sleep.

The next step involved adding a profile picture. Laura chose one showing a happy moment in her life. Her hair was being brushed by a light wind, and behind her the blue sea shimmered.

She'd been in Italy at the time and was laughing at Matt, who'd nearly fallen over trying to find a good position to take the shot.

Staring at the picture, Laura realised that time was frozen in that laugh. The life she had now was completely different.

What are you doing? How can you just ignore all those years?

The questions went off like a horn inside her head.

Her own eyes stared back at her from the computer screen, forcing her to look down. Faces and hands were rising from the ground, screaming and pulling at her. Panicking, she sprung up and crossed her arms around herself.

"It's not real," she said. "It's in my head."

She breathed deeply, still frozen in terror, before extending her hand out and reaching for the off button. The screen turned dark. She pulled away, leaving her guilt inside the electronic box.

She was in desperate need for air. Stepping out onto the porch, she hoped to steal a peaceful moment from the night. Curling up on her bench, she wrapped her arms around her knees and looked up at the sky. It was very dark and the moon was fighting with thick clouds to reveal her face to the earth.

11

"How did the meeting with the Hamptons go?" John asked. It was later that evening when Laura received a call from him.

"It went well," she replied. "I feel much more confident about what I'm going to do. They seem like a very nice couple."

"Yes, they are," replied John. "I know his father. We used to be members of the same golf club."

Laura picked up on the sign that followed. "Why don't you go to the club anymore?" she asked, but her question was met with silence.

Eventually, John thought of a way to answer. "I didn't see the fun in it any more," he explained. "I found some more interesting things to do and divorced myself from the club."

Laura could tell that he was trying to make a joke, but his voice was strained, his speech forced. She knew all too well why he'd given up his hobby and his friends. It was because he wanted to be with his wife every second and minute of the day, before he lost her completely. Laura knew only too well how hard it would be to close that chapter of his life, to see his happy memories wiped away.

"Call me whenever you feel like talking to someone," she said. She was surprised by her own offer, that, as fragile as she was, she able to offer someone else her support.

"Laura, thank you. That means a lot to me. You are a very special lady."

John's voice was soft and sounded so familiar to Laura, so fatherly. It was a voice she had missed for a long time.

"It's so hard," John continued. "So painful to see someone you love getting lost every day. I feel so lonely knowing that in the other room is a stranger, and hoping and waiting for a lucid moment. We have this thick wall, full of dementia, between us."

John's voice trembled, then he went silent. Laura could hear his heavy breathing as he strained to force back his tears. His pain was born from an everlasting commitment to his wife. The knowledge of this tore Laura's heart to pieces. She knew how he was feeling, of course she did. She was not free from pain and never would be.

"I know how you feel, but try to enjoy the good moments," she soothed. "When she is with you, every second is precious."

"I miss her, oh God do I miss her," John replied. "She was my lover and my best friend. I used to take her with me to the golf club on Sundays, and we enjoyed so many sunny days together until she got sick. Now I can't face anyone there. It hurts me when they ask after her."

Laura had found that difficult too, she'd found the sorry expression on people's faces so irritating. How could they know how she felt? Her pain was unknown to them.

After they'd said their goodbyes, Laura felt wounded and fatigued. She wrapped her wool cardigan more tightly around herself and sank deeper into the cushions of the sofa.

Grabbing the remote control next to her, she turned on the TV. Some distraction would be good, she needed to take her mind off the conversation she'd had with John. But the images on the screen were all blurry and she realised that her eyes were full of water. Her throat was tight, too. Loneliness and sadness were her only companions.

"I miss Matt so much," she said out loud, folding her knees up, and sinking her face into a cushion. Her shoulders and body trembled and she felt as if she was going to explode into an uncontrollable sob. Giving into it, she wept until her voice was weak and she was overcome by fatigue. But this time, her tears were for her, not for the dead.

Outside it was raining and the wind howled like crazy, a perfect accompaniment to her cries. Soon, sleep took her away.

***

With three weeks to go until the deadline, Laura found herself constantly zigzagging across London, ordering the best materials and even trying her old contacts so she could acquire made to measure furnishing. Her phone was always buzzing in her pocket, but at least she was now used to the routine of work.

The morning had got off to a chilly start and prior to leaving the house she enveloped herself in a soft wool shawl. Once outside, she rubbed her hands in front of her face before breathing her warm breath against them. Then she leapt inside her car and headed to the office to drop off some receipts. She'd already rung John to let him know she'd be stopping by.

"It will be so lovely to start the day seeing a beautiful lady like you," he'd said, sounding happy.

But their previous conversation had left Laura feeling wretched. She couldn't stop John's words swimming around inside her head. Facing his pain meant dealing with hers, too.

When Laura entered John's office he stood up and directed her to a chair by the window. Holding her gaze, he smiled and picked up his phone. "Two coffees, please," he said to his secretary.

Laura placed her handbag on the coffee table next to an elegant glass vase filled with fresh white magnolia flowers. She unwrapped the shawl from her neck before taking her seat and looking out of the window.

"What a spectacular view from here," she said. The day was overcast and they were so high up that Laura felt at one with the clouds.

The secretary brought in their coffees and John took a seat in front of Laura. The smile on his face had disappeared. Laura was full of concern.

"How are you keeping?" she asked.

"I am feeling sloppy," John replied. His voice sounded tired and there were dark circles beneath his eyes. He looked older.

"She is getting worse every day, I am losing her."

Laura stared at John, speechless. What could she say? What words could reach his pain?

"Why don't we go out and have a coffee somewhere else?" she said, transferring her gaze to the untouched cups on the table.

"Okay, why not? What a very good idea to get out of here!"

John followed Laura out of his office like a faithful old dog. When they got outside, he took over the directions. "There's a nice coffee place right around the corner," he said.

They navigated their way through the tiny gaps between pedestrians to the soundtrack of drills plunging deep into the ground. Repair work on the pavement was in progress. It was so loud that it was a while before Laura noticed that her phone was ringing. She pulled it out of her bag and stopped outside the café door, gesturing for John to go in ahead of her. Carla's name was flashing on her screen.

"Hey, curly head, what's up?"

"Everything is wrong," Carla replied. She sounded as if she'd been crying.

"What's happened?"

"I've never been like this before, never. It's Tom, he's going to India as part of some exchange programme with his college. I don't know what the hell they're doing sending him there."

"And?"

"And...? And how can he go? He's still a boy, for Christ's sake. He's never been outside London without me. The worst part is that the ticket has been booked for a month. Larry knew all about it, he was hiding it from me. I'll never forgive him, he's betrayed me."

"Calm down, Carla. They just knew how would you would react, that's why they didn't tell you."

"I want to go with him. If he went to France or Belgium then maybe I could have coped, but India? One month, Laura, one long month. He's never been away from home before. What is he is going to eat? He's not used to Indian food."

"He won't be alone," Laura reasoned.

"But he won't be with me!"

"Calm down, Carla, please calm down."

"I can't, Laura, I can't. My heart wants to explode."

There was a pause as Carla wiped her nose. Laura was thinking more about Larry. He was a wise man, but he had a soft nature. He wasn't able to stand up to Carla when she was angry.

"What should I do? Should I stop him from going or go with him?"

"Don't make things worse. It's happening, just accept that and let it go. Now, please take a deep breath."

Laura waited until she heard a change in her friend's breathing.

"Okay, now get some fresh air. It'll make you feel better. And don't upset Larry, okay!"

It made a change to be the one telling Carla what to do. When she entered the coffee shop she felt relieved to be getting away from the noise of the road and Carla's complaints.

The interior was decked out with red leather seats and it resembled a large train carriage. John had already ordered an espresso and a glass of water for himself, plus a skinny latte for Laura.

"It was my friend," she explained, dropping her phone back inside her bag.

"Is everything okay?"

"Yes, it's just that the bird is getting out of its cage, that's all," Laura smiled. "It's her son, he's going to India."

John remembered how it felt when his own children spread their wings.

"It's inevitable," he commented before taking a sip of his espresso. He stared at Laura for a moment.

"Your pretty face just reminded me of my happy days," he said, his eyes turning gloomy.

Laura didn't know what she could say to ease his pain.

"My home just doesn't feel like home anymore," John went on. "Everything looks strange. This dementia business is driving me crazy. Nothing makes sense anymore."

Laura could see herself reflected in John's pain. He had the look of sadness that she'd worn for years.

"The worst part is that you can only observe it without having the power to change anything. You can only bow to the rules that life has chosen for you."

John sucked in the air deeply before exhaling forcefully. Lost in his own unhappiness, he continued. "I dreamt of retiring with her," he said. "Spending our quiet years sitting on the porch, watching the sunset. Seeing our grandchildren playing on the beach, holding each other's hand as our feet got splashed with water. But now…it is all gone."

"You have two beautiful daughters and your wife is still alive and needs you," Laura said.

"Not like me," she thought to herself bitterly. "I can only count dead people."

Laura's words struck a cord. John momentarily forgot his own sadness.

"How about you, dear? How are you getting on?"

"I don't know," Laura replied honestly. "Sometimes I feel like I don't know myself any more, and I don't know what I want. I feel so lost, like I am living in someone else's time and mine stopped a long time ago."

"Don't say that," John said. "You are smart, beautiful and courageous, and this *is* your time. Grab it and hold on to it. You will be fine, and you have to admit it, you are doing a very good job."

"But I feel so stuck, I can't move on," Laura protested. "It feels like I was chosen to carry around the curse of the deaths of the people I loved. I often ask why this happened to me, but I know I'll never get an answer to that."

"No, my dear," responded John. "You make your own luck and you have all the opportunities to make your life a good one."

He was so gentle with his words and a very good listener. Laura felt comfortable around him and was relieved to be sharing her feelings. It felt as if a mountain of snow was drifting from her shoulders.

"Maybe this is the time for me to reconstruct my life," she thought.

The cafe was overflowing and all the tables next to them were filled with people laughing and talking. One conversation in particular caught their attention.

"Do you know why I am so happy?" a man asked his female companion. "Because I keep the company of weird people. Does that make me a weirdo?"

"Yeah, silly," the woman replied, laughing. "But that's why I love you."

Their joy was contagious and John and Laura couldn't help but burst out laughing, too.

Just then, John lifted his head up. He was looking towards someone in the distance and instinctively started waving. Laura followed his gaze to a blonde haired man holding a briefcase in one hand and a cup of coffee in the other.

"There's Adam, one of my friends," John explained. "Actually, he's related to my wife. He's her favourite nephew, I mean was, because she doesn't recognise him anymore." John breathed in sharply before adding: "We get along well when we see each other."

He caught Adam's eye and the young man headed over to join them.

"Is it okay if he sits with us?" John asked.

"Yes, it's absolutely fine."

John moved over to make a space for Adam before politely introducing him to Laura.

Adam was very handsome and seemed bright, dynamic even.

"So, you must be the beautiful designer," he said, looking intently at Laura.

She dropped her head down with embarrassment and John interrupted to stop his young friend saying anything else foolish.

"What are you doing here, Adam?" he asked.

"Sorry," he said, realising his mistake. "Only they mentioned it in the office when I asked for you. They said that you were here with the beautiful designer."

"Okay, that's enough, I get it."

"For your information, I had a meeting round here and I figured I would drop by and see you. How's Kate?"

John sighed and shook his head. "Not good, not at all good."

Adam put his arms on the table and rested his head in his hands. A silence veiled them. Laura looked back and forth between the two men and saw that they were lost in despair. She felt so bad for them.

John's phone buzzed and the trio instinctively got up to walk out. Kissing Laura gently on the cheek, John turned his back on her and went to answer his phone. She thought how vulnerable and alone he looked, there on the street.

"He's a really good man," she mumbled.

She knew how close to the edge he was. But today, weighing the sadness of the others, such as Carla and John's, Laura felt free from the heavy pain and grief that she'd been carrying with her for years.

When she turned around, she saw that Adam was still there. They were facing each other and it would have been rude of Laura to turn away. Adam pulled a packet of cigarettes from his pocket and offered her one. When she refused, he put the packet away.

"Would you like to have breakfast with me tomorrow morning?" he asked.

The invitation took Laura by surprise. Suddenly, as if out of nowhere, a man wanted to spend time with her.

Adam had even surprised himself with his bold proposition.

"We could have a big breakfast at McDonald's, or just a coffee…"

Laura laughed. She felt playful. "What if I don't like coffee?"

"Then you can just have water…and dinner later on."

"Hmmmm, I don't know," Laura replied, frowning.

"Can I do that?" she wondered. She suddenly felt as if she should run away as quickly as she possibly could. But then, she reasoned, she couldn't spend her life constantly running.

Her heart was pumping hard and the words yes and no rolled around her mouth. She couldn't work out which one to let out.

"I will call John's office for your number," Adam went on. He wasn't about to leave any space for Laura's indecision.

"Can I drop you off somewhere?" he asked, glancing at his watch.

"Oh no, my car is parked down the road," Laura replied. "It was very nice meeting you, Adam."

As he strode away, she stood there watching him like a statue, unable to move. Again, she asked herself: "Could I do this? Could I let my past go?" She reasoned that she'd been hurt enough already, had kept herself locked indoors for years, too long. She knew that her family were not going to come to her. Maybe it was time to accept that another life was out there for her.

As she walked towards her car, two little girls holding McDonald's balloons bumped into her. She had to grab one of them to stop her from falling.

"Whoa, darling, watch out," she said.

Climbing into her vehicle, she looked up through her windscreen at the clouds above. Were they clearing? Might the sun break through? As she drove off she ruminated on the weird day that had just passed.

12

Laura's first thoughts upon waking were her deadline *and* her possible date. She wondered whether Adam was going to call her and then grinned, tracing her fingers over her lips as she recalled the sensual dream she'd just enjoyed.

The sky was filled with dark clouds that didn't seem to be letting any light through, and an icy current ran through Laura's body, making her shiver. Before leaving the house she raised her collar and tightened her shawl around her neck.

"Come on, Laura," she said to herself. "You don't have time for this. Move your ass to the car and get going."

She pulled out her car keys from the big pocket of her coat and climbed inside her vehicle. Today was a big day, one that would take her all over London. The marble worktop she'd ordered was still in the workshop ready to be cut, the chandelier she'd wanted was delayed and she had to check up on the handmade blinds she'd commissioned.

The Hamptons were on holiday, and they were expecting to move straight into their mansion once they returned. Laura had to finish up by then.

By the time she got home that evening, she was too tired to even think about getting her dinner ready, let alone of Adam's strange breakfast proposition. Was he out of his mind? The question had been bouncing around in her head all day.

Later, the sound of the phone ringing jolted her awake. It was dark and all the lights were off. It took Laura a while to register where she was. She must've fallen asleep on the sofa. Her eyelids still felt heavy. Releasing a tired groan she reached for the phone on her table.

"Yes."

At first she could hear only heavy breathing. It was John. She braced herself for bad news.

John's voice was trembling so much that it took him some time to get the words out.

"I'm in hospital, dear. I'm losing her."

"I'll come straight over," Laura said, without hesitation.

"No, you don't need to come. I only need someone to talk to."

"Which hospital?"

"King's College, but you don't..."

Laura dropped the phone, grabbed her coat, slipped on her boots and jumped into her car.

The night was a chilly one and Laura was overcome with a strange feeling. All her energy and hope from the day had been sucked from her.

Arriving at the hospital's reception area, she breathlessly asked for John's wife.

"Second floor, room 201, follow the blue line," the lady behind the desk informed her.

Laura strode towards the lift. An elderly couple clutching sticks lumbered in front of her, slowing her down. When she finally reached the right room, she found the door half open ready for her arrival. John was seated by his wife's bed, he was clutching her hand and his eyes were glued to her.

"I can't do it," Laura murmured. "I can't steal his final minutes with her."

She found the visitors' room and took a seat. A TV was fixed high on the wall and she gazed at the images on it without interest. Near to her, a curly-haired woman was rocking back and forth, her head buried in her hands. The young boy next to her put his arm around her shoulder in a futile attempt to offer comfort.

Laura inched up her seat to be closer to them.

"I hope you don't mind me asking," she said to the boy in a low voice. "But what's happened?"

The boy looked directly at Laura. His blue eyes were red from crying. He was holding too much pain for one so young.

"It's my brother…" the boy said.

"…My son," the sobbing woman interjected. She twisted a piece of tissue paper around in her hands. "He's had a heart transplant. The doctors don't know yet whether his body will accept it."

As she spoke, her other son covered his face with both hands. Tears rolled down the woman's face. Laura moved back, unable to find any words to say. She felt her heartbeat quicken as her mind jumped from one room to another. Here, the line between life and death was so easily crossed. The thought brought Laura out in a cold sweat. She stood up and ran from the visitors' room and into the hall, where the fluorescent lighting dazzled her eyes. Feeling dizzy, she stumbled towards a nurse.

"Are you okay, madam?"

"I need air," Laura gasped.

Grabbing her arm, the nurse led Laura to the staff room, where she ducked her head out of the large open window and took a deep breath in. The nurse offered her glass of water, which she gladly took, taking a big gulp from it.

"Do you feel better now?" the nurse asked.

Laura nodded and said she needed to find her friend. When she arrived back at room 201, she found John outside, walking up and down the corridor with slow, unsteady strides.

"What happened? How is she?" Laura asked.

John simply shook his head. He swallowed the lump in his throat and said quietly: "She had a stroke and she's not coming out of it."

"Don't give up," Laura said. "She will be fine."

"No," John replied simply. "She's weak and she doesn't want to fight any more…"

His voice trailed off. He seemed to be gathering the strength to continue.

"I can't bear to look at her. It hurts me here," he said, forming a fist and placing it on his heart. "She used to be such a happy and beautiful soul. All of this seems terribly unreal."

Laura gripped John's arm, but part of her was still thinking of the mother and her desperately ill son, both praying for a miracle. Unable to hold back her tears, she buried her head in John's chest. She was crying for John, crying for the mother, crying for Matt and the little one she'd lost.

***

Two days later, John's wife slipped away on what was a bright, cold February day. The icy air seemed to hold the bitterness of death. John had lost the love of his life, but at the same time he was free of the ghost of his wife, a person he'd barely recognised any more.

Laura went to the funeral, which only added to her pain. The smell of the graveyard was so familiar to her. As she walked among the gravestones the images of the caskets containing her loved ones were fresh in her mind. When she joined the funeral party around the hole in the ground where John's wife was to be buried, she was struck by the harsh reality of the proceedings…just another dead body waiting to be eaten by the earth.

"I'm so sorry," she said to John, knowing that her words were not nearly enough to console him. John nodded in response, closing his eyes, which were circled with black. In those moments, silence was more fitting than words.

"I will try to look at the different colours of the sky," John said with a weak smile. A week on from the funeral, he had decided to fly out to see his daughters.

"I just want to be a granddad for a while," he said.

He was in his office, taking things from his desk drawers and boxing them up. Laura stood watching him, trying to swallow the pain of separation from the man who, in a short space of time, had become such an important part of her life.

"It's been an honour to work with you," she told him.

"You are a very good friend, Laura."

"I'm going to miss you so much," she replied, unable to mask the desolation in her eyes.

"You take care of yourself, kid," John soothed, pulling Laura towards him, feeling her wet tears on his shirt. "And catch your time, darling...promise?"

Laura nodded. She was about to be left alone again, and without John's presence she couldn't even feel enthusiastic about finishing her project at the mansion. She had a new job lined up, but it had failed to feed her curiosity.

Leaving John's office, she felt intensely uneasy and lonely. She walked restlessly, feeling as bare as the leafless trees. It was so cold that it was as if the city's smile had been swiped away. Just when she'd thought that her life was beginning to flow in a normal direction, something had happened to shift it out of balance. John's weak gaze, the beloved son on the threshold of death, the smell of the graveyard...they were all fixed to her memory like nails in a cross.

13

THAT night in bed, Laura found it difficult to get comfortable. The pillow felt like a hard rock beneath her head. Her body was longing for sleep but it was betrayed by her mind. It jumped from one thought to the next, causing her to panic.

Rolling over, she pulled her head out from beneath the covers and flicked on her bedside light. The clock had already ticked past midnight. Feeling the need for some fresh air she trudged to the window and opened it wide, filling her thirsty lungs with big gulps of air. She lifted her gaze up to the full moon, which magically lifted her spirits. In her mind's eye she started to replace the stars that were hidden from view by patches of cloud.

Climbing back into bed, she reached for her laptop and switched it on. It was her small attempt to rid herself of loneliness.

An explosion of messages, accompanied with names and photos, spread out from her computer screen. She pushed her back harder against the headboard, distancing herself from the monitor. She was thrust into the flames of an unusual panic. She could barely even remember entering her details into a dating website.

"What did I get myself into?" she thought. "How could I have acted so immaturely?"

She had opened herself up to the world, but the response seemed unreal. She didn't know what to do about it and felt defeated, lost.

"I have to try," she told herself firmly.

She turned her attention back to the screen and started reading the propositions she'd received. Sadly, none of then appealed. The world of internet dating was new to her and she felt embarrassed to have entered the charade. The strangers who'd contacted her had the potential to cause her more trauma.

Taking a deep breath, she started to delete the requests one by one. But one message caught her attention and her fingers hovered over the delete button as she read it.

> *"Dear Laura, my name is David. You don't know me but something really weird happened to me and I have been looking for you ever since. When I recovered from the shock of finally seeing your picture, I simply had to get in touch. For nearly a year now, I have seen your face in my dreams.*
>
> *I know I am just a stranger to you, but please believe me; you MUST come to America to meet me because I have something important that I need to tell you."*

"What an idiot," Laura muttered under her breath. "Who does he think I am?" Putting aside her laptop she lay down and hugged her pillow. Even though she had already dismissed the email, it had irritated her so much that she found it difficult to fall asleep.

***

"Wow, it hurts," Laura gasped, putting her hand on her tummy, where a slitting was tearing through her. She didn't know whether it was day or night; her heavy curtains were blocking the morning sun.

"Oh, I am pregnant," she said, surprising herself. She felt the baby start to kick. The jabs were becoming stronger and she was now in agony. Beneath her still hand, her tummy bounced.

"Help, help…my baby wants to come out," she cried loudly. "Please, somebody help."

Then her voice became weak, as if it was being pulled back into her mouth. She closed her eyes, started to drift into unconsciousness...

When she came round again, the first thing she did was look down at her tummy.

"It's flat," she said. "Where is my baby?"

She heard the sound of someone running nearby and caught a glimpse of a child racing through the half open door.

"Wait, don't go," she called as the steps grew fainter.

Grasping the bedframe, she tried to push herself up but her legs were like jelly.

Someone knocked on the door. Laura squinted at the digital clock. 8am. *Who could be calling at this time?* Her mouth released a tired yawn as she looked down at her toned tummy once again.

"Oh, I was dreaming," she signed. "What a dream!"

Still dressed in her pyjamas, she padded downstairs to open the door.

"Mimo!" she exclaimed, gazing fondly at the white ball of fur in Sylvia's arms before turning her attention to his owners. Behind his wife, Martin was hauling a big case into the back of their car.

Laura's sleepy eyes were now wide open.

"We're going to our daughter's house in the south of France for a couple of weeks," Sylvia explained. "Her baby is due this week and we want to be there for her. I know it's short notice, but our dog sitter's let us down. Could you look after Mimo for a couple of weeks?...Martin said not to bother you, but I don't want to send her to kennels."

"Actually, it's a splendid idea," Laura said. "Mimo will be my special guest."

Ducking down, she pulled the little dog from Sylvia's arms. "We are going to be great company for each other," she said, nuzzling her face into Mimo's fur.

Mimo wagged his tail in appreciation and Laura felt very

happy to have been given a temporary present. In fact, it was one of the best things that had happened to her recently.

"I hope you will like it here, boy," she said, setting him down in the direction of her hallway. He moved inside a little stiffly as he looked around and sniffed his unfamiliar surroundings. Laura followed him with her eyes, smiling. His presence had lifted her mood so much. She went into the kitchen and turned on the kettle, eager to start the day.

***

The excitement of having Mimo around gave Laura the confidence to unseal the envelope containing the details of her new project. She felt lost without John, but she had promised him that she would take a look at it. So that afternoon she regretfully left her new companion behind and went to see the building that she had been asked to transform. The traffic was heavy and it took her a full hour to get there. Something was bothering her, but she couldn't put her finger on what was making her feel so bad. She felt lazy and unenthusiastic as she padded around the building, jotting ideas down in her notebook. She worked quickly and on her way home she decided to stop in Greenwich and go for a walk.

The noise from a passing party boat drew her to the edge of the river. She heard laughter and saw the shadowy shapes of people dancing. It gave Laura a view into a very different world.

"I want to be like that," she thought.

Tiny drops of rain brushed against her face. Her fellow walkers speeded up in order to get away from the shower, abandoning the river path. Laura jammed her hand inside her pocket and pulled out her phone to check the time.

8pm.

Then she saw the date.

March 20th.

"Oh, perfect, it's my birthday today," she said out loud, looking up towards the sky. "Okay, let's just pretend that this party is for me."

Running her hands through her hair, she followed the boat until it disappeared around the bend of the river.

"Today, I am 41," she sighed.

The number frightened her. Coupled with her loneliness came a feeling of being ancient. Her initial enthusiasm for rebuilding her career was fading. After all, she had no one to share the joy of her success with.

Moving away from the riverside, she felt tired and empty.

"What a life...what a way to celebrate my birthday..."

Walking on, she didn't feel the need to hurry. She had no one waiting for. No husband or boyfriend, no children...just a furry dog, her temporary houseguest.

"That reminds me," she thought. "Better stop off and buy some food for him."

In the shop, she picked up a bottle of red wine for herself as a birthday present. Back at home, she heard Mimo jumping and scratching at the door as soon as he heard the sound of her key turning. When she stepped inside she felt his fur brushing against her legs.

"I missed you too, boy, but guess what? It's my birthday. Do you think we can celebrate together?"

She fed the dog and then poured a glass of wine for herself, taking a seat at her long dining table.

Looking around her perfect home, happier memories from the past challenged her.

"I have an announcement to make," she said, lifting up her glass. "Happy 41st birthday to me. Cheers to my years of devotion to this ridiculous life."

With that, Laura laughed hysterically until her giggles transformed into violent sobs. She crossed her arms on the table and sank her head into them. She felt exhausted and remained seated until pain crammed into every inch of her stiffened body. Eventually, she dragged her feet upstairs where her enormous bed was waiting for her.

***

As Laura made herself a coffee the following morning, Mimo fought with her handbag, which she'd left on the sofa.

"What are you doing, boy?" she asked.

She realised what had piqued his interest. Her phone inside it was dancing and he was trying to get it out. She quickly pulled it free and swiped to answer.

"Hello," she said.

"Hi, this is Adam. I hope you remember me?"

Of course she remembered. Adam was one of the few people with whom she'd had any social contact lately, and they had exchanged a nod of recognition when they'd seen each other at John's wife's funeral.

"The breakfast man! How could I forget? Breakfast invitations aren't that common."

"Well, then allow me to change it to a dinner invitation. Don't let this poor man live with his guilt."

Laura laughed and then paused. She was thinking about how to phrase her words; she wanted to be polite and not say anything that she might later regret.

"Adam, thank you, but tomorrow I have plans to visit an art gallery."

"Then allow me to come along and be your body guard. Afterwards, I'll take you to the best place in London to eat dinner."

Laura took a deep breath before replying, "Seems like an irresistible proposition."

"I'm so happy," Adam said, with genuine gratitude.

Laura hung up the phone and sauntered around the house,

tracing her fingers around her lips, which had formed into a mischievous smile.

"Hmmmm, maybe some spice in my life wouldn't be such a bad idea," she mumbled and strode up to her bedroom to survey her wardrobe.

"This one, or this…or maybe this," she said, sifting through her outfits. She threw the few she deemed as potentials for her date over a wide chair by the window. "I'll decide later," she said to herself.

Closing the door of her mirrored wardrobe, she stared at her reflection, taking in her full length. Shaking off her loose cardigan, she slipped the slim straps of her camisole off her shoulders to expose her braless breasts. Scooping them into her hands, she closed her eyes; her body felt full of fire. Her nipples hardened under the light touch of her fingers and she opened her mouth to let out a long, slow groan. Oh, how she longed for a man's hands. She could picture them in her mind's eye, feel them on the curve of her stomach as her innards melted to lava. As her breath quickened, she moved her hand down and ran a finger across her clitoris, then up into her vagina.

"Oh yes…yes."

The lava inside her was boiling. "Oh, it feels so good," she cried out, her finger working faster as her thighs tightened against each other.

"Oh…yeah…oh," she cried out loudly, her body turning to jelly.

Inhaling, she opened her eyes. In the mirror, she saw what a mess she was. Her breasts were hanging out of her top, her knickers were halfway down her knees.

"Oh shit," she said, pulling up the lacy material and running quickly to the bathroom.

14

Laura glanced at her watch and peeked out at the street from behind her bedroom curtain. She saw Adam pull up in a green Jaguar – he'd arrived right on time. Laura was reminded again how handsome he was and quickly withdrew from the window to finish applying her makeup. She put on some pink lipstick and smiled at her reflection in the mirror; the blue Dior dress she'd finally settled on perfectly showed off her figure. Her hair was pulled back and diamond earrings added sparkle to her look. She slipped on some black heels and grabbed the Chanel bag that her mum had bought her from Harrods years earlier. Stepping outside, she felt attractive and hungry for everything. She hadn't felt like this for such a long time.

***

Adam smiled when he saw Laura walking towards him. He was looking good too, freshly shaven and dressed an elegant black suit.

"You look stunning," he said, getting out of his car.

"Thank you," Laura blushed.

He opened the passenger door and Laura climbed into the car, getting a whiff of her date's expensive cologne. Pulling on her seatbelt, she fixed her gaze on the window indicating that she was ready to hit the road. Adam jumped into his own seat, gave her a gentle smile and started the car.

***

The art gallery used to be one of Laura's favourite places in London. Here she got to peek into the minds of some completely different people via their work. She hadn't visited for more than three years, and remembered the last time, when she had argued with Matt over whether to attend an exhibition opening or go to a party that one of his friends was throwing to celebrate his promotion.

That evening, the work of a new American talent was being presented. Looking around the space, Laura felt exhilarated to be back at a place that was connected to her former life.

She was so engrossed in viewing the pictures that she almost forgot about Adam's presence at her side, though his hand never left her arm.

"Aren't they amazing?" he said.

"Yes, they are," Laura replied, smiling up at her date.

She stopped before a larger than life picture of woman dressed in a greyish white dress that flowed down, becoming one with the air around her bare feet. The image captivated her. The subject's hands were outstretched and her penetrating gaze seemed to speaking to Laura directly.

"Laura, come here...take my hand."

The woman's face seemed familiar, almost alive. To Laura, this was more than an image - the painting seemed to grasp her soul. It was drawing her in with an unfathomable force.

"Laura, are you okay?" Adam asked, touching her shoulder from behind.

She turned to face him; her eyes were far away, she seemed in a daze.

"Er, yes," she replied. "But please hold my hand."

"Was I hallucinating?" she wondered.

"This is an interesting picture," Adam said. "The artist has put a lot of soul into it. His named is David Boyer. Have you ever heard of him?"

Laura knew she'd come across the name before, but where?

The painting was dated, and it was less than a year old. Looking at it intently again she gasped, raising her hand up to her mouth. The image of the woman had changed. Now her back was turned and her face was in profile.

What the...?

Gathering herself, Laura turned to walk away from the picture, her delusion, but her mind was still fixed in its frame.

After the gallery, Adam drove her to the restaurant. As he parked up, Laura could see which one it was and smiled.

"I told you that this place was unusual," Adam said, with obvious satisfaction.

The restaurant was built out of stone and surrounded by exotic trees. The yellow glow of sunken lights gave it a magical feel.

Adam gently touched Laura's back as they headed inside. She looked up at him and they smiled at each other. Everything about this place was glamorous and it felt so inviting. Laura's presence didn't go unnoticed.

"Look who's just barged in here," said a woman. She oozed affluence and was wearing a black dress, a sparkly silver shawl and drop earring that touched her shoulders. Her black hair was loose and wavy. She was in her 50s but could have easily competed with a woman half her age. She had a smack of red carpet glam, could have stepped straight from the pages of Vogue magazine.

"Laura, I haven't seen you in such a long time," she said, opening her arms and pulling her close for a hug.

"It must be around eight years. It's great to see you, Irina, you look so good."

"Thanks. I get younger as my husband gets older."

Irina was Russian and owned the restaurant. Her husband was a French businessman.

"You look good, too," she told Laura, before leaning in to whisper something in her ear. "He's handsome. Is he your new partner?"

Laura managed a dry smile. She didn't want to go through her list of bereavements.

"Who is the lucky man?" Irina asked again, this time so both of them could hear.

"His name is Adam," said Laura.

"Pleasure to meet you, Adam, and are you aware that you have by your side a very talented designer? She's the one who created my magical cave here."

"Whaaaat," Adam replied, his eyes widening in astonishment.

Laura took her mind back eight years, to when she was working on the restaurant. The combination of stone, glass and water features made the place feel otherworldly. The walls were stone and spaces had been carved within them to store the restaurant's expensive wine collection. Light dropped from the walls, resembling icy stalagmite forms. A wide glass staircase, with water flowing from each side, led to the second level of the restaurant. Walking up it felt like stepping over a waterfall.

After a brief conversation, Irina took Adam and Laura to their table and wished them an enjoyable evening.

"This place is incredible," Adam said, continuing to look around him. Then he turned his attention to the wine list.

"Do you like Chardonnay?" he asked.

But Laura was so overwrought that she didn't register the question.

Lost between the lines of the menu, the image of the woman in the gallery was coming alive in her mind.

"Hmmm…what…sorry?"

"What about Chardonnay?"

"Oh, yeah, great," Laura smiled.

"I am so impressed by your work," Adam went on. "You are truly blessed to have this talent."

Laura's lips curved into a sly smile. Adam couldn't stop looking at her.

"Your eyes are so mesmerising," he said, causing his date to blush uncomfortably.

Once the waiter had come over with their wine and taken their food order, Laura decided to flip the conversation to the subject of Adam.

"So what about you?" she asked. "How do you spend your days?"

"I'm a lawyer, you could say it's a family tradition, we follow each other's steps. Some of us defend and some of go chasing criminals, so we've been on both sides of the law, so to speak, for generations. I am more involved in adoption cases and work with social services. But this must be boring for you…" Adam trailed off.

"Oh no, not at all. Finding the right home for a child is very noble."

"Yes, it's a very good feeling. When you see a little boy or girl with their new parents the feeling is indescribable. You know that their entire future has just changed."

"Do you have kids?" Laura asked, suddenly remembering that John had mentioned that Adam was divorced.

"Yes," Adam replied. The question caused a sudden change in his mood. He looked away and took a sharp breath in, the action of someone who has been under tremendous strain.

"I have a daughter, she's ten," he said, clearing his throat. "Tomorrow I have promised to take her to the aquarium." He barely smiled as he spoke and Laura found it impossible to tell whether he was excited or sad.

A strained silence passed between the couple. Adam grabbed the ring he was wearing and started twisting it with his finger nervously.

Laura took another sip of wine, her gaze asking a silent question.

"My wife and I are getting a divorce," Adam went on. "But we can't reach a settlement. We are both too strong headed, too proud. Sometimes we are fools to ourselves."

As he spoke he ran his palms over the table and started tapping his fingers on it - another nervous habit.

"I'm so sorry," Laura soothed. "It must be so hard to go through all of this."

She could tell that even though this evening was his attempt to escape what was happening in his life - to contemplate starting a new one even - the separation from his daughter and the divorce were playing heavily on his mind.

"It hurts a lot," Adam admitted. "The hardest part is being away from them. I spend every minute wondering what they're doing. We may be bound by strong chains of love and a shared history, but we are divided by a wall of stupidity and pig-headedness."

Adam appeared to be looking at Laura, but his mind was somewhere else.

"At least he can talk about his family," Laura thought. She wondered about giving him an example of what it really feels like to lose your family, but no, it was too depressing. Besides, Laura's feelings were incomparable with Adam's. She'd lost her husband and son forever, while his wife and daughter were just a few miles away.

"Anyway, more about you," Adam said. "Any brothers or sisters?"

It was a dull question, but he already knew the rest of Laura's story. She was 'the beautiful widow' - that's how they'd described her at John's office.

"No, I'm an only child."

A strange thought crossed Laura's mind. If she did have any siblings, would they be dead now too? A cold shiver shot through her body. Her shoulders trembled and the muscles in her face tightened. She took a deep breath and forced herself not to think about that any more.

"And I'm the only one left from my family," she added.

Just then, the waiter brought the food. It provided a welcome distraction from their rather sombre conversation.

When they'd finished eating, they stepped out on to the balcony and Adam asked the waiter to bring their desserts to them there.

As Adam looked at her hungrily, Laura's gaze drifted down and then away, up to the sky where she tried to pick out images of the night.

"It's a perfect spot," Adam said.

"Do you see anything?"

"As much as I keep trying, I can't see a damn star."

It was nearly midnight by the time they left the restaurant. When Adam had dropped Laura off, they stood for a moment by the metal gate of her house.

"Thank you for being my date tonight," Adam said.

"It's been a wonderful evening."

Gently, Adam slid his hands over Laura's arms and tried to pull her towards him, but she remained frozen. She was smoke; the fire wasn't there.

Adam was such a handsome man; in fact, he was everything a woman could want. But he wasn't for her. She still felt so absent. And while she was on the way towards accepting a new way of life, Adam was wrestling with whether he should hold on to what he had. He belonged to someone else. As for Laura? For now she belonged to a dream only.

She looked down, watching her hands tighten around the handle of her bag. Her whole body was tense.

"Look, Adam, you're a wonderful man and we're both looking to find love again, but please don't let go of something that you already have. Sometimes, a steep step backwards is worth it for the people we love."

Adam closed his eyes, nodded and sighed.

"Thank you again for the good time you gave me tonight."

With that, he kissed Laura firmly on the cheek and went back to his car. Laura dashed inside the house and leaned her back against the closed door. She stayed there for a moment, relieved to have ended her first official date after such a long time. She forced herself not to think about what she'd left behind.

Mimo came rushing towards her, rubbing against her feet, ready to be in her company.

"I had a date, boy, but you are the best one for me so far."

Laura crouched down, patting Mimo's head as his tail danced happily.

With the dog following close behind, she walked through to the living room and opened the French doors on to the garden. Leaning against the frame, she realised that for now, only the silence of the night would provide her with the peace of mind she craved. Closing her eyes, she crossed her arms over herself and hugged herself tightly.

"Is there anyone out there for me?" she whispered.

She thought about the mysterious message she'd received from the man in the States. What a joke that was. But she had to admit something to herself. Regardless of how her date had just concluded, or who had sent her that strange email, she felt like a different person. She had the sense that something would soon change.

Laura stayed there for a few minutes staring up at the sky. It was only the sound of Mimo growling by her feet that brought her back to earth again. He was staring at her, his eyes pleading for something.

"Oh Mimo, you must be so hungry. Sorry boy, I forgot your dinner... come on, follow me."

Laura hurried to the kitchen and quickly filled Mimo's plate with tinned dog food.

"There, boy, enjoy your dinner. Now I need to have a bath."

Before Laura had even finished her sentence, Mimo had sunk his face into the food. Leaving him to it, she padded upstairs to her bedroom, got undressed and dashed naked into the bathroom. She'd already showered that day, but she wanted to wash away the burden of all the emotions she no longer wanted to haul around.

While the water was running she lay in the bath and squeezed a jasmine scented body wash over her body. The smell was dazzling. Running her fingers over the cold gel, she started lathering the soap over her body. The cascade of water from the taps splashed against her toes and the steam from it formed a thin mist around her. She closed her eyes, and the image that formed in her mind was one of cosy white clouds. As the water level rose, covering and tickling her, hundreds of butterflies fluttered inside her. Pushing both her legs under the water, she grabbed some foam and ran it over her neck and down to her breasts. The water reached the top of the bath as her hands moved quickly down from her belly to between her legs.

"Oh, it's so hot," she cried as slight waves formed on the surface of the water.

A mass of lava began to boil inside her clitoris. White foam covered her mouth and her heavy breaths sent bubbles flying upwards. The waves moved faster as her body erupted, ready to explode beneath the water. Pushing her fingers deep inside, she pressed her bottom down, creating an arch with her body. Her head ducked under the water, sending a wave out over the edge of the bath and on to the floor. Such was her ecstasy that Laura didn't even notice the minor flood she was creating. A high voltage current travelled from her the folds of her sex right down to her toes. Feeling her limbs go weak, she struggled to catch her breath before opening her eyes. Water was still flowing out of the bath like a waterfall.

"That was incredible," Laura murmured, moving to turn the tap off.

She closed her eyes again, extending the moment until finally scrambling out of the water, leaving the scent of her guilty pleasure behind in the hot steam.

***

Laura spent the following morning lounging around in her living room. She flicked through some magazines, enjoyed the warm sun that was invading the room from the open window. In the background, music from the TV pulsed in her ear.

She was just about to open a new mag when the buzzing sound of her mobile changed the direction of her hand. Carla's name flashed up. Laura smiled before swiping the phone to answer.

"My Tom's back from India," said Carla, sounding hysterically excited. "He's home."

"Such good news," said Laura, mirroring her friend's happiness.

"We are all chatting in the kitchen," Carla continued. "I can't believe how grown up he looks. Larry is cooking his favourite meal later and I am making pancakes while he tells us lots of interesting stories about India."

Laura could hear the sound of chatter and clatter in the background. Carla, it seemed, had the busiest kitchen in town.

"Now, I hope you will accept his new status of grown up son," Laura chided.

"Hmmm...nah, he is still my baby," Carla giggled in response.

After Laura had hung up, she spent a few seconds staring at the receiver as if she was still holding the happy voices of Carla and her family. How ridiculous the noise from the TV now seemed; it would never fill the empty house. Tightening the belt of her kimono, she walked into her office. She'd started sketching some designs for her new project and got out her notebook to take a look. But after gazing at two random pages, she realised that her concentration was zero. Putting her work away, she wandered over to her computer and logged on.

"Let's see what's new today," she said before sighing: "Oh, nothing!"

She felt drawn to look at the strange message she'd received a few days earlier from a man named David.

"You MUST come," he'd written. Laura said the words out loud, feeling their urgency. She stared at them until her vision blurred and the letters twisted out of view. Then something made her focus her attention again. She leaned closer to the screen. A pair of green eyes appeared, staring back at Laura for a mere split second.

"Wow!" Laura exclaimed, shooting back into her seat. Her heart was pounding and she quickly turned her computer off.

"What was that?" she said, holding a hand against her chest. She ran from her office and up the stairs to her bedroom, where she fell into bed. With her face pressed against the pillow, her breaths quickened. The image from the screen was still inside her head.

"What is happening to me?" she wondered. "Am I going crazy?"

She rolled over until she was looking directly up at the ceiling, then she sprang up. "I'm not crazy!" she announced and forced herself to go back down to her office. She switched her computer back on, focused her eyes. The message was still there, nothing else. She reached out to touch the screen, imagining the intense eyes she'd just seen appear there.

"What is going on with me?" she thought. Her head was growing heavy and she felt dizzy. "Is my mind producing illusions?" The question forced her into a snap decision to leave the house before she lost her mind completely.

"I have to find some serenity and learn to control my emotions," she said out loud.

Her gaze fell on Mimo, who had climbed on her office chair and was trying to dig his way under the blanket she'd left on it.

"How do you feel about me kidnapping you and taking you away from this madness?" she said. "We'll have a nice relaxing time together, just you and me."

She logged back on and after a quick search found just what she'd been looking for: a room in a beautiful sandstone self-catering cottage with no restrictions on pets. She clicked to book it immediately, feeling an enormous sense of relief. This would be a perfect escape.

15

FOLLOWING a sleepless night, Laura rose early and quickly packed a bag full of comfortable clothes for her and one filled with enough food for Mimo. Dressed in black velvet trousers and a cotton t-shirt, she climbed into her car, letting Mimo jump into the back seat.

It was late afternoon by the time she arrived at the cottage, which was five miles away from the village of Hoarthwithy in Herefordshire. Stretching her legs as she got out of the car, she gazed at her surroundings. Everywhere was so quiet, fresh and pristine.

At the entrance to the cottage, Laura was greeted by a petite woman with jet-black hair. She introduced herself as Christina. Laura noticed how she was dressed for the country in a fleecy sweater decorated with pictures of snow leopards.

"I'm sure you're going to like it here," she said. "It's incredibly calm."

"Just what I need!" Laura replied with a smile.

"Another family is staying in the cottage," Christina explained. "You'll be sharing a kitchen with them. They came down yesterday, from London too.

"And we are two," Laura said, dropping her gaze down to Mimo, who was scampering about by her feet and wagging his tail enthusiastically.

"Do you like biking?" Christina enquired.

"I haven't tried since I was a kid."

"Well, you can now. There are bikes in the garage and many routes to try in the area. Oh, and we have a brilliant local pub, The Harp Inn – it's next to the River Wye.

Laura thanked Christina for the information and went to get her bags from the car. As soon as she opened her boot, Christina called out to someone called Gary. A shaved head duly poked around the door of the cottage's garage. "New guest?" said its owner. "I'm coming."

"Gary is the handyman of the house," Christina explained. "He'll start a fire on the stove if you're cold or would like to cook over it."

Wiping his dusty hands over his jeans, Gary came over to greet the new guest. "Welcome to our beautiful countryside," he said. "I hope you will like it here…it's a very healing place."

"That's why I came," Laura mumbled, more to herself than Gary.

"Let me help you with your bags. I'll take them up to your room."

Inside, Laura saw that the entire cottage had been furnished with period antiques and oriental rugs. The floorboards were dark wood and the ceilings were supported by exposed beams.

Up in her room, Laura ducked her head out of her tiny window. The back garden was full of exotic, tropical plants and a stone barbeque was surrounded by wooden garden furniture. Beyond that, the cottage commanded some of the best views in Herefordshire.

Laura was delighted with her choice and followed Christina on a guided tour of the property.

★★★

The kitchen was large with a stunning original brick arch, granite work surfaces and a wood burning stove with a slate hearth. French doors opened out on to the patio, and a big American style fridge stood in the corner.

"Oh, and before I go," Christina said. "We have an internet connection, but the computer of the house isn't working, so if you need to log on I can lend you my laptop."

"That's not necessary," Laura replied, thinking to herself how the very reason she'd come to the cottage was to escape her computer. "I'm sure I'm not going to need it."

"The mobile reception here isn't always good, either," Christina added, "but you can use the landline if you need to."

"Thanks," Laura replied. "But I'm not going to need that either."

She went up to her bedroom, which was furnished with dark wooden drawers and a matching wardrobe that contrasted well with the bright white windowpanes. She sat on the mattress, testing its softness.

"Very comfortable," she mumbled before turning to Mimo. "Now, I have to make you comfortable, boy," she said, getting up to unpack the blanket she'd brought to use as his bed.

She felt the need to freshen up and quickly rid herself of her clothes and got under the shower. Closing her eyes, she felt her muscles relax as the warm water cascaded over her body.

Wrapped in a bath towel, her wet hair dripping over her naked shoulders, she went to open her bedroom window.

"Hmmmm, it's so peaceful," she said, inhaling the fresh air and taking a moment to appreciate the stunning view. The dazzling lights and throb of London felt like years away.

"Tomorrow I can explore," she decided as she climbed into bed. It wasn't long before she fell into a deep, undisturbed sleep.

***

As Laura padded down the stairs the following morning, she heard a woman's voice.

"Stop jumping on the bed, both of you. It's time to get ready for breakfast."

"One more round, Mum," a child replied amid giggles.

Laura realised it was the family that Christina had mentioned the day before.

Once in the kitchen, she started going through all the cupboards and doors to familiarise herself with where everything was. Then she grabbed a mug and put the kettle on.

Two children, a girl and a boy, both blessed with adorable faces, entered the kitchen, closely followed by a woman with red curly hair and a lovely figure. The little ones immediately made a beeline for Mimo.

"Can we play with him?" the girl asked in a pleading voice as she looked up at Laura.

"Yes, of course," Laura replied with a smile. "Mimo will be delighted to have your company, but first you have to tell him your names."

"I'm Nick and I'm seven," butted in the boy, flashing a toothless grin at the dog.

"I'm Pamela and I'm four," the girl said. "Can we take him now?"

"I'm sure he'd love to go and play in the garden with you," Laura reassured her.

The pair stormed out, chattering about their new friend and beckoning Mimo to run after them.

Then it was their mum's turn to give a name.

"I'm Julie," she said to Laura. "It's so nice to meet you."

The two women looked towards the kitchen door as a heavily built man with grey eyes entered the room.

"That's my husband, Mark," Julie explained.

Once the introductions were over, Laura found out that the couple were both teachers from London. She gave very little away about herself, telling them only that she was an interior designer from the same city. She left out the bit about being a widow, couldn't bear to see any more pitying faces.

"It's our first time here and the views look amazing," Julie said, gazing out of the window.

"We definitely picked the right place to enjoy our Easter holiday," Mark added.

The kettle had boiled and Laura went to grab a couple more mugs for her new friends.

"Leave that," Julie said. "I'll make my special tea. I don't think you will have tried it before."

She was just about to get started when Mark butted in. "Why don't you let me do that," he said. "You two get to know each other."

"Okay," Laura smiled, and she followed Julie into the living room where they perched by the window and ducked their heads to watch the children playing outside. Nick and Pamela were busy throwing a tennis ball for Mimo, who enthusiastically chased it. Then the pair exploded into laughter and rolled on the grass, with the dog jumping on to them.

"Your kids are lovely," Laura commented.

"Yes they are," Julie smiled. "They're a real blessing. I can't thank God enough for what I have."

For a few minutes, a strained silence passed between the two women. Laura sensed that Julie was hesitating over an obvious question. She wanted to ask Laura about her own family, see whether she had a husband or children, but it obviously wasn't the case. Surely, if she had either of those she wouldn't be at the cottage alone.

"Tea's ready," Mark said, entering the living room with the drinks on a tray and breaking the awkward silence in the process.

Laura took one of the steaming mugs and thanked Mark for it.

Taking a sip, she noted that Julie had been right about it being like nothing she had tried before.

"It's so refreshing and smells so good," she said. "What's in there?"

"It's called Masala chai," Julie explained. "It's an Indian recipe and it's flavoured with cinnamon, ginger, cocoa and milk. I learned how to make it when I visited Asia. It helps with the flu, but hopefully you won't be getting that while you're here!"

After they had finished the lovely refreshing tea, Laura went to wash their mugs up in the sink while Julie and Mark joined their children in the garden.

Looking at their happy, smiling faces from the window, Laura's mind flicked back. What if her life hadn't been broken by fate? Would she have...? Tears pooled her eyes as a big lump tightened in her throat. She'd hungered all her life for a family. Had it been too much to ask? She imagined the sensation of two little arms coiling around her neck, and then stronger arms gathering mother and child up into a tight embrace. Laura gave into her emotions as she imagined how wonderful this would feel. Then she felt guilty for picturing something that she would never be able to have. She had allowed herself to feel the future calling, imagined that destiny had plans for her - perhaps the feel of a man's touch - but now she realised that it was just a joke, a trick of the mind.

"Forget about that now," her inner voice told her. "You did what you had to do, restarted your career, made new friends, went on a date, but don't expect that some magical end to your pain will somehow drop from the sky. Accept, accept, accept. You lost everything and never will get it back."

"Is Mimo going to eat breakfast with us?" asked Nick, interrupting Laura's inner voice.

"Does he eat cereals? chimed Pamela.

Laura managed to dry her tears and plant a smile on her face. As she thought about how to answer Nick and Pamela's questions, Gary entered the kitchen carrying a pile of chopped wood and whistling a tune. He'd come to set up the fire, which immediately drew the kids' attention away. They were captivated as it started to flicker and crackle inside the mouth of the stove.

"You mustn't go near it," Gary warned. "You don't want to burn yourselves."

Laura found herself gazing into the flames too; once again she was wrestling with her past and future.

"Would you like anything from the market?" Julie asked her. "Mark's going."

Laura turned towards her new friend. Her face was numb and her eyes still carried the image of the burning flames.

"Want what?" she asked.

"Anything from the market," repeated Laura.

"I don't know…hmmmm…maybe some…"

"Don't worry," Julie responded softly. "I'll ask Mark to pick up some extra vegetables. I'll cook for us all."

As she thought about whether to accept Julie's kind offer, Laura glanced around the room. Gary and Mark were laughing about something and the children were running in and out, with Mimo in tow. The atmosphere was electric. For a few seconds, Laura almost felt as if she blended in with this happy domestic scene.

"Don't screw it up, Laura," she told herself. "Not this time. Just forget everything and enjoy the moment."

Over the coming days, Laura and her new family got on so well. Julie happened to be a wonderful cook and never set the table without asking Laura whether she wanted to join them. The children proved to be the best companions that Mimo had ever had, and every morning Gary would come in whistling the same melody as he set up the stove.

At lunch, the gang would head out to the river with a picnic. Julie took care of every detail, filling the basket with delicious sandwiches, croissants, a strawberry cheesecake, sparkling wine and blankets in case anyone wanted to lie on the grass.

Laura also adhered to Christina's suggestion to go biking and it was the best fun she'd had in a long time. Peddling through the woods, she felt as if she was entering the magic tomb of nature.

Back at the cottage, she felt very comfortable in Mark and Julie's company. They talked mainly about work: the trials and pleasures of teaching and Laura's recent design projects, tiptoeing around any personal questions. In fact, Mark and Julie never asked Laura about her life, which suited her. She was content to live in the present, after all, that was why she had come away.

***

On their last evening, the adults decided to go for dinner at a local pub. The children, unwilling to leave Mimo alone for a second, chose to stay behind and Gary agreed to keep an eye on them.

"We're going to miss this place," Julie volunteered as Mark drove them. Laura took a deep breath and gazed out of the window. "I'll soon be back to my emptiness again," she mumbled, softly enough so that no one else could hear.

When they arrived, Laura slid out of the car and looked up to the sky. The night had already taken over and the chilly wind made her shiver.

The pub was surrounded by trees and had an open terrace with wicker tables and magnificent river views. Unfortunately, the early spring evening wasn't warm enough for alfresco dining so they opted to sit inside.

"It's so exotic," Laura said, taking a seat near a fire blazing in a stone hearth.

"It's romantic," Mark added.

The trio's faces glowed under the soft light of antique chandeliers.

"Good evening and welcome. May I take your order, please?" asked a smiley faced man in his mid-sixties. He was wrapped in a blue and white apron, which told them that he was the chef as well as their waiter. It was a very small pub.

Sensing their indecision, the chef suggested the speciality of the day. "It's duck with a spicy sauce," he explained. "Served with grilled vegetables."

Laura, Julie and Mark were unanimous in their decision to order the dish.

"And what will the charming ladies like to drink?"

"Don't you mean, 'what would this charming man and the ladies like to drink?'" Mark joked.

The chef laughed and replied with another exquisite suggestion of a French vintage red served with strawberries and grapes to enhance the flavour.

"Sounds truly irresistible," Julie said.

"If I'm busy in the kitchen then my wife and lover of 40 years will attend to you," the chef continued, noting down the order.

"Now tell me," Mark said, looking across at Julie with a playful glint in his eye. "How have you managed 40 years with the same woman?"

"It's easy," replied the chef. "When I get fed up I send her to the hairdressers for a new hair colour and we start all over again."

"My darling," Marked beamed, turning his attention to his wife. "Would you mind changing your hair colour for me?"

"Only if you do the same," Julie replied. "Then we can be equal."

They all laughed loudly at this and as the chef left them, Laura gazed towards the table next to them. It seemed that the adrenaline was running even higher than on theirs. Hands were clapping and heads were bent down over the table in unstoppable laughter.

Laura felt like she was floating along the same river as her friends. For so long she had existed outside the doors of society. She now realised that this feeling hadn't meant to be a lasting one. Although she dreaded returning to her hollowed out life, for now there was food, wine and good company.

"I will remember these days," Mark said, tucking into his duck.

"Just imagine," Julie said. "The day after tomorrow we'll be back in the classroom."

"And Laura will be back to her designs," Mark replied. "At least it will be quieter."

A pained expression momentarily appeared on Laura's face. She inhaled deeply and her gazed drifted away from her companions. She was lost in her own thoughts.

Eventually, Mark broke the silence by rising from his chair and declaring a toast.

"This is not an end but a beginning," he said. "I look forward to more days like this, and a continuing friendship."

"Thank you for giving me such a wonderful time," Laura added, raising her glass.

On the way back to the cottage, Laura barely spoke. The following day would take her back to reality and her week away would soon be forgotten, like a dream. She would be lost inside her loneliness again. The night was still young and she didn't want to bring it to a close just yet.

"I want to stay out a bit longer," she declared when they pulled into the driveway. Running into the cottage, she wrapped herself in a soft wool blanket and went to sit at the garden table. The sky was embellished with only a few stars and Laura was left to contemplate them as Mark and Julie went to tuck the children in. She slipped off her shoes and moved to a swinging chair. It was so quiet that she could hear the leaves rustling in the trees. She felt so peaceful, never wanted this moment to end. Closing her eyes, she felt herself drifting away…

When she opened them again, it was so dark that she couldn't see a thing, though she could hear a voice. It belonged to a child.

"Where are you?" it said.

"I'm coming, honey," a woman replied, her voice someway in the distance. "Wait for me."

"Mama, Mama," the child cried.

"Honey, grab my hand."

Laura looked down. She could just make out the outline of her own hands; they were stretching out to reach something. Then the soft hand of a child gripped one of them.

"Don't let me go, Mama…"

Laura was desperate to see his face. Squinting, she tried to pull the image from the dark. Before her, a face flickered into view before the blackness took over again.

"Wait, wait," Laura cried. "I have to see you."

She could hear footsteps behind her and a hand pressed over hers, the one with the child's curled inside it. It was a big hand and she knew instinctively that it belonged to a man. Twisting her head back, she could see the outline of his large shoulders and felt his breath on her cheek. He moved his hands onto her shoulders. Oh, this touch.

Millions of electrolytes charged under her skin, penetrating deeply. Laura couldn't deny this magical feeling that was pulling her from the dark.

Raising her head, a strong light made her squint. A woman in a bright dress was walking backwards. She seemed strangely familiar.

"Don't go," Laura cried. "Wait a minute – you are me!"

She heard the child crying out for his mama again and thrust her eyes open. She sprang up so fast from her chair that she left it swinging behind her. Jumping a wooden gate, she ran into the wood adjacent to the cottage, sprinting until she was so out of breath that she had to stop. She was lost now, disorientated amid the expanse of woodland that stretched out endlessly in front of her. The coldness of the grass beneath her feet made her shiver all over, and she felt the chill right down to her bones. The world was spinning around her, making her unsteady, and she fell down on to her knees, where she stayed until the sound of her breathing quietened.

"What is happening to me?" she wondered. Yes, she had heard voices before, but nothing like this. The people and the voices were so real. Laura knew that they were coming from somewhere, an unknown distance.

The confusion between dreams and reality was truly daunting. She felt the wind that had passed through the green souls of the trees blow across her face, drying her tears. Slowly getting up, she made her way through the dark and back to the cottage.

★★★

"Oh, I must have overslept," Laura mumbled the following morning, stretching her arms and swinging her legs around to the floor.

By the time she made it downstairs, Julie and Mark had already packed and were ready to hit the road.

She felt so bitter over having to leave and wanted to cling to every last minute of her holiday. She swapped numbers with her new friends and they came up with a plan to meet at the cottage again the following year.

"What about Mimo?" asked Nick. "Will he come too? I'm going to miss him so much."

"I will too," Laura replied. "He belongs to my neighbour and he'll be going home soon, but I'll plead with them to let him join us next year. Look how happy he is with you. I am sure that he is just as sad to let you go."

Heads down, the children dragged their feet to the car and looked longingly out of the rear window as Mark pulled out of the driveway. Mimo gave a sad little whimper as he watched his friends disappear, and a lump formed in Laura's throat. She dashed back inside to do her own packing. The house was deadly silent now, making her feel uncomfortable, and she hurriedly gathered up her things and tossed them into her bags. On the way to her car she thanked Gary, who was whistling his usual melody, for his hospitality.

"I wish I didn't have to go back," she said, opening the backdoor for Mimo to climb inside. "We both had a splendid time."

Above them, the clouds were wrestling in the sky and rain seemed imminent.

"Typical," she murmured, slamming her door and turning on the ignition, ready to hit the road.

16

As soon as she pulled into her driveway, Laura spotted the lights on in her neighbours' house. She turned her head round to Mimo, feeling disarmed.

"I'm sorry, boy, but it looks like I'm going to have to let you go," she said, patting his head.

Knocking gently on Martin and Sylvia's door, it soon flung open. Laura could hear the sweet cries of a baby in the background. Flabbergasted for a moment, she leant against the doorframe without even acknowledging Martin's presence.

"A baby?" she eventually spluttered.

Martin turned his body to the side so that Laura could see inside the hallway. His daughter Anita waddled towards them like a duck, proudly carrying her newborn in her arms.

"Let me introduce you to our lovely neighbour," she said, jamming the baby's face towards Laura. Laura ducked her head to get a better view of the little girl, who had crystal clear blue eyes. Her face was pink, the same colour as the clothes she was wrapped up in. Safe in her mother's arms, she gurgled like a bird in the nest.

"Congratulations," Laura beamed. "You have such a lovely baby."

"We couldn't let this little jewel out of our sight," said Sylvia, appearing in the hallway. "Anita and her little Sara are going to be staying with us for a while." As she spoke, she shook a bottle filled with warm milk.

"She's like an angel," said Laura, rubbing the back of her finger over the baby's soft, cotton-like skin.

"We are truly blessed," said Martin, who already had Mimo twisting around his legs, eager to take some of the attention away from the baby.

Laura stepped back, feeling like an intruder in this intimate family moment. She said her goodbyes and, feeling utterly lost, dragged her feet back home.

With a taste of despair over leaving Mimo behind and the smell of milky baby's skin still lingering, she entered her empty house.

"If my baby had lived he would be four by now," she thought. In her mind's eye she pictured him with a shock of black hair and clever eyes. Wondering about the life he would never have she felt a jab in her belly and placed both her hands on it. Sometimes her emotional pain made its presence known physically.

Moving slowly from the door, she switched on the lights, slipped off her shoes and, leaving them scattered on the floor, made her way to the living room. Reaching out her hand she touched the wall, which felt icy cold. The room was quiet and clean and everything was in perfect order - Laura felt suffocated by it.

"What am I doing here?" she said. Upon hearing the sound of her own voice, she took a step back. She felt unconnected with everything in the house, even her presence within it.

The joy of the previous few days...her vivid dreams and visions, the strange email she had received, they'd all left a mark on her. In her mind, she was mapping out a new path to follow. It was time to face up to things now, even the strange email. With that, she strode into her office. She took a seat by the computer and, extending a forefinger out, pressed the on button.

The screen lit up and Laura logged on to her email before she had chance to change her mind. There were a bunch of new ones, mainly junk, and one from the new company she was working for, briefly informing her of the progress of the project.

Building work at the site was still ongoing. She also spotted a message from John and, moving her mouse, she positioned it over his name in order to read it. But her finger froze just as she was about to click down and her eyes dropped one line below. There was a new message from the mysterious man called David. It had been sitting in her inbox for five days.

For a long time she sat and stared at the name.

"What's new now?" she said out loud, her voice trembling. "Have you got something important to tell me again? Please don't play with me. Don't let me get lost inside my illusions. I'm so crushed, I can't carry any more disappointments."

Unable to read the message straight away, she clicked back on John's.

Dear Laura,
I hope you are doing well. You have tremendous ability and I'm sure you are. Remember what I said to you? It's time to move on...

As for me? Well, I'm playing the granddad role rather well. My granddaughter is two so she is keeping me pretty active, as you may well be able to imagine. I'm also enjoying the sunshine out here. Actually, I'm having the best time of my life.

"Good for you, John," Laura said, smiling. Slowly, she led the arrow key to the next email and inhaled deeply.

Dear Laura,
There's not much time left for me; I'm like a weak bridge about to cave in. Please hurry and come. I know this request will be the strangest thing that you have ever heard, but please believe me...you have to.

You will find something here...trust that it's a good thing.

Don't try and contact me by email. The answers to all your questions lie here. I've included my full name and address.

Laura read the email again, going over every single word. This was so unexpected and weird. As she got up from the computer, she realised that she was shaking. She decided to pour herself something strong to help her calm down. On her way to the kitchen she paused and leant against the wall.

"I have to go," she told herself. "I have to break up my pointless days inside this house."

Slowly looking around her surroundings once more, she made her final decision. "I'm going to get the hell out of here," she said, feeling suddenly brave.

The walls that surrounded her, the loneliness they brought, didn't satisfy her needs any more. Her house was like a box full of her memories of the past. She decided that maybe it was time to fill a new one.

Retracing her steps back to her office, she booked a one-way ticket to New York on the next plane available. Feeling emotionally supercharged, she stood up. Her inner voice was talking to her, but this time it was different, stronger.

"You may be making a mistake," it said to her. "But you'll never know if don't go."

She felt as if she was protected by an invisible superpower.

Hearing the soft tingle of her phone she realised that it was on her person and reached inside her trouser pocket. It was a message to tell her that she'd missed 12 calls from Carla's mobile. She remembered Christina warning her that the reception was poor at the cottage and immediately called Carla back.

"I need to see you," she said as soon as her friend answered.
"Where are you?"
"I'm at home."

"Okay, then what if I bring the boys out for a pizza? You can join us."

"I need you alone."

"What?"

In the background, Laura could detect the rumble of the tumble dryer - then she heard a door close. Carla had moved to somewhere quieter.

"I need to see you on your own," Laura repeated.

"Oh, you sound serious."

"Yes, I am."

"Is everything okay? You seem different…is something bothering you?" The worried tone had returned to Carla's voice.

"No, I'm okay. Well, there is something, but it's nothing to worry about. I'm fine."

"But where have you been? I've been trying to reach you all week."

"I was on holiday."

"You do surprise me. How wonderful!"

"Yes, I was in the countryside…Herefordshire…I had a nice time."

"I'll stop by tomorrow afternoon," Carla promised.

Bidding her best friend goodbye, Laura ended the call and wondered how Carla was going to take the news. The prospect of sharing it with her didn't bring much relief. It was time to pour herself a stiff drink.

***

By the time the hour of Carla's visit approached, Laura was feeling agitated and she couldn't stop glancing at her watch. She needed her friend. Even though she knew that Carla wasn't going to approve of her decision and would surely question it, it was a heavy burden to carry alone.

She meandered through the house, clenching her fists as many thoughts swirled around her head.

"Why do I feel like this?" she wondered. What she was about to do was crazy, yet it still felt right. Still, she knew she was about to plunge into the unknown.

Down in the kitchen, she made herself a ham and cheese sandwich, but then discarded it after just one bite. She'd lost her appetite. "Along with my mind," she thought dryly.

Thinking about what was ahead had given her butterflies, but that wasn't going to stop her going to New York. Her house, the dullness of her days and the cold dark nights were more frightening for her.

She poured herself a gin and tonic and took a big gulp. Her throat was dry and tight. As she drank, the sound of an unfamiliar horn caused her to stand on her tiptoes to peer out of her kitchen window. In her driveway stood a cherry red Mini with an English flag painted on its roof. She smiled as Carla climbed out of it and hurried to the door.

"I won it!" Carla explained. "On a scratch card, would you believe?" As she spoke, she opened her arms wide and punched the air with her fists. She sounded so excited.

Laura couldn't help but share her friend's joy. She led Carla into the house, wondering how to bring up the subject of New York and preparing herself for the barrage of questions that her friend was no doubt going to ask.

"The kids won't let me drop them off at school in my beautiful new car," Carla went on. "Can you imagine? They get Larry to take them."

But when she turned around, she saw that Laura was somewhere else entirely.

"Do I smell trouble?" she asked, raising an eyebrow.

Laura sat down, her emotions unmasking her. She couldn't hide anything from her best friend for too long.

She took a deep breath and quickly got the words out. "I'm going to New York."

"What…another holiday?"

"No, nothing like that. It's for something completely different."

"Well, then tell me," Carla said, scrutinising Laura's face. "What have you got to do over there?"

"I don't know yet," Laura tried to explain. "I just know that I have to go. I am just as surprised."

"Wait, wait, rewind a little. I don't understand. What are you talking about?"

"I have to see someone or something," Laura said, digging her fingers into her hair and scraping her scalp nervously with her fingernails.

Carla jumped to her own conclusion. "I'm so happy for you," she said. "At last you've made room for someone. This is monumental news."

"It's not quite as simple as that," Laura replied weakly. "I put my picture on the web and…" Her voice trailed off. How could she explain?

"But it's still good news. Where did you meet him?"

"The strange thing is that I haven't met anyone yet…if there is an 'anyone'. I just had an email."

"What? You must be fucking mad."

"Maybe I am. But since the day I received the first email, strange things have been happening to me. I see images and hear voices…they follow me everywhere I go. And he said that he knows something and it's very important that I go over. I'll find something there."

Carla listened, unblinking, clearly shocked, and Laura felt the need to continue. "This something…I feel it, a part of me is out there somewhere. I feel like I am a missing piece of a puzzle. I need to find an explanation for what is happening to me. I know I'm not insane…actually, I feel incredibly…charged."

"It's okay, take it easy," Carla said. "But you did hear voices before, remember?"

"Yes, but they were the voices of people I knew. It was my memory playing tricks on me. Now I am different…this is something else. I don't know what and I can't explain it. It's something inside me, I feel it flowing through my blood."

"What about trying to get some more information?" Carla suggested. "Do you even know why he wants to see you?"

"I have no idea. I just have an address in New York."

"And you think it's a good idea to just go there? You're joking, yeah?" The tone of Carla's voice was critical, just as Laura had known it would be.

"Yes, I am going to see a stranger…I have to find out what the email is all about and I'm going whether you like it or not. I wanted to tell you, not get your permission."

Laura's own tone was a little angry. Silence passed between them, with only the sound of Laura's heavy breaths audible. She decided to try and explain herself one last time. "I am uncertain," she admitted. "But I also feel confused here, and trapped. I'm unable to sleep at night. I have to resolve this before I really go crazy."

Laura swiped her hair out of her face before placing her elbows on the table and holding her head between her palms. Her lungs were pumping forcefully and rhythmically.

"But it's such a risky venture," Carla argued. "What if you don't find what you're craving? What if this is all just your fantasy and it's actually some fucking crazy maniac that's written to you? Are you sure you need *this* kind of distraction?"

"I don't know how to explain…it feels like something is hidden inside me, it's in the corner of my mind and it won't leave me alone. I will go and take my chances. It's better than staying here and hurting. Besides, I've already bought the ticket."

"You do worry me," Carla shrugged, reaching over and scooping Laura's hands into her own. "I just don't want you to get hurt any more. But if you think that this will bring some serenity to your mind, then go."

"I am scared," Laura reiterated. "But not as much as I will be if I stay."

"You're so damn headstrong at times," Carla said, leaping out of her chair and going over to hug her friend. "I just want you to be happy," she added. "I wouldn't be able to bear seeing you get any more hurt by life."

By now the pair were so overcome by emotion that they had to get tissues to dry their watery eyes.

"If you remember," Carla said, her tone much lighter. "I asked you to jump out of the cage, not into another continent!"

Laura laughed. Her still damp eyes were sparkling more than usual.

"I'll take you to the airport," Carla said before she left. She hugged her friend once again before climbing into her car.

Laura closed the door feeling a little bit relieved: she had taken the first step, now she just had to cross a few thousand miles. Re-entering her house, everything seemed different. For years she had the nursed ghosts and the spirits of her dead loved ones; now suddenly she felt free, free and infused by unfamiliar feelings.

17

Padding up the stairs, Laura opened the door to her storage cupboard, which almost fell off its hinges in the process, thanks to a loose screw.

"I always forget to fix this," she mumbled. Holding the door in place, she bent her head under the shelves crammed with her belongings and pulled out a suitcase, which she took to her bedroom and rested on the bed. Seeing it there made her nostalgic for the last trip she'd taken with it.

"The three of us," Matt had said, his hands on Laura's pregnant belly, "will have the best adventure ever."

They'd gone to Norway, in what was to be their last holiday together. Laura had just finished a project and they'd decided to get away before the baby arrived. She remembered how beautifully the earth, water and sky seemed to blend with each other, and could still picture the wild pristine landscapes, snaking rivers and lonely fjords. Laura took a deep breath and it was like inhaling the fresh air from that holiday. But now was not the time for dwelling on the past; she had to decide what to take to New York. Sliding open her wardrobe door, she couldn't avoid catching site of her reflection in the mirror.

"How could I have forgotten to do the conditioning treatment my hairdresser gave me?" she thought to herself, before turning her attention to her exquisite clothes collection.

"It's not necessary to take many things," she told herself, selecting some trousers, a skirt and some tops that would go with either. Moving to her underwear drawer, she couldn't resist picking up the jewellery box that she kept on top of her chest of drawers. She slid it open, making a beeline for a blue sapphire bracelet, which instantly opened a door to the not so near past.

"Oh, Grandma, I do miss you," she muttered. She was 13 when she first fastened the bracelet over her slim wrists, in shock from starting her periods. Her grandma, finding her sat on the bed, her head sunk between her knees in hatred of the body that had become a stranger to her, knew exactly what to do.

"Come on, darling, don't be like this," she'd said gently, scooping Laura's hand into her own. "You have become a woman today."

"But I don't want to be, I hate it," came Laura's reply.

"You are going to be a beautiful woman," her grandmother soothed. She patted Laura's hand with her wrinkled old fingers then pulled the bracelet from her pocket. "The gemstones will protect you," she said. "You will need them, especially from now on. One day you will be a wonderful mother and wife, just as you are a wonderful daughter and granddaughter right now."

Laura was dazzled by the gift, and the flawless beauty of the stones affected her eyes, which began to sparkle. Her confidence in her body had been restored.

Back in the present, Laura put on the bracelet and silently thanked her grandma again, seeing her in her mind's eye wearing an immaculate white shirt, with not a single grey hair out of place. The memory gave her the courage to continue with her packing. But the burst of confidence didn't prevent the night from being an unbearable battle between her need for sleep and her uncontrollable anxiety. Switching on the bedside lamp she stared at the ceiling, visualising the strange journey that she was about to embark on.

"What will I find there?" she asked herself, painfully aware that all she had was a name and an address. But then another feeling took over, and this told her that something magical would guide and protect her. Hearing her breath amidst the quietness of the night, she felt a sudden surge of excitement and power overtake her fear. She drifted off again and the night passed, the daylight bringing a new path for her to follow.

When Carla arrived the next morning, Laura was waiting with her suitcase by the door.

"I'll take this," Carla said, carting it to her car.

Laura stood still for a moment, holding her key in her hand and staring at the keyhole. She was about to lock up the place that held all her grief, all her dreams. Deep down, she knew those walls no longer needed to hold her too.

"Is everything okay?" Carla asked.

"Yes…I'm coming," Laura replied, climbing into the passenger seat and pulling on her seatbelt.

Carla hesitated, her fingers and thumb on the key in the ignition.

"Are you sure you're ready for this?" she finally asked, noticing Laura's agitation at their stationary status.

"Yes, I am, just hit the road," Laura replied, trying to sound calm while nervously clenching her fists and trying not to meet Carla's gaze. She forced herself to look into the distance, pushing her thoughts in the same direction.

Not one word passed between the two friends. They were both thinking different things, but their thoughts often crossed.

A mile before they reached Heathrow, Carla pulled off the motorway to fill up her car with petrol. Seeing a carwash she decided to extend her time with Laura by going through it. She paid and climbed back into the car. Colourful feathers began to foam and run over it.

Laura laid her head against the seat, oblivious to the dazzling waves in front of her. Carla looked at her friend in anguish. So many unsaid words were flying around in both women's heads. Their eyes met each other for a moment and they acknowledged a mutual understanding: there was no need to talk any more.

Following a white foam rinse, the motion of the feathers stopped and Carla turned the ignition.

When they reached the parking bay at Heathrow, Carla breathed deeply and tried once more to get her words out. But her throat had a big lump in it and her eyes were wet.

"I know, I know," said Laura. "It is scary. I feel like I'm spinning in an empty space with nothing to hold on to. This is a big task for me but I already have the steps in my head. I've taken them in my dreams, now I have to take them for real."

"Don't you think you might be pushing your luck a bit?" Carla asked, unable to help herself.

"Maybe," replied Laura. "I just have to hope that my senses aren't leading me towards disaster."

"I care about you, Laura. You deserve the best out of life. I'm just asking you to give this some more thought."

"I will be fine," Laura said.

"Are you sure?"

"I may sound like a fool, but I feel that a kind of miracle will somehow be out there for me."

"No, you're not a fool," Carla reassured her friend. "You are bold."

Carla didn't make any further attempts to change Laura's mind. "We better get moving," she said instead. "It's time for you to check in."

"I'm ready," Laura replied, trying very hard to believe in her own words.

"Promise me you'll be careful and stay in touch?" Carla said.

"I promise," Laura replied, holding and squeezing her friend's hands. Taking her suitcase from the boot, she blew Carla a kiss before joining the crowds entering the airport. As she checked in her suitcase, she reminded herself of the promise she'd made not to look back.

18

ONCE on the plane, a stewardess directed Laura to her seat. As she lifted her hand luggage to place inside the overhead locker, she heard a voice behind her.

"Let me do that."

Turning her head, she saw a tall, handsome man dressed in a marine's uniform standing behind her. After he'd helped Laura with her bags he took the window seat, which was next to where Laura was seated.

"Thank you for doing that," she said to him with a smile. Then she untied her hair, slipped off her jacket and started to make herself comfortable.

"I'm Denis," the young marine said, extending his hand. He had shaved hair and dark eyes. Laura guessed that he was in his mid 20s.

Laura introduced herself and the pair started chatting about the six-hour flight stretching ahead of them. To Laura's left sat a young girl with braided hair and a pregnant belly. As the plane's engine's started to howl, she bent forwards, clenching her firsts and muttering prayers.

Laura felt her own stomach turn as the plane lifted off the ground. She decided to introduce herself to her other neighbour. "Afraid of flying?" she asked her gently.

"Yes," she nodded, sounding terrified. "It's my first flight. I've never been on a plane before. Well, actually, this is my second flight...London was my transit stop. I flew there yesterday from Latvia."

As she spoke in somewhat broken English, Laura could see

her lips tremble. She angled her body so she could reach inside her pocket for some chewing gum. Pushing a stick loose, she offered it to the girl. "It will help," she said. "For me it's a habit to chew gum when I fly. And you have no need to worry, we'll be fine."

She turned her gaze forwards, leant back on the headrest and wondered about the girl's story. She didn't look more than 16 and was pregnant and alone in a foreign country.

A child carrying another child.

Laura dropped her gaze down to the girl's stomach and her maternal instinct kicked in. The baby's heartbeat throbbed inside her head and she quickly turned her gaze to the window, where clouds appeared to swim in the blue sky. The staggeringly beautiful sight took her away from her reality and memories for a moment.

"What's taking you to the States?" Denis asked. "You sound English."

"Yes, I'm from London," Laura replied.

Why was she going to New York? She was constantly asking herself the same question. It could simply be because she was desperate to feel something different.

"It's going to be my first time in New York City," Laura replied, deciding to dodge the question. "In my mind I've visited a hundred times, though."

She wished that she was really visiting the city for a holiday - then she could really absorb its spirit. For now she had to find the root of the rope that had pulled her from her home so powerfully. Only then could she begin to do any of the stuff that tourists do.

"This is my girl," Denis said, thrusting a photo of a young and beautiful girl towards Laura's face. "We're getting married next week."

"Wow, congratulations," Laura replied. "She looks so pretty."

"She is, and she's pregnant too. We're having a little boy."

"Do you know for sure that it's a boy?" Laura asked.

"What else could it be?" the marine replied, his lips curling into a wry smile.

"Is that a military order?" Laura teased. She absent-mindedly picked up a magazine from the pocket in front of her and scanned the cover lines before turning her attention back to Denis. He was no longer smiling.

"I'm so lucky that I will see my son born," he said. "I came back from hell...back from Afghanistan." The muscles in his face tightened as he thrust his head forcefully against the seat. "I saw him..."

"Saw who?" Laura asked softly.

"My friend...his body all messed up. I can still feel his fingers clenching my hand, his broken body reduced to dust...he was my best friend; we even shared the same birthday. He was supposed to be best man at my wedding. I can still smell his flesh..."

Denis bent over, his elbows against his knees and his hands covering both ears as if he was shielding them from the thunderous blast of a grenade. "I was covered in his blood," he mumbled. He began to dig his fingers into his short hair, scrubbing his skull as if the action could help take the pain away. Then he laid his head back against the seat again and stared out the window, unable to meet Laura's gaze.

Laura was shocked by Denis's outburst. In her mind's eye she could see a field scattered with bodies and fresh blood; the horrifying images brought hot tears to her eyes. Shaking her head in an attempt to dislodge them from her mind, she turned her gaze to the Latvian girl next to her. Her eyes remained clenched shut, and she was oblivious to the arrival of a stewardess at their row.

"Would you like something to drink?" she asked, directing the question at all three of them.

"A black coffee for me," Laura replied. Denis ordered vodka on the rocks while the young girl shook her head.

Laura already felt worn out, as if she'd escaped a battlefield herself. Tightening her hands around her plastic coffee cup, she focused on the bubbles that had formed in the centre of the steaming beverage.

"My fiancé works as a nurse," said Denis, who was still clutching her photo in his hand. It was as if his little outburst minutes before had never happened. Meanwhile, Laura was still recovering from the terror his words had induced, words that had filled her mouth with the taste of blood.

"What?" she asked.

Denis repeated himself and then added, "Pretty soon she'll be nursing my son."

"Can you hold this for a minute?" Laura asked, plunging her cup into the Latvian girl's hand. She undid her seatbelt and stood up, feeling desperate for air. She felt as if she'd been hit on the head by a brick. Taking a second to regain her balance, she made her way unsteadily to the toilet. Bending over the stainless steel sink, she splashed water on her face and then shook her head, trying to erase the last ten minutes from her mind; the bombardment of blasts and bloodshed.

"What a nightmare," she said, freeing a tissue from the metallic box by the sink and drying her face.

When she arrived back at her seat, the Latvian girl handed Laura her drink and introduced herself as Anna. Laura's gaze travelled down to her belly once again, and Anna pulled her hands up inside the long sleeves of her jumper to hide the fact that they were trembling.

"I'm going to America to give birth to my baby," she confided.

It was an answer to the unspoken question that Laura had possessed since she first took a seat on the plane. But there were so many more. "How many more months to go?" she asked.

"Three more and he will be out of me," Anna replied.

Laura was shocked by her brusqueness. This girl was shaking the roots of the pain inside her. It was as if someone had shone a flashlight on the dark corner of her mind. The memory of her loss made her stomach turn somersaults. She felt dizzy again as she thought of her child, the cord that had connected her to him. What she would give to have another heart beating inside her. She couldn't help but feel envious of the young girl.

"Have you got family waiting for you in New York?" she asked.

Anna shook her head and thought for a moment before placing her hand on the mountain of her belly and replying weakly, "I was scared. This terrible, shameful thing happened to me and I tried to pretend it hadn't. I didn't want to think about babies."

Laura wondered how she could possibly refer to her child, a new life, as something shameful. If she'd had a magic wand she would have used it to transfer the young girl's baby into her own body.

"I was so stupid," Anna continued. "I was in love. I never thought I would get pregnant. This is my punishment for trusting him. He turned his back on me, didn't give a damn…"

"Don't call yourself stupid," Laura soothed. "Love isn't stupid."

"But he lied to me," Anna protested. "When I told him that I was pregnant he ran away and I never saw him again."

Her eyes glowed with anger as she recalled recent events. "I spent hours waiting for his call. I was afraid to go home and tell my brother. I felt so trapped and desperate."

"You poor thing," Laura murmured. "I can't imagine how shocked you must have been. Couldn't your parents have helped, though?"

"I don't remember my father," Anna replied. "I haven't seen him since I was three. My mother remarried and my elder brother took care of me. He's married now, with his own family. My only way out was an abortion, but I couldn't go through with it. I contacted an adoption agency and they found a couple for the baby, but I am so scared."

Laura patted the girl's arm. "Don't be afraid. You are a very courageous girl, think of it that way."

"I had different plans for my life," Anna said sadly. "You dream about things in such beautiful detail and then bam, everything changes." She swiped her hand through the air to demonstrate this, then added, "With one shot your life is shattered. The dreams gone, wiped away like a sandcastle when the tide comes in."

"But you don't have to give up on your dreams," Laura argued. "You will catch your time."

She noticed that she was echoing the words of John, and realised how right he'd been.

"My mother once told me that a dirty spoon can poison your life forever," Anna said. "She was talking about herself, but now it's real for me too."

Laura's face fell as she felt the girl's pain. She was so young and pretty, like a flower picked from the garden in the fresh dew of the morning. Now she was about to give up her baby, would carry a wound for the rest of her life. There was no doubt about that.

"I try not to think of the baby, but I love him, I really do. I hope his mum will be…will be as good as you. You seem so kind."

"I'm sure they will be good parents," Laura said, hoping and praying that her words would prove to be true. She squeezed Anna's trembling fingers in a soft, protective touch. It was only then that she realised she was old enough to be her mother.

Anna gazed at Laura, managing a smile before whispering in her ear: "I have to use the bathroom now."

Laura watched her waddle up the plane's narrow aisle. The sight of her thin, fragile legs supporting such a heavy load induced in her a rush of sympathy. On her other side, Denis was snoring, his head resting against the window. It was as if his head was being carried by the white clouds on the other side of it. He looked so calm and carefree but Laura could only begin to imagine what was happening in his dreams. Were the bombs still blasting, or was sleep a chance for him to lick his wounds? She was struck by the contrast between the two people seated either side of her. Denis couldn't wait to hold his unborn son and Anna was giving hers up.

"What about me?" she wondered. "Where do I stand?" She had no idea where her journey was taking her and there was something cosy about where she was now, miles above the ground, soaring between the clouds. As much as she wanted to reach her destination, part of her wished the journey could last forever. She was afraid of what was waiting on the ground.

Her eyelids began to grow heavy and she managed to drift off, despite her aching muscles. But once in a deep sleep, her eyes opened again. In front of her was a face, just a breath away. It was her own face and she was staring right into her own eyes, seeing her entire soul encased inside their green sparkle. Then the face became blurry and was replaced by a smaller one. Two warm little hands started tickling her cheeks. She cupped the face with her own hands, taking in the soft fresh skin, the silky black hair and milky white teeth. Slowly, she slid the boy's fingers from her cheeks to her lips. It was an exchange full of warmth and love.

Next, she felt a man's touch, could smell his scent. He whispered Laura's name, "Come on," he beckoned. "Come with me..."

"Miss, we are landing," said another voice. She felt someone poking her elbow, was pulled back to reality. Bewildered, she sprang from her seat and turned her gaze towards Denis. He buttoned up his jacket and then secured his seatbelt. On her other side, Anna was sat up straight, her eyes squeezed shut again, clenching the material of her trousers.

The cabin lights were turned off and only the seatbelt symbols continued to glow. Laura tried to recapture the man's scent, the sound of his voice, the feel of his touch on her skin, but she was unable to pull anything out of the darkness. She wondered why she was having the same dream, and why it was giving her the same feeling. Fastening her seatbelt for landing, she closed her eyes and, as the plane descended, her psyche was lifted by an unknown power. The feeling was beyond her comprehension. It felt as if her mind was racing at the same speed as the aeroplane. The countdown to her future had begun.

19

AFTER passing through security, Laura speculated once again whether this journey would help her to shake the burden she'd been carrying from her shoulders, or lead instead to destruction. Either way, she knew it wouldn't be long before she discovered the reason for her journey to another continent. She was just about to enter the throng of people waiting for their loved ones in arrivals when she felt her arm being gripped. It was Anna.

"I'm so scared," she said.

"You will be fine," Laura replied, wondering what on earth she could do to help the young woman. She had an idea, and with a swift movement slipped the blue sapphire bracelet from her wrist and fastened it around Anna's.

"It will make me happy if you take this," she said. "And it would make my grandmother happy too. She gave it to me. I hope it brings you luck."

Looking down at the bracelet, Anna quickly wrapped her arms around Laura, clinging to her tightly as if she was the only thing left to hold on to in a whirlwind. Laura felt the young girl's heart thrumming next to hers; she was like a bird out of the nest and her entire body trembled. Struggling to hold back her tears, Laura pushed Anna gently away from her and scooped her beautiful white face in both her palms, as if it were a snowball. "Be brave," she said. "You are doing what is best for the baby and your life will be crammed full with other possibilities. Just remember to take care of yourself."

As she spoke, Laura couldn't help wondering: would she take her advice, or be haunted by her actions for the rest of her life?

Anna nodded in response, her eyes full of tears, which caused Laura to pull her into her arms again and kiss her hot, wet cheeks. Then she released her to follow the river of her fate and destiny. Even though she'd only known Anna for a matter of hours, she felt as if she'd lost another member of her family. She watched as Anna went to join the couple that she presumed were going to adopt her baby. They couldn't conceal their excitement and the woman looped her arm in Anna's while the man took hold of her suitcase. Neither of them could help stealing glances at her belly, just as Laura had done. Anna let them lead her away to her temporary new nest and Laura pulled her eyes away. She'd witnessed one sad show, now she had to deal with her own.

"Good luck in New York," Denis said, overtaking her like a hurricane, his large bag slung over his shoulders. He twisted his body in order to look at Laura, his eyes sparkling, his white teeth glowing. Laura smiled back until he turned around again, at which point he spotted his fiancé. He opened his arms as he approached her and after they'd kissed and hugged he span her around in a pirouette. Their joy was almost tangible.

Night had already fallen by the time Laura stepped out of the airport doors. A cool breeze brushed across her face and she was relieved to breathe some fresh air into her lungs. Hailing a taxi, she gave the driver the name of the hotel and exhaustedly slumped back against the seat. Her mind swam with images of Denis's wide smile and Anna's watery eyes. Staring at the bright lights surrounding her, she momentarily forgot why she had come to this city; the only thing on her mind was having a long hot shower.

★★★

Stopping in the middle of the hotel's huge reception area, Laura noticed how the reflections from the chandelier above her head danced over the shiny marble floor beneath her feet. Fighting her jetlag, she went to the front desk and, too tired to speak, pushed a piece of paper containing the details of her reservation at the receptionist. She followed the directions she was given to her room and discarded her clothes as soon as she had closed the door behind her, leaving them sprawled on the floor. Untying her hair, she grabbed the white bathrobe that had been left carefully folded on her bed and turned on the shower, waiting until it was at just the right temperature before stepping inside it. The powerful spray succeeded in relieving her tired, cramped muscles. After getting dried, Laura wrapped herself in a bath towel and squeezed her body between the plush white sheets of her enormous bed. It was the best place to rest her stiff body and empty her mind. Within seconds, she had drifted into a deep sleep.

***

The following morning, a knock on the door caused Laura to spring from the pillow. It took her a few seconds to figure out where she was. Her head felt heavy, in contrast to the feel of the luxurious linen on her legs. Releasing a yawn, she fully opened her eyes. Her room was contemporary, fresh and spacious – a true sanctuary.

Slipping on her robe, she opened the door a little and craned her neck in order to see who was behind it. It was a Latino man and he was clutching a tray upon which were croissants, little dishes filled with strawberries and honey, and a glass of orange juice.

"Room service!" he announced, still smiling.

"Oh yes!" Laura replied. She'd been so jetlagged that she'd forgotten about ordering it the previous night. She stepped back from the door to give the waiter room to step in. Then she reached for her handbag and pulled out a five-pound note, which she pressed into his hand.

"Thank you," he said, looking at the note with a vaguely puzzled expression.

"It's English," Laura explained. "You just need to change it at the bank."

"Thank you," he said again, before bending his head and pulling the door behind him.

Laura stretched out her arms and tightened them around her body.

"This is for real," she said out loud. "I'm in New York."

The morning sun was shining into her room, which had floor-to-ceiling windows. She went to close the blinds and spent a moment gazing at the view over Central Park. She couldn't even recall what floor she was on and had to search her mind for the number. She congratulated herself for such an excellent choice of hotel, and transferred her gaze to the Metropolitan Museum of Art. If her purpose for coming here had been different it would have been her first port of call. Turning from the window, she reached for her breakfast tray, but she couldn't keep her eyes away from the mesmerising panoramic view for long and was drawn back to it as she popped a strawberry into her mouth, squashing it so that the juice ran down her throat. As she did so, she imagined that she was surrounded by a magical and colourful aura. She felt ready to tackle the boisterous noises of New York. Withdrawing from the window, she went into the bathroom, washed her face with cold water, combed her hair and applied some light makeup. Amazingly, after such a long journey the day before, she looked fresh, rested and ready to go.

★★★

For her first day in the Big Apple, Laura chose to wear a black bomber jacket and a patterned skirt made of a soft, swishy fabric. As she made her way across the marble floor in the corridor outside her room, her snakeskin shoes clicked rhythmically.

"I can't believe I've come this far," she said, feeling a smile come to her lips. Stepping into the lift, she pushed G for the ground floor. Travelling down, she couldn't help but admire the walls; three of them were upholstered in red velvet and brightened by hundreds of tiny ceiling spotlights, which also reflected from a mirrored wall. There was no part of the hotel that didn't ooze luxury.

Just then, she heard a mellifluous whisper behind her ear and felt her heart skip a beat. Wasn't she the only one in the lift?

She twisted her head around until she was facing the mirror; the bright light coming from inside the glass stung her eyes, but she could immediately tell that the reflection staring back at her wasn't her own. Instead there was a woman in a white, flawless dress. A mist veiled her. Laura moved closer to the mirror, feeling the coldness of the glass. The image before her began to oscillate. She stepped back, pressing her fingers over her eyes. When she opened them again she saw the image disappear, leaving warm steam in its wake that coiled around her, tickling her face. She had the feeling that someone was next to her, someone with whom she had a connection, and the scent of the steam filled her with desire.

The ping of the doors opening brought her back to reality. All the fragmented pieces from her delicious reverie disappeared and she realised that someone was holding on to the doors and was waiting for her to get out. Bewildered, she took one last look at each of the elevator walls, searching in vain for a spectral silhouette – a sign that what she'd just seen wasn't the product of her imagination. Eventually, she stepped out into the enormous hall, questions flooding her mind. *Had she been hallucinating? And if so, why had the experience felt so real?* She could only have been in the lift a minute or so, but it had felt like hours. Heading for the reception desk, the sound of a man laughing pierced her ears like a drill. She searched for the source of the noise, no longer sure what was real and what was imagined.

"Good morning, madam, did you enjoy your night?" the receptionist enquired. He was wearing steel-rimmed glasses and his teeth were showing slightly behind a thin-lipped smile.

"This morning I barely noticed where I was," Laura replied honestly.

"What?" the receptionist asked, which made Laura realise that she was expected to sound more positive. "I meant to say that I had a lovely time," she went on. "The view was amazing and as for the breakfast…"

The receptionist's smile grew wider. He was happy now. Laura clocked his name from the badge pinned on to the pocket of his red wine coloured jacket.

"I need a taxi, Horatio," she said, returning his grin.

"Yes, Madam, let me call one for you."

As she made her way towards the bar to get herself a drink, she noticed a bunch of people coming into it. She stepped sideways to give them more room, her eyes dropping down to their shoes. She rested her gaze on a pair of men's brogues. They were black and shiny and positioned next to some high heels, whose owner had long, elegant legs.

"That went better than expected," she overheard someone in the group say.

"All thanks to Evan," a woman replied.

At the mention of the name, Laura gasped uncontrollably, feeling a rush of air whistle around her ribs as her stomach muscles contracted. She raised her head and saw a strongly built man with jet-black hair. He was wearing a light grey suit and the sight of him sent a shiver through her body. Conversely, her cheeks flushed with heat. She noted that the woman with him was stunning.

"Am I missing something?" she wondered. "Is fate running with me or am I reading things into nothing, my mind playing tricks? Why am I having all these sensations? Right now I can feel the touch of man. It's making my skin tingle and giving me butterflies."

Taking a deep breath, Laura vowed silently to herself to pretend that she had felt nothing and headed to the bar where she ordered a strong black coffee.

20

Evan

"DID you forget something?" Gloria asked Evan, touching his elbow. He had stopped dead in his tracks but didn't know why.

"I'm not sure," he replied. "Why do I feel as if I have left something behind?"

It was typical of Evan's actions lately. He'd been acting weird, feeling nervous, sometimes lost. Maybe it was because his memories were becoming stronger now. The one-year anniversary of Alison's fatal crash was approaching and he felt himself stumbling through his days towards it.

Gloria was standing in front of him, holding the straps of her handbag in both hands and letting it swing against her thighs.

"I was wondering if we could go out tonight," she said. "What do you think? We have the right to celebrate after that agreement. We deserve to give ourselves some credit."

As Gloria spoke she lifted her gaze so that she was making direct eye contact with Evan. The expression on her face was clear, she couldn't hide her feelings about him - she was besotted.

In contrast, Evan's expression was blank and his mind wasn't on the person with him. He was indifferent to Gloria's suggestion but couldn't bring himself to tell her no. As he searched his mind for a reply he felt the collar of his shirt constricting his throat.

It didn't take Gloria long to get the picture. She dropped her gaze and pursed her lips in disappointment. Evan's silence was like a slap in the face.

He'd spent the last year committed only to his work, leaving no room for anyone. Obviously, he was not yet ready to share his life, his son, his grief with anyone.

"It's OK, Evan," Gloria said softly, touching his arm. "I do understand. I will be here for you when you are ready."

Gloria was not the type of woman who was usually turned down. She was beautiful, charming, intelligent, and she had a promising career.

What else could she possibly need to make a man fall under her spell?

As an afterthought she added: "But sometimes you have to pick up things and run with them." Then she turned her back on Evan and went off to join the other members of the team.

She left him standing there in the middle of the hall, his shoulders slumped as if the pity he felt for himself bore a physical weight.

Why couldn't he just follow his male instinct? It was still there, if hidden deep inside. And he couldn't escape the strange feeling that he had left something behind, as if something had been lurking right beneath his eyes.

21

HORATIO waved at Laura from the entrance of the bar, signalling that her taxi was ready. Before getting into the car she held her head high and took a deep breath. She felt so different from the way she had earlier while looking over the city from the safety of her room. All her confidence had fled.

"West Hurley please," she said, handing the driver a piece of paper with the full address of her destination on it.

As the driver zipped through the city's back streets, Laura felt hollow inside. She had no expectations of what she was about to find. After all, all she had was a name. How could this man possibly know what her future held?

"Oh God, where am I going," her inner voice was shouting. By the time the car pulled over she was perspiring badly.

"This is the house, Madam," the driver said, twisting his head to look at her as he spoke.

Laura was gripped by so many emotions as she gazed at the bungalow in front of her. It was covered in vine leaves that seemed to hug every corner, invading the edges of the window and twisting around the pillars at either side of the front door.

It took Laura a few moments before she could gather herself enough to get out of the car. Clutching her bag tightly she willed herself to go forward, stepping carefully as if she were walking across a field littered with landmines. At either side of the path stood planters filled with thistles that cried out to be attended to. Straightening her jacket, she climbed the steps up to the front door, keeping her gaze fixed on it. Wires poked out from the doorbell, telling her that it probably wasn't working. Her final step was the heaviest and she slowly stretched out a fist to knock on the door. She had a feeling that even the lightest touch would cause the wood to scatter and break in front of her.

Her first knock was met with silence so she tried again, taking one step backwards and resting her hand against one of the pillars. The straight lines of shingles, visible beneath the vines, went wavy in front of her eyes.

"I'm so stupid," she said to herself. "What do I want? What am I going after?"

In that moment she felt so unbalanced, her dreams so unreachable. Why was she wasting her time following a path that was not going to lead anywhere?

Maybe one more knock...

She formed a fist but her hand lost its power as soon as it made contact with the door. She dropped her gaze to the floor and noticed a glass sitting there with some paper underneath it. Bending over she picked it up and read the note written on it.

"Sorry, I've had to go to Wyoming...come and see me there, David."

Laura felt her breath get stuck in her throat. Resting her back against the pillar she couldn't help feeling deflated.

After travelling all this way...

She wondered whether it was a joke, then questioned whether the note could even be meant for her. How could it be? But upon closer scrutiny she was sure that it was her name scribbled at the top of it.

Gripping her stomach, which felt empty, she stumbled back towards the road, droplets of sweat running down her face. What was next? Why Wyoming?

She'd asked the taxi driver to wait for her, but before climbing back into the cab she caught site of a grey hat bouncing up and down behind the bushes of the house next door. Then its owner, an old woman, emerged into view. She was looking in Laura's direction curiously. Laura forced herself to smile.

"Hello, I was just next door," she explained. "I'm looking for David."

"Oh, David," said the woman, slowly dragging her feet towards the porch of her house. She slipped her gardening gloves off, revealing her small, wrinkled hands, and then the hat, beneath which her silvery hair had been flattened down.

"He's a very nice man, do you know him?"

"Not really…"

A thudding noise sounded from the front door of the old woman's house and Laura turned her head. A black and white cat had jumped from the gate, closely followed by another one, which was as white as snow. Both cats stopped at their owner's feet, pressing their soft fur against her ankles. The old woman bent down to stroke their backs in turn. Then the white one turned its attention to Laura, looking at her straight in the eye with a questioning gaze.

"My babies!" exclaimed the woman. "They can understand me without words. They can heal better than humans."

"Yes, that's correct," Laura replied with an approving smile.

"As for David, he's a very good man," the woman continued. "What happened to him is so sad"

A strange expression crossed her face, leading Laura to enquire further.

"Oh, you don't know? He had an accident, ended up in a wheelchair. That poor man, his tall strong body forced to rely on four wheels. His house has been so quiet since, I've barely seen anyone cross the threshold. They say someone died in the accident. I guess he was lucky just to end up in that wheelchair."

Laura's eyes widened at the revelation. What did this tragic man have to tell her?

"I miss having him around," the woman continued, lost in her own memories. "He used to do funny sketches for me…of the cats."

"Sketches?" Laura repeated, failing to hide the astonishment in her voice.

"Yes. David was an artist, a painter. Come, I will show you. I have one of his works inside."

The old woman pushed open her front door and then looked back towards Laura, her smile repeating the invitation. But Laura remained fixed to her spot on the middle of the porch. Her throat was dry, but she already knew that she had to see the painting.

"Can I offer you something to drink?" the old woman asked as Laura followed her into the house.

"A glass of water, please," she replied, searching the walls of the house for the painting. Every surface was covered with a souvenir so it took a while for Laura to fix on a picture in a wooden frame. It was a beautiful painting of a spring day, and so full of life.

"That's David's picture," the old woman confirmed.

"It looks like a very happy painting."

"It is indeed. And my cats are in there. Can you see? They're behind the flowers."

Laura smiled, scrutinizing the canvas even closer. But instead of finding the cats, her gaze fell on the signature in the corner of the painting. The image of the picture she saw at the London gallery flashed through her mind.

Is he?...Did he?...Was this the same artist she'd seen in London?

"What are you here for?" the woman asked, handing Laura her glass of water and interrupting her chain of thought.

"Oh, nothing important," she replied. "I was in New York and I decided I'd like to meet David in person. I met him online. He left a message for me."

"Online?"

"Yes, through the internet."

"Oh, the modern world. Everyone talks online these days, they even marry online. That's why nobody knocks on doors anymore. I thought you were an insurance person!"

"Why would you think that?"

"They often turned up after the accident. But lately it's been an ambulance…" The woman paused. Laura thought she seemed tired and out of breath. "And his friends stopped coming too. Everyone except one young man; blonde, very good looking. Even his fiancé left him after the accident. She was very beautiful but I never liked her. She had a certain look, I couldn't trust her."

"How awful," Laura commented.

"Yes, it's not fair. She fled right after the accident. Poor David, so full of energy, always smiling. He used to call me Mama Dolly. I miss him. He came over in his wheelchair only the other week, but he looked so different. It was the first time I'd seen him since his accident a year ago. He said he was going to Wyoming…mentioned something about his roots."

The word roots struck a chord with Laura. David was chasing his roots too, but unlike her at least he knew what they were.

"Shall I put the kettle on and we can talk more about David," the old woman offered.

"Oh, thank you, but I have a taxi waiting for me and I bet the driver is getting fed up of sitting there."

"He can come in too, my dear."

Laura was astonished by the benevolence of her host, but insisted that she had to leave. "Maybe next time, Mrs Dolly, or should I say Mamma Dolly?"

"The second one, it warms my heart to hear that again."

As she left the woman's house, Laura felt her anxiety grow. She'd learnt so much about David yet she still knew nothing about why he wanted to meet her.

Stepping into the taxi, she murmured the words under her breath: "I have a flight to catch."

22

"There are a few storms on the way this evening and after a mostly cloudy start to tomorrow, the sun will be making a reappearance…"

"Would you like me to change the channel, Madam?" Laura's taxi driver asked, reaching for the dial of his car radio. "Maybe some music?"

"No, it's okay. Hearing about the storm is fine with me."

In truth, it suited her mood. She gazed out of the window, at the uninterrupted views of white rock. Winding down her window, she felt the brutality of the dry air in her lungs.

"All this dry wind means a storm is definitely coming," the driver said.

But Laura didn't allow herself to be drawn into a conversation about the weather. She continued looking out of the window, this time focusing on the purple grass on the verges, which was being combed by the hot wind.

The driver pulled up. "From the address you gave me the house is supposed to be here, but I can't see any buildings."

Laura took in her surroundings. A few yards ahead stood an old church. The colour of the shingles had faded and she could almost hear its wood cracking. The house had to be behind it. Getting out of the car, she felt the tension grow in her body. At once, the gladiator-style sandals she was wearing became covered in thick dust. She became aware that she was being watched and noticed that there were lizards sheltering beneath clumps of wild bushes. Apart from these scaly-skinned creatures, there wasn't another soul around and the bright sun made her squint and attempt to shield her eyes with her hands. She decided to see if there was anyone in the church. As she neared it she became aware of the silence of the place, which was interrupted only by a cloud of dandelion stems blowing over her head.

Walking in the middle of this desert, enveloped by the hot winds and thousands of miles away from home, Laura's empty life among the crowded houses and jolly people of London somehow faded away.

She stood in front of the church for a few seconds. Its wooden door was slightly open and making a creaking sound in rhythm with the wind.

Inside she slowly walked up the path between the old wooden pews. She stared up at the big cross nailed to the wall and muttered a prayer.

"Dear God, give me strength. I need you today to find the person who dragged me all the way here. I feel so lost. Please give me a sign. Why am I here? What should I do? What am I really chasing?"

She heard the clanking sound of a door opening. At the side of the church a grey-haired head emerged from a narrow door. The owner straightened up, revealing his face, and Laura noticed a deep scar on his forehead, resembling a crater. Surrounding it, his wrinkles were visible even from such a distance.

He was clutching a toolbox in one hand and used his other to grab hold of one of the pews, stretching his legs and back with a groan. Then he slowly walked towards Laura, every feature in his old face posing a question: who are you?

"Hello," Laura said after a deep breath. "I'm looking for the house of David Boyer."

The man instantly looked as if he recognised the name, but a second or so later he shook his head slowly. Laura read fear in his expression.

"Where have you come from?" he asked.

"London."

"You've travelled a long way to this desert," he commented, clearing his throat.

Laura managed a short smile but kept her gaze fixed on the man, determined to stay put until she got an answer out of him.

He started to rub his chin, pondering what to say. Dipping his hands into the pockets of his loose trousers, Laura could see that he was hesitating to let the words come out of his mouth. Eventually, he moved closer to Laura and said in a hushed tone: "Yes, I know about him, his house is just around the corner."

It was what she had been waiting to hear, but she didn't feel happy, something was bothering her.

"Come on, I will take you there," said the man, waving his hand in the direction of the entrance, whilst still seeming hesitant.

Laura followed him to the door, which was still swinging in the wind. At its threshold the man froze, placing his hand against the frame and looking back towards Laura as if he wanted to say something. Then he sighed, shrugged and stepped outside, letting the dry wind take his unspoken words. He dragged his feeble legs forwards and Laura followed, concentrating on the footsteps he left in the dust.

"I have a taxi," Laura said. "We can drive there."

"You don't need a car, it's just around the corner," the old man said. "Besides, the road that leads up to it is covered by bushes. You can only walk."

Waving at the driver to signal that he should wait, Laura quickened her steps behind the old man, who was scratching his scrawny neck. Her knees felt weak. She had the feeling that something wasn't right.

Eventually, they crossed a pathway relatively undisturbed by pedestrians.

"Oh my God!" Laura exclaimed.

Before her stood a decrepit house, the foundations of which were surrounded by clumps of ferns, bunches of burdock flowers and American beautyberries. Naked tree branches overlapped the roof, and on the side of the path an old tree stump that had been placed there as a bench was covered in vine leaves. Next to them stood a collection of rusty buckets and an empty water trough with only one leg. The house was in a seriously weathered state.

The old man walked a few steps ahead of Laura, shouting croakily for someone called Liz. The front door of the house was wide open and eventually a woman with a round figure, short blond hair and big grey eyes appeared. She was wearing a knitted blue jumper and loose denim trousers; her shabby appearance reflected the state of the house.

"She's looking for Dave," the old man said, pointing his thumb in Laura's direction.

Liz's face crumpled as she looked towards her visitor. Meanwhile, the old man was digging his fingers into his scalp through his thin grey hair. Unspoken words were passing between them. Laura, feeling disconcerted, stepped forward.

"I'm Laura," she said, her voice trembling with emotion. "I'm from London and I'm here to see David. Is this his house?"

"This is his house, but he's not here," Liz replied.

Laura felt disappointment tug at her. She'd come all this way for nothing. She was following a nobody.

"You said your name was Laura, right?" Liz asked.

"Yes, that's me."

"He left something for you. A letter."

"But where is David?"

Liz shot the old man a look before clearing her throat and lowering her eyes. Taking a step forward she pulled a leaf from one of the juneberry shrubs that had taken root in the cracks of the decaying steps of the porch.

"He died, two days ago."

"Whaaaat?" Laura cried out. Her face contorted with anguish, her insides churned and her knees went weak. It was as if the earth had begun to shake under her feet. Instinctively she reached her hands forwards, looking for something to hold on to if she fell, but there was nothing in front of her but empty space. Losing her balance, she slumped into the side of a bush until the old man reached out his veiny hand to grab one of hers, releasing a deep groan as he did so. Liz jumped down the two steps of the porch in one swift movement, grabbing Laura's other hand. Together, the two of them pulled her up in one go.

"I better get you inside," Liz said, picking some leaves out of Laura's hair.

"I will leave you two alone," the old man said, letting Laura's hand go free. He walked away, coughing over the blowing dust.

Liz led Laura into the house and plonked her down on an uncomfortable sofa. She still felt dizzy and emotionally disturbed. *Was this the result of her long journey? Conjuring a ghost from a desert?* How pathetic. What had she been thinking? Had she been expecting someone to come from nowhere and gather her into their arms? It was time for her to surrender, give up on her unfounded dreams. Her instinct had let her down. The embers inside, fired by hope, had finally been extinguished. Once again, death had slammed the door in her face.

Her mouth was so dry that she couldn't speak a single word. Still, the urge in her was to get up and run the hell out of this ramshackle house. But as much as she wanted to she felt rooted to the ground, as if she was being controlled by something else, something she couldn't understand.

She gazed around. The sun was poking through the ripped net curtains covering the windows, shedding light on the cobwebs that had formed in every corner of the colourless walls and over the decrepit furniture. Everything looked ancient and was veiled by layers of dust. A stained brown teddy bear had been carefully placed in the corner of the sofa, and it looked like he was in charge, keeping record of the savage effects of time. A pungent smell lingered, making Laura sniff.

"Drink it," said Liz, thrusting a glass of water towards her.

She jammed both hands on the glass, clutching it tightly in an attempt to gain some control over her trembling fingers, then she drank the water in big gulps.

Liz walked over to the dining table, the floor creaking beneath her feet, and stretched her hand out to reach for something. Striding back, Laura noticed how her bust, cheeks and every curve of her body undulated in union with the desolate house. She handed her an envelope with her name written on it.

Holding it for a few minutes, Laura felt as if it was burning her fingers and swiftly dropped it inside her handbag. After all, it wasn't important any more. David was dead like everyone else. Gone forever. She didn't know how much more of this she could take.

Liz took a seat in front of her and opened her mouth to speak, though no words came out.

Laura cast her eyes over the room again. Underneath the cobwebs and the layers of dust she could see glimpses of bright colours, which hinted that the house had once been a happy home.

"He came back a week ago, after 30 years, just to die here," Liz said, clenching her hands together. "I guess he wanted to be buried close to his parents' grave.

Grave? Just hearing the word alone made Laura shiver. But the house itself was like a giant tomb. She felt a lump in her throat, tried to swallow it but found she couldn't.

"Did you know David well?" Liz asked curiously.

"Not really. So far I've seen two of his paintings and received some emails from him. That's why I came here, I wanted to meet him in the flesh."

"And you've come all this way from London? I'm sorry you didn't get the chance to meet him."

Laura nodded and didn't say anything else. How could she

possibly explain in a way that the woman would understand that she had been drawn here by a spiritual connection, something that wouldn't leave her alone, day or night.

"Dave became an artist, a painter," Liz went on. "Not so long ago I heard that he had sent a dozen or so of his paintings to a school here. The two of us were the same age. He was a very good looking boy and I had my first ever crush on him…"

Liz paused to smile at the memory, but kept her eyes down, away from Laura's gaze. Then she took a deep breath and continued.

"I remember the day they came for him. He was just ten years old. It was a man and a woman, they were from social services, and they took him away in a black car. It was just a few days after his parents' funeral. They both died in a fire, they were away at the time. David locked himself in his room, refused to come out…"

By now Liz's voice was trembling with emotion, but she gathered herself, carried on.

"It was two hours before he emerged – such a gruesome day. He walked towards the car with his head down, only turning once to take a last look at the house. He didn't cry though, I imagine that he forced himself not to. I saw his fists clenched. I guess you could say I cried enough tears for him. I hid behind the bushes to do it, only stopped when my dad slapped me across the face. David was an only child, just like me. I hated that he left me all alone in this shithole."

"Did he have any other relatives?" Laura enquired quietly.

"Yes, an auntie, but she was sick and wasn't able to take care of him. Sometimes she'd come down here and sit on the porch and talk to herself. That was until a stroke took her away. Poor lady, she never dried her eyes from the tears. Her husband had died a few months after they were married and she never remarried. David was all she had. She went to visit him once. A family in St Louis, Illinois had adopted him. They had ten other orphaned children and she found him sleeping in the garden. He'd been sharing his food with a stray dog. She hoped to take him back but her health never improved. Poor David, his childhood was devastating."

Laura didn't know what to say. The pity for her childhood friend was etched in Liz's face. She was close to tears.

"Oh, I'm sorry, it slipped my mind," she continued, rubbing her eyes. "Can I offer you a cup of tea or coffee? I brought some here last week, when David was here."

Liz was already getting up from her chair when Laura answered no thank you, and she swiftly slumped back down again.

"I was so surprised when I saw a light coming from his house. I ran straight over and what did I find? He was already half dead. He reminded me of a candle that you just know is going to extinguish at any moment. He spent most of the time looking out of the window, said he wanted to take in every fragment of his surroundings, the rock, the bushes. He barely talked but he did tell me that he should have died in the accident he was in, but that he'd been spared for one more year for a reason. He wouldn't say what that reason was though…"

***

By the time Laura stepped outside again the sky was turning grey. Dark clouds were gathering above the ramshackle house as if they wanted to gobble it up. She walked away, gripping her throbbing stomach with her hand. The door had been opened to another life, but all she'd received in return was another death to add to her list of tragedies. Again, she was left with the feeling that a normal life would always elude her. She wanted to escape, but where to? It felt as if death was following her everywhere she went.

She walked to the taxi and reached for the door. But just as she was about to pull the handle, she felt a current move through her body. A spiral of leaves and dust rose up from the ground and twirled above her head. A thunderbolt exploded in her mind and she heard a voice scream in a clear voice: "Follow it and find it…you have to find them."

She felt dizzy and could see only bright, white shapeless images before her eyes. No longer having any control over her body, she felt herself lifting off the ground, floating in the air. A moment passed, no longer than the blink of an eye, and she was back with her feet firmly on the dusty ground again. The dark clouds were dropping down, coming closer and closer. Desperately unsettled, Laura reached for the car door again and this time climbed inside. But she held the door open for a moment as if she wanted to throw her delusions out into the wind.

"None of this is real," she muttered to herself, laying her head against the seat and forcing herself to close her eyes.

The driver ducked his head out of the window to get a better look at the darkness above. "We better get moving before the storm batters us."

Just then a series of heavy raindrops hit the ground and the driver quickly started the engine.

"Did you find what you were looking for?" he asked. But when he caught sight of his passenger's face in the rear view mirror he got his answer. He could see the sadness in her eyes and knew not to press her to talk.

"Take me to the hotel, please," Laura said, slumping down further into her seat. All she wanted was to sink into a deep sleep and not be disturbed for a long time.

23

It was almost dark by the time the taxi pulled up outside Laura's hotel. She stepped outside the cab and her feet were immediately sprinkled by a slush of red-coloured water. She lifted up her head, allowing her face to be hit with the heavy droplets of rain that were coming down all around her. The air smelt like earth and she was in no hurry to escape the downpour. She looked up towards the mountains surrounding the hotel, they seemed to be beckoning all the thunder and lightning from the sky. Hearing the Green River gurgle she hugged her drenched body, but felt her insides crackle with the fire of bitterness.

By the time she got inside she was wobbly on her feet and her unsteady footsteps left wet, uneven footprints in the heavy carpet of the lobby. Her sodden fingers were trembling as she put the key in the door and let herself into her lonely room. It was dark inside but she didn't bother switching the light on. A flash of lightning outside showed her the way to her bed. Throwing her handbag down she barely noticed when all the contents spilled out. Finding a place next to them, she clenched the pillow, pushing her face into it.

"Go back to London," her inner voice told her. "There is nothing that you can do here any more. It's over."

Yet part of her still felt that she didn't belong there any more. In her desperation, she decided to call Carla and switched on her bedside light. Even the dim light emerging from the blue lampshade hurt her eyes. Her wet hair was flat against her face, merging with her tears, and she knew she looked a mess. She began to dial Carla's number but then changed her mind, putting down the receiver before entering the final digit. She knew she wouldn't be able to cope with her friend's questions and buried her head in the pillow once again.

Rain was cascading down the window and she allowed the sound of the wind against it to send her into a deep sleep, a sleep she wished could be endless.

***

By the morning the rain had stopped and a rainbow was visible from Laura's uncovered window. Her eyes followed the sun's rays to the picture behind her bed, and she sat up and twisted around in order to get a closer look. For a moment she was lost in the deep blue ocean depicted in it. It looked so calm and peaceful. Her head and body felt lighter somehow and she turned her attention to the items scattered all over the bed, her hand reaching for the white envelope. She took it to the window in order to look once again at the rainbow, which had drawn a breathtaking picture of its own over the clear blue sky. Pulling her eyes away she gazed down at the envelope. Her name was written on it in big capital letters. She tore it open, speaking out loud as if its author might somehow be able to hear.

"What was so important, David, that you had to drag me from London?"

Inside the envelope was a piece of paper covered in handwritten words that seemed to convey the exhaustion of the man who had composed them. Without further hesitation, Laura began to read.

Dear Laura,

I have been anxiously waiting for you to come, and as you're reading this it must mean that you have. I realise how strange it must have been for you to receive my emails, and I am so happy that you acted on them. This has been really important to me in the year since I was involved in a horrific crash that put me in a wheelchair.

Even while I was unconscious, and every night since, I have seen your face. Sometimes you are serious, sometimes sad, and it's driven me to try and explain something very important to you. In truth, I don't know exactly what it is about, but I believe that it is going to be important for your future happiness. I hope it will eventually make some sense to you, even if I will never fully understand it myself.

I knew I wasn't going to last forever so I turned the visions I had of you into a number of portraits. You should see these as postcards to you from your future.

I am not sure where all of this has come from, but I know that it has something to do with my accident, and that I recovered enough to be able to reach out to you. In fact, I think this was my main reason for living.

When I saw your profile and picture on your web page, I immediately knew that I had to get you to come here.

I am so weak now that I can hardly hold a pen. The accident didn't kill me but I also have cancer of the spine, which I'm not going to beat. It's a shame that we never had a chance to talk face-to-face, but now that you are reading this I can be content in knowing that I have been able to do what I was meant to.

Go Laura and find your own happiness. I have started your journey and now you must continue it. You will carry all my love while you find the person you need to share yours with.

David

Laura placed the letter carefully on a mahogany table and slumped into a chair, resting her elbows next to it and holding her head in her palms. This dead man obviously felt some kind of mysterious connection with her. But what had he meant by going to find her happiness? This was completely outside the orbit of her understanding. She picked up the envelope again and a newspaper cutting and another small envelope flew out. The headline of the report read, "Fatal Accident on Route 53". She read on.

A woman was killed and her three-year-old son left fighting for his life after their vehicle collided with an oncoming motorcycle. The driver of the motorcycle remains in hospital in a serious condition.

Next to the print was a hazy picture depicting the scene, but somehow Laura could detect every microscopic element from the image. But it wasn't just her vision that was super sharp. The scene was unfolding in front of her like a clip from a movie, and it was enveloping her too. She could hear the blasting sound of the crash inside her head, feel the pain experienced there at the moment of impact...a head hitting the hard ground, fingers scraping along the gravel, blood flooding from a mouth, a last breath drifting away.

A moment later, Laura had her head out of the window and was gasping for air between coughs. Her throat was dry and tight and tears burned in the corner of her eyes before rolling down her face.

"Oh God I was there," she heard herself muttering. "I felt everything."

Deep in her subconscious she had touched death. Pulling herself away from the window, still with the cutting clenched in her hands, she sunk down on to the bed. It was as if part of her soul had flown away with that last breath, which she knew couldn't have come from her own lungs, even if it felt that way.

But there was more. She reached inside the smaller envelope and pulled out a photo. A beautiful boy's face smiled up at her from it. His brow was covered with jet-black hair, his eyes were sparkling, his skin pure, his pearly white teeth perfect. Laura couldn't help smiling back as she ran her fingers over the image, which seemed to give off a positive energy. This boy was the cutest little thing she had ever seen and she drew the photo to her chest as if she would somehow be able to hear the boy's heart beating. She felt warm inside, content even. Closing her eyes she took a deep breath and exhaled. She was feeling something like never before, as if a living thing with a real smile and a real touch was in the room with her.

Turning the photo over she saw some words written on the back of it.

"Murray Topillow. D.O.B. March 12, 2010."

A gasp jumped from her throat. She buried her head into her folded knees. Her stomach muscles clenched as if she was experiencing the contractions of giving birth. That date was seared into her memory. It was the date of her miscarriage.

***

Everything was moving fast around her. She felt as if she was caught in the midst of a hot storm. Even the view from the window, the mountains and the dust and the blue sky, was out of focus, like oil colours being mixed together. Eventually they switched to black and Laura lost all sense of time, lying in her bed for hours.

Later, she slowly got up and looked out of the window, which now revealed a beautiful orange sunset. Her mind was clear and she knew exactly what her next step would be.

24

One Year Earlier, New York
David

THE sound of the phone ringing in the sitting room startled David, causing him to drop his brush, which he'd already used to mix the pastel oil colours set out on a thick wooden work table. He lifted himself up, gripping his lower back while casting an eye over his unfinished painting on the easel. He walked backwards in order to carry on scanning his composition, his gaze moving to the empty red wine bottle and two glasses next to it. He grinned, recalling the previous night and the chaos they'd created: how she'd silently crept up behind him while he'd worked. She'd placed the wine bottle and the glasses on the table then squeezed his big shoulders from behind. Her long, curly black hair had brushed against his face, and with one swift movement he'd been able to spin around, gathering her delicate body into his arms and sitting on the chair, pressing her down into his lap. He'd moved a clump of velvety curls from her face and rubbed a finger over her plump lips, struck by how much her blue eyes shone.

"Oh God, you are so pretty," he'd said. "Beauty has only one other name, and that is Kaitlin."

"Mmmmm, I appreciate the eyes that see me this way," Kaitlin had replied.

"Let me do a picture of you," David had suggested, moving his fingers from her face down to her shoulders, then to one of her breasts.

"But you've done that already. I sat for you for a week."

"But that was a long time ago."

"Surely I haven't changed in six months?"

"Yes, you have become a wrinkled old lady!"

"Oh, shut up," Kaitlin had said, turning her head to check out his latest painting.

"What have you named this one?"

"Symphony of the Dry Land."

"Can't you find something more attractive to paint? This looks too earthy."

"But this interests me."

"What does?"

"The fact that it's about feelings, the things that we humans can't see but feel instead…the energy, movements and vibrations that come from the rocks, the greens, the cracks in the dry earth and the steam that rises after the rain. It's as if a symphony is being played by all the features of nature."

David had grinned, before adding: "But for now we have to conduct our own symphony."

Grabbing the bottle, he'd filled each glass in turn. "God, you are really beautiful."

"Do you know that you are the most romantic man in New York?"

"Hmmmm, tell me more about that."

David had pressed his face into Kaitlin's neck and put his hands up the back of her t-shirt. In response, she'd twisted her body round until she was facing him, wrapping her legs around the back of the chair for balance and pressing herself into his chest. The feel of her breasts brushing against him drove David wild, prompting him to stand up while still holding onto her. He'd rested her against the wooden table and soon open cans filled with paint were splashing over the dozens of sketches laid out on it. David didn't care. He'd slipped off Kaitlin's t-shirt while she'd hurriedly unbuttoned his shirt. Grasping at her hips he'd pulled her closer, his lips burning with passion as he ran them over her naked torso. Kaitlin had dug her fingers into David's hair, pulling him closer still, inviting him to enter her. As he did so, wine poured from the bottle and the glasses, mixing with the oil paints. Meanwhile, their own bodies became covered in paint and they drew a colourful abstract composition of their own as they moved together.

The memory caused David to instinctively reach into his trouser pocket for the ring, which he rotated over one of his fingers. He'd so wanted to put it on Kaitlin's own finger, but the timing had been wrong.

The ring meant so much to him; it was the only physical thing he had left from the first ten years of his life, when he'd been blessed with the unconditional love of his parents. Their deaths had left him jumping from home to home, school to school. The ring had belonged to his mother and until recently he'd kept it on a chain around his neck. Now, clenching it between his fingers, he felt his mum and dad watching over him from heaven.

He could still hear the voice of one of his neighbours declaring right after the funeral, "Good thing they didn't have more children, that they left only one orphan."

He'd often wondered since how different his life would have been if he'd had brothers or sisters. Of course, it would have meant that he'd have been able to say, "I have a family".

But it wasn't too late for him. He could start one with Kaitlin. Why not? He was 40, she ten years younger, and there was a great chemistry between them. She was smart, beautiful, everything that a man could dream of. Kaitlin, a dancer, shared his passion for the arts and they both respected each other's careers. David never missed any of her shows and she attended all of his exhibitions. But the topic of children had somehow never come up. Their love was strong, though, and David was convinced that Kaitlin would share his desire for a big family. He threw the ring in the air, catching it in his palm and enclosing it in a fist.

"I have to find the right moment to free this from my pocket," he whispered under his breath.

The sound of the phone cut through his daydream. He reached for the receiver just before the caller rang off.

"Can I speak to Mr David Boyer?"

"Yes, this is he."

"Hello Mr Boyer, I'm calling from Hurley Hospital. Your physician has arranged an appointment for you here, it's tomorrow at 10am."

"But why? Do I have to attend?"

"Yes, Sir, you ought to come."

David put the phone down, confused by the call, which had come relatively out of the blue. A few days earlier he'd had some tests done. He'd been suffering from back and neck pain, and a little weakness in his arms, but he'd figured that it was to do with the longs hours he spent painting. He had an exhibition coming up and had been working around the clock to prepare for it. He couldn't imagine it was anything serious because he'd always been robustly healthy, rarely even got the flu. He was as strong as an ox.

Rubbing his palm against the slight stubble on his jaw, he went to the kitchen, took a bottle of dry gin from the cupboard and pulled off the top. But as he lifted it towards his mouth to take a gulp, he lost his grip and it fell from his hand, smashing against the tiled floor. Taking a deep breath, he left behind the mess of glass and liquid and walked back into the studio where he took a seat facing his unfinished painting and stared at it for a long time, without blinking.

***

As the nurse read out his name, David was sending a text message.

Sorry I can't make it today. Something has come up. I'll call you later.

The text was for his friend, Fred, a fellow artist. Once a week they'd haul their easels, paints and a bottle of wine to a different spot, each new location bringing fresh excitement. Fred had become an important part of David's life since they'd first met at the opening of his first exhibition.

Fred had been standing with both hands dipped in his jeans pockets, looking closely at each painting, as if trying to detect their soul. After analysing each one he took a seat on the concrete steps outside and pulled out a sketchbook and pencil from his bag. David had slipped outside for a breath of fresh air, had noticed one of Fred's drawings.

"Very impressive," he'd said.

The sketch depicted a narrow street stretching back to a narrow point in the distance.

"What's at the end of the road?" David had asked.

"The things that I like to imagine and want to see."

The two artists introduced themselves and upon hearing David's name, Fred immediately clicked.

"I just saw your paintings," he'd said.

"Any good?" David had asked wryly.

"Of course they are. I like them. You can find your lost soul in those paintings."

"Wow, that's the best compliment ever. Thanks."

Then David had stood up and announced: "It is time to celebrate lost and found souls. Do you have time for a beer or have you got something else to do?"

Fred's eyes had crinkled into a smile. "I don't have anything better to do than talk of lost souls."

Since that day their friendship had blossomed naturally. They were both orphans and Fred had never known his parents, moving from one orphanage to the next throughout his childhood. The two men could sense each other's pain. Spending time together allowed them to find peace and consolation, becoming for each other the family they had never had. Each of them knew that any of their offspring would automatically have an uncle.

But for now their weekly meet up would have to wait. David took his place behind the nurse, following her steps and watching her long, straight ponytail as it swished back and forth. She led him into the office of a doctor by the name of Thorn, promptly dropping his file on his desk and exiting the room, closing the door quietly behind her.

David laid his motorbike helmet on the desk and took a seat, his eyes focusing on the folder. Seeing his name on it made him edgy and he could feel the throb of his pulse in his neck. Unzipping his fitted leather jacket he transferred his gaze from the folder to Dr Thorn, who was seated with his fingers crossed over each other, rotating his thumbs. His grave expression told David that what he was about to say was serious.

After a lengthy silence he gave the patient a brief smile before clearing his throat and pulling the folder closer to him. As he read the contents he ran his finger through his hair. Sunlight shone through the window behind him causing David to squint as Dr Thorn met his gaze. Putting his palms flat over the folder, the doctor exhaled and went straight to the point.

"The results show an anomaly in the function of your central nervous system."

It felt like thousands of flies were buzzing in David's head. He clenched the leather of his trousers.

"The cells of the spine keep dividing, forming a lump…"

The doctor stopped, as if to measure David's reaction so far.

"Lump?" David said. "What kind of lump?"

"A tumour, it's a tumour."

David felt the colour drain from his face. A surge of emotions rose up inside him and it felt as if his chest would burst open at any moment. He rested his elbows on his thighs and his head in his hands, the shock making it instantly too heavy to hold up. When he finally lifted it up again, his eyes were bloodshot.

"What type of tumour is it, Doctor?"

"It's malignant. I'm sorry, David, but we have to do a number of tests before we can decide on your treatment. We need to find out the size and position of the tumour."

By now David felt dizzy. The immaculate office whirled around him. His brain may have been pre-programmed with all it needed to live and survive, but this sudden news was taking him in the opposite direction of life, and he was finding it very difficult to swallow.

"We'll do a CT scan. It will help us to build up a picture of the tumour."

In his mind's eye, David visualised a creepy tree planted inside him. Soon it would take over his body, spreading out branches like the long nails of a witch's finger from a dark fairy tale. But while fairy tales usually have a happy ending, he had a different fate.

As Dr Thorn gave him further details about his spine cancer and the different treatment options, David felt that it was just a matter of looking at how easy or complicated the march to his own funeral would be.

"What's the prognosis?" he demanded to know.

Dr Thorn inhaled deeply and pressed his lips together, absent-mindedly tapping a pen on the desk.

"How long? How much time is there left for me, Doctor?" David pushed on.

"With the right treatment we may be able to slow down the growth of the tumour. It could be a year."

***

David pushed himself through the hospital doors feeling numb. The sun's warm rays continued to shine from the blue sky but they felt icy on his face. One more year to live. What was that? A gift or a favour, like a bank postponing a credit card payment? The beating of his heart now felt like a clock ticking inside him.

He walked towards where his motorbike was parked and

struggled to put on his helmet. Switching on the ignition, he had no particular destination in mind as he exited the hospital; he just wanted his wheels to take him as far as they could. He had limited days on the calendar left and time had absolute control over him. The right to make plans, have dreams, no longer belonged to him.

25

Evan and Alison

"Hmmmm, I want a few more minutes in bed with you," Alison murmured, pressing herself into Evan's back and resting her golden head on his shoulder as he covered his chin with shaving foam.

Evan stopped what he was doing and looked at his Santa Claus image in the mirror before turning to face Alison, kissing her and covering her face with white froth. Taking one step backwards he studied her closely.

"Missed a bit," he said, taking some of the foam and rubbing it onto her nose.

"Oh, you are funny," Alison said, covering his mouth with a kiss. "I'll go and put the kettle on and make you some pancakes with honey."

Grabbing a hand towel from the radiator, she began wiping the foam from her face.

"I'm sorry, honey, but I'll have to skip breakfast today. I need to send some quick emails before I go to the office."

"Can't you do that later?"

"You know how important today's meeting is. There's a very good chance it will take our firm to the next level."

"Does that mean I have to see your picture instead of you at the dinner table?"

"Come on, honey, don't make that face, it's only for the short term."

Once he'd finished shaving, Evan slapped his face to alleviate the burning sensation and picked up his laptop from the bedside table. He hesitated before turning it on, aware of Alison's gaze on him.

"Both of us can't have an office here in the house."

"Yes, I know that," Alison replied. "I'm the lucky one."

"And you insisted on working here. We both made compromises there."

"Yes, I did, and I don't regret it. It was the best decision for Murray, at least he has one of us around all day. I couldn't leave him with a nanny, but sometimes I miss being out there."

Evan was all too aware of the sacrifice that Alison had made by turning down the position of cardiac nutritionist at New York University health centre. Instead of taking the esteemed role she'd opened a private practice, building an extension next to their home in Richmond.

Evan had helped her to set it up, and things were going well, both for the couple and their son.

"I promise you I will be there for dinner," Evan said. "I bet Judith's already got the muffins in the oven."

"Oh, I do like your mum's muffins."

"Well, I know she's at the cabin," Evan went on. "I called them yesterday. She and Arthur had already arrived. Mum is trying to keep herself busy."

"It's good that they both retired at the same time," Alison commented. "This is like a long-term honeymoon for them."

"Maybe, but I doubt it," said Evan. "If I know my mum as well as I think I do then she'll not be able to resist going to check up on Jason. Oh, and he's coming to the cabin tomorrow."

"How is he?"

"He's excited about taking over the clinic. But you know my little brother, ever the extrovert."

"He'll be fine running it on his own."

"I know that he's fallen for his new assistant, but he's nervous about committing. You know the male ego."

"So, he's found a new fish in the sea."

"Yes, and I hope this one will be the real thing."

"Well, if he brings her to the cabin then she'll be in his trap for sure," Alison giggled.

"Oh, yes..."

"Like you trapped me!"

"First you trapped *my* heart, and then I trapped you in that cabin."

"I better get Murray's bag ready before he wakes up," Alison said, turning her attention to more practical concerns. She pulled a big holdall from the wardrobe and started filling it with the clothes they'd need for their short vacation.

Evan's parents' cabin in Woodstock was the place they traditionally escaped to. Tucked away in the Catskills Mountains, Evan loved to go mountain biking in the labyrinths of the surrounding woods. He'd ride until the sweat was dripping from him before cooling off under the nearby waterfalls. He also liked nothing more than to watch a storm unfold from the canopy bed on the porch. Here, he could almost feel the breath of the trees under the noise of the rain. The best days of Evan's life had been spent at Woodstock.

***

Trips to the cabin became a favourite for Alison too when she became a member of the Topillow family. The bond of love they shared constantly amazed her, and during the seven years she'd been married to Evan she'd become part of that bond. They called Woodstock 'The Enchanted Place', and it was where Evan had first taken Alison to meet his family. It was snowing then, and their agenda for the week was skiing.

Just before they had gone inside, Alison had grabbed hold of Evan's arm to prevent him from entering.

"Wait, wait a minute," she'd said, taking a deep breath. She was rubbing her chilly hands together but at the same time her body wrapped inside her coat felt boiling hot.

"You look good, baby, don't worry," Evan had soothed, curving his hand around her back and pulling her closer to him. "They will love you."

Her nerves had soon vanished with the warm welcome she had received, and since that day it had felt like she had been with the Topillow family all her life.

"Oh honey, don't forget Murray's bike," Evan called from behind his laptop. "I left it in the garage, but I don't want him to see it. It's going to be a surprise."

"Like father like son!" remarked Alison.

"Oh yes, he's inherited the good bits."

The garage in Woodstock was chock-full of Evan's bike collection, including his first mountain bike which Arthur, his stepdad, had bought for him. That one would always be special for Evan because of the excitement he'd felt that day as he rode through the woods on his first proper bicycle. Judith had married Arthur, who had been her attorney, years after Evan's father had died following a long illness. Evan was nine at the time, Jason six, and they'd been happy to have a new father figure in their lives. Arthur was an active man and took the boys hiking, kayaking, biking and skiing to their hearts' content.

***

Alison crouched down, clearing some of Murray's toys from the floor and picking certain ones out to take on the trip. Then she swiftly slipped off her t-shirt and silk pyjama top to change. As she did so, she felt Evan's eyes on her from behind. Her body was like a delicate flower, so fragile and perfect. Shaking her head, she felt the heavy waves of her hair brushing against her back and turned to look at her husband. Feeling the power of her own sensuality she moved towards Evan, standing before him and bending down, covering his head with her long, golden hair. He raised his head up and their lips soon found each other.

"Hmmmm, you smell so nice," Evan whispered, the sound of his voice alone sending a charge of butterflies through Alison's tummy. He ran his fingers through her hair, gently kissing her neck before moving his hand down under the waistband of her sweatpants. Then he lay down on the bed, pulling Alison down with him and wrapping his legs around hers.

"Hmmmm, don't you have to send your emails?"

"Yes, but they can wait a bit longer."

Just then, a rumbling noise came from the corridor. They both recognised the noise – a toy bus on a rope. Murray was pulling it towards their bedroom. A second later he had pushed the door open and entered, rubbing his sleepy eyes.

"Your emails can wait but he can't," said Alison, easing herself out of Evan's grip.

Evan buried his head in the pillow and chuckled as Murray climbed up to join them, bringing his toy bus with him, which he rolled back and forth between his parents. His soft milky cheeks were soon covered with their kisses.

***

Dressed in a blue navy t-shirt and white linen trousers, Alison walked out of the front door clutching Murray's hand. With his free hand he was holding on to his purple Barney dinosaur.

"Mum, will Grandma be waiting for me?" he asked.

"Yes, honey, and guess what she's making for you?"

"Chocolate muffins!" Murray replied, jumping up and down with a look of pure delight.

"And we are going to have lots of fun," Alison said, squeezing his hand. Each time she felt her little boy's hand in hers it reminded her how gratified she was, how content. She had the man of her dreams and in her son, the family she'd never had. Growing up, she'd held her nanny's hand more times than her own mum's. Both her parents had worked in law, had been focused heavily on their careers.

"Mum, will I see the pecker bird?"

"Its proper name is a Red-Belly Woodpecker," Alison replied. "If we leave some food in the garden then maybe he will pay us a visit."

She glanced at her watch and saw that it was a quarter to nine. Looking up towards the sky she noticed white clouds, like balls of candyfloss, were moving quickly, leaving the sun exposed for the first time that morning.

"Mum, mum, give it to me…that beep thing."

"Yes honey," Alison replied. She dropped the car keys into his hand. Murray pressed the button on them and as the electric locks clicked open he squealed with delight. His exuberance was infectious and Alison grinned as she helped him into his child seat and pulled the belt over him.

"There we are, all ready," she said, scrunching his hair. "Now give me a kiss."

As Murray kissed his mother's cheeks he began to count. "One, two…"

"And where's the third one?" Alison asked.

"Here," Murray giggled, throwing his arms around his mum's neck and pressing his lips against her one more time.

Alison slid into the driving seat, diving into her handbag for her sunglasses, which she discovered weren't there.

"Oh damn, I must have left them inside," she muttered. "But we're late already, I'm not going back for them."

Placing her bag on the passenger seat she put on her seatbelt. It didn't seem to click into place properly so she pushed it in again.

"That's better," she exclaimed, putting her key in the ignition. Just then, her phone buzzed with a text message. She pulled her phone from her bag and swiped the screen to read it, her eyes sparkling as she did so.

I love your pretty face. You're the best jewel of my life.

Her lips flickered into a tender smile and she ran her fingers over the screen, reciting Evan's message in her mind.

"I love you too, honey bear," she said out loud. "Thank you for allowing me to start each day happier than the one before. No words can describe the boundless love I have for you."

Dropping the phone back into her bag she inhaled deeply. Her eyes were watery and she felt full of emotion. She could still feel Evan's touch, his breath on her soft skin. Taking one last glance in the rear view mirror at Murray, who was holding his dinosaur tight, she started the engine and hit the road.

***

After passing route 87 she stopped for a refuel before taking a right turn on to West Hurley Road. She was now just fifteen minutes away from Woodstock, and despite the warm sunny day she felt the fresh breeze coming through the trees from The Ashokan Reservoir.

"Spirit of the woods, I talk with them," she said out loud.

It was what Evan often repeated after returning from one of his bike rides, his sweat smelling sweet to her.

"Did you talk with your woods today?" she'd teased him once.

He'd just ridden his bike from Belle Ayres Mountain to Ashokan.

"Today I was in a bit of a hurry to break my speed record," he'd replied.

Alison knew that it was in the woods and the mountains where Evan could feel his spirit running free. His relationship with nature had become an important part of her and Murray's lives too.

"Why don't they talk to me?" she'd joked that day. "Or is there a special language I have to use?"

"Baby, when the woods realise how beautiful you are, the

kind of spirit you have inside, they will talk to you and you will know about it."

As he'd spoken, Evan had held her arms and kissed her forehead.

Now in the car, Alison felt embraced by the pristine perfection of nature. She glanced at the time. It was 10.30, not that she had to watch the time today. It was a habit she couldn't shake, even during holiday time. Evan would be joining them in the evening and until then she had a whole day in which to relax at the cabin.

As she signalled to overtake a white van, she glanced at Murray who was still happily playing with his dinosaur friend, moving him through the air as if he could fly.

A split second later, a thunderous noise broke their peaceful silence. Alison saw the wheels of a motorbike moments before they smashed through her front window, scattering tiny cubes of glass all around her head. The last thing she saw were the cyclist's eyes through the visor of his helmet before it smashed into her face.

As the billions of links between Alison's neurons disintegrated and her essence collected itself to leave her shattered body, it seemed to pass through David's own flesh, his helmet still buried in her face, his motorcycle leathers covered in her blood: an unnatural intimacy.

For the two strangers, all that was left was the quietness of death and near death whilst all around them metal ground against the road as the car spun away, hitting a post on the side of the road. Meanwhile, David's motorbike, its engine still running, flew out from under him, rolling over and over until coming to a stop in a field next to the road.

Inside the car, Murray fought for breath, feeling tightness in his chest and the taste of blood in his mouth from where his teeth had sunk into his tongue. By the time the emergency services arrived on the scene he had already slipped into unconsciousness.

26

THE sound of applause and of champagne corks popping filled the air as fizzy white foam spilled on to the floor of Evan's office in Manhattan.

"You did it," said one his colleagues, Liam, holding his glass up in a salute. Evan held his own glass aloft and chuckled in response. All his hard work had paid off. It had worked out well having one foot planted firmly in the Manhattan business world, the other in the solid base of his family.

It seemed he had a glittering future ahead, and today he was the centre of attention, with all of his colleagues discussing his strategy, which had helped the firm win the biggest contract in its history.

"Your approach was brilliant, we're all so proud of you," Liam added. Someone else came over to congratulate him, occupying the space between Evan and Liam and extending her slim wrist to clink his glass. It was Evan's other close colleague, Victoria.

"To the most charming man of the day," she announced.

"Steady there," Liam joked. "He's a married man."

"Hmmmm, well, had I been twenty years younger I would have stolen him for sure."

"What about me? I'm twenty years older than him?" Liam piped up, rubbing his baldhead.

"Do you think that qualifies you for what you so covet?" Victoria shot back, looking at Liam, one of her eyebrows raised.

"Lady, don't make me do a hair transplant at my age," Liam said.

"Oh, now, if you do that you'll definitely get me."

Evan smiled at them benevolently, clasping a hand on each of their shoulders, careful not to spill any of his champagne.

"Now, in my opinion you deserve each other," he grinned.

Victoria and Liam had been with the company since its launch and had been dating each other ever since, but, afraid of disturbing the cosiness of their lives, had never taken the next step. When Evan had joined the team, the couple both agreed that he'd add the spice the company needed and now, on his office desk, was an envelop containing the details of his promotion; he had been made a director of marketing. But it was a day of celebration for everyone as they were all due pay rises.

As more drinks were being poured, Irene, the company secretary, appeared at the entrance of the conference room where they were holding their impromptu party. She scanned the room for Liam, catching his eye and beckoning for him to leave his colleagues and come over. Liam noticed the look of gravity on her face and left Victoria holding his freshly filled champagne glass. She was talking to Evan about his new office, but Evan's attention was somewhere else now, on Irene and Liam by the door. They looked as if they were debating whether to leave the room or come further into it.

Evan gave his own glass to Victoria, leaving her with three to juggle, and strode over to them. "What's going on?" he asked.

Meanwhile, Victoria, who was starting to spill the champagne, dumped the glasses on the nearest bit of furniture she could find, a chair near the enormous oval conference table, and ran after him, rubbing her hands on her skirt to dry them.

Liam was rubbing his palm over his jaw and looked as if he was struggling to find a solution to an irksome task. Irene next to him had her eyes fixed to the floor.

"There's been a..." she began in a quiet voice.

Evan flinched. He knew something had happened and turned to Liam with a questioning look. His colleague moved forward, gripping his arm.

"Evan, there's been an accident."

"Accident," he repeated, his throat tightening. "What accident, where?"

"On the way to Woodstock…I'm sorry."

Evan clenched his tie and forcefully pulled it down. Two of his shirt buttons pinged loose in the process.

"Oh God. Murray, Alison?"

He felt the power in his legs cut off and lost his balance, staggering slightly until he found a wall to lean against. As soon as he made contact with it he slid down until he was resting on his haunches.

Liam bent over and reached for his arm while calling for Victoria. "Help me to hold him up," he said.

But his girlfriend was frozen with shock, covering her open mouth with her hand. A moment later she gathered herself and the pair of them grabbed Evan under his armpits, straining to pull him up.

"Evan, come on, we don't know anything yet," Liam said. "You have to go to the hospital. We'll come with you."

Such was his state of shock that Evan couldn't reply.

27

As soon as they arrived at the hospital they were directed to the surgical ward. Evan's heart was pumping hard in his chest. When the doctor came out to see him a white mask was still hanging from his neck.

"Your son sustained a severe head injury," he explained. "We had to perform surgery to drain the blood from his brain. Now we have to wait to see if the swelling goes down. The rhythm of his heart has also been affected. We are monitoring that too."

"Alison, my wife, how is she?" Evan asked.

The doctor sighed. "Sorry Evan, she died before she arrived here."

Evan staggered towards the nearest chair and slumped into it. For a moment he was pure animal and had no thoughts or plans, just pain and rage. His face was soaked with tears, snot and saliva and he thrashed his arms out when Victoria and Liam tried to comfort him.

Eventually, one of them managed to press a glass of water to his mouth, which he gulped down, immediately feeling that he wanted to sick it back up again.

A short while later his mum Judith and brother Jason arrived. Grabbing his shoulders, Jason pulled Evan into tight hug, holding him until he'd finished retching and heaving. His mum wiped his wet face with her scarf and stroked his hair as her own tears flowed. An element of calm returned to Evan and the nurse who had been waiting patiently in the wings stepped forward. "We can take you to see your son now," she said.

As Evan lifted his head he became aware of the people around him as if for the first time. Testing his legs he stood up, supporting himself on his brother's shoulders, and the two of them made their way to the post-operative recovery room.

Evan's little son, the most precious thing in his life, was lying on a trolley and was attached to various tubes and wires; a ventilator was pumping air into his tiny lungs.

Evan stroked his soft warm cheek below the bandage swaddling his head.

"Oh God, please, please," he cried before laying his head on his son's hand until it was wet with his tears.

"We expect him to make a full recovery," the nurse said. "It is amazing how strong youngsters are."

Evan turned his head, his eyes pleading for a miracle. He wanted the nurse to repeat herself, needed to be sure that he'd heard her words correctly.

"Really? Will he survive?" he asked, wiping his face with his palms.

As if hearing his question the doctor entered the room. After seeing that the boy's cheeks were pink and feeling his face for warmth, he checked the heart monitor.

"His rhythm is now normal," he declared. "This is good news."

Evan felt a flood of relief surge through him. His son was going to live. He didn't want to think about Alison. The idea that she was dead was too much for him to fully absorb. He'd start to come to terms with that later. For now he was holding his son's hand and nothing else mattered.

***

Night came. The preceding hours had felt like years. Evan sat in the visitors' waiting room staring at the darkness outside, his head full of terrifying thoughts and the image of Alison's face. In a nearby ward, under hot fluorescent hospital lights and wrapped in bandages and jabbed with tubes, lay his son. Life and death were so close to each other and Evan felt so feeble, too exhausted to even cry anymore.

He felt a touch on his shoulder from behind but didn't react. It was only when the person persevered, touching him with greater force, that Evan turned around.

A pale-faced, handsome young man was stood before him. He was tall with untidy blonde hair and he was dressed in jeans and a sleeveless black t-shirt splattered with paint. Evan's own hair was all over the place and his eyes were bloodshot and underscored by dark rings. Feeling uncomfortable, the man unconsciously took a step backwards. He felt so useless, unsure of where asking for help from this man would get him, but he persevered anyway.

"Sorry, Sir, I just...I just wondered if..." He took a deep breath before continuing. "My name's Fred. It's my friend, he needs a blood transfusion but he has a rare blood type, AB +, and I'm searching for people who may be a match to donate their blood."

Evan kept his eyes fixed on the young man without saying a single word. He sighed, feeling deflated until his instinctive humanity took over.

"Yes, I have that type," he said in almost a whisper.

Fred's relief was palpable. A big smile spread across his face.

"Thank you, Sir, I can't begin to tell you how grateful I am. He's my friend and he means everything to me. In fact, he's the only family I have. When I heard about the accident near Woodstock I was so afraid for him. Someone died in it."

"What did you say?" Evan asked. "An accident in Woodstock?"

"Yes, that's what they told me," Fred replied, shrugging. "My friend is still in a coma."

Evan's face darkened and his breath became unsteady, his chest rising and falling as he took quickened intakes of air. He felt a mixture of emotions, ranging from pure hatred to sympathy for this stranger in need. He wished he could crumple up in a ball on the floor but instead he forced himself to stay upright in his chair. His fixed his gaze on his hands and said: "Life's a bitch sometimes, it can put you in some awkward situations, but I guess that's one of the aspects of being human."

Taking a deep breath in he clapped his hands together once, wiped his face with his sleeves and stood up.

"Yes, I will do it," he told the expectant stranger.

28

David

DAVID'S eyelids flickered before suddenly opening wide. He found himself looking straight up at some bright strobe lighting, which immediately made him want to close them again. But then he noticed that there was something else there too: two jade-coloured eyes were peering down at him. He sucked some air deep into his throat and with a wince moved his head, trying to get a better view of his surroundings. Looking down at his own body he saw that half of it was swathed in bandages. His fingers were stiff too, and one by one he tried to move them.

Pressing his palms flat against the mattress, he strained to lift himself up, using his body weight to swing his legs around until they were dangling from the bed. Reaching out to grasp the wheelchair next to him, he slid down into it and headed towards the door. The wheels of the chair squeaked as he moved down the deserted corridor, the ceiling lights flickering above his head. He found himself coming to a halt outside one of the hospital rooms. The door was open and he saw a woman standing over a little boy in a hospital bed. She was stroking his head while he slept peacefully. Beneath his arm he was cradling a toy purple dinosaur. In the corner of the room a man was sleeping in a chair. The room was dark but the boy's bed was surrounded by light. Perhaps sensing his presence, the woman turned and their eyes met.

"Have I painted those eyes before?" David wondered to himself as his gaze remained locked on the woman. They were a deep, dark green and there was something so familiar about them. They seemed to be able to see straight into his soul.

He opened his mouth to ask the woman who she was, but the words wouldn't come out. She came closer to him, took his hand.

"You have to find her, David," she whispered in his ear. Then she dropped something light into hand. When David looked at it he saw that it was a photo of a cute little boy with a big smile on his face.

"Wait a minute," he said. "Is this the boy who is sleeping?"

He raised his head to try and see for himself, but noticed that the woman was gone. Then he heard a voice in the distance that gradually became louder.

"Doctor, come here quickly. David is waking up."

He blinked his eyes and tried to focus on what was happening. It took a moment for him to recognise a familiar face among the medical staff: the beautiful face of Kaitlin.

"Welcome back," she smiled. "The doctor tells me that you have been very, very lucky."

David lifted his head from the pillow, groaning over the ache in his ribs. The white room around him was unfamiliar and on the table next to his bed stood a bunch of fresh flowers and lots of cards. He tried to lift himself up but his body wouldn't obey his will and he slumped back down again, powerless and full of pain.

A thudding noise sounded in his ears and he felt his head making contact with the hard ground with force as glass shattered all around him. Squeezing his eyes shut the image of a woman's face invaded the darkness. The feel of his eyelids being forcibly opened and a flashlight being shone into his eyes interrupted the memory.

"Do you remember what happened?" asked the doctor.

David squeezed his eyes shut trying to recall earlier events. Some fragments started to flow over him, but he wasn't able to separate his delusions from reality.

"Kaitlin," he said, his voice weak. As he focused on her face he saw pain etched into it, moisture around her eyes. But she managed a smile when she noticed David looking at her and stepped closer to him, grabbing his hand.

"Do you remember what happened?" The doctor asked again.

"I remember the sound of a blast," David said. "My body hitting the ground. And a woman. I remember her face, her eyes. How long have I been here?"

"Forty-eight hours," the doctor replied. "You're in a very bad way. Both your legs are fractured; you have deep cuts in your arms and bruises all over your body. But on the bright side your vital organs are stable."

David wondered whether the doctor knew about his recent tests. His organs might be okay now but soon they would be eaten away by the cancer. The cancer! It was the first time he'd thought of it since the accident. He closed his eyes and sighed with anguish. His time living above ground was only temporary so why had he survived the crash? What difference would an extra year make?

The nurse walked around to the other side of his bed and gently pulled up his hospital gown so that the doctor could press his stethoscope on to his bruised skin and listen to the action of his heart and lungs.

"Where is the wheelchair?" he asked, his eyes scanning the room.

"Wheelchair? There isn't a wheelchair here," the nurse replied with a frown.

"What is it, David?" Kaitlin asked, concern in her voice.

"Oh nothing," he said with a faint smile. "Maybe it was just a dream. But as he spoke he was thinking, but the squeaking sound the wheels made was so real.

As soon as the doctor and nurse had left the room, Kaitlin moved closer to him, stroking his hair and gently kissing his bruised lips. "A welcome kiss back, my love," she said.

David inhaled the scent on her neck. "You smell so good," he said. "At least my sense of smell is still awake."

A strand of curly hair fell over Kaitlin's forehead, brushing her eyelashes.

"I want so much to feel you close to me, but these damn arms won't let me," David said, before turning his gaze to one of the biggest cards on the side table. He could see inside it, recognised the writing.

"Come back soon from wherever you are or I will not forgive you. I love you, even though you're a pain in the ass, Fred."

He chuckled and then winced in pain as the movement squashed his lungs.

"I love you too, brother," he mumbled, switching his gaze to his beautiful Kaitlin.

"And I love you too," he said to her. "I should have said this to you more often, and I'm going to say it a lot more before my time's up."

"What do you mean, time's up?" said Kaitlin. "You're going to get better soon. It's nothing too serious."

David breathed in deeply, feeling the air slitting his ribs. He hesitated before telling her about his diagnosis. For a while the silence hung over them. He knew that what he was about to say was going to change everything.

"I went to the clinic just before the accident," he began to explain, forcing himself to look Kaitlin in the eye.

"Why? What's wrong? You've never had any issues with your health before."

"It's my spine. It's out of control."

"I don't understand."

"Cancer. I have cancer. I've only got one more year to live."

The shock of it caught Kaitlin by surprise and she let out a scream, the colour draining from her face. Struggling to breathe, she stood up, holding her hand on her chest as she gasped for air. Moments later she slumped back down into her chair.

"I'm sorry, Kaitlin," David continued. "You're the best thing in my life and that hasn't changed. My limited time won't alter that."

Kaitlin's eyes filled with tears and her lips trembled as she struggled to take in the shocking news. Her heart was torn apart and a big knot formed in her throat, preventing her from speaking. She wouldn't have known what to say anyway.

An awkward silence ensued. They were standing on the threshold between life and death, both of them witnessing the obliteration of their dreams.

Kaitlin felt glued to her chair, was unable to move an inch as her limbs stiffened. Death? She wasn't ready to think about that, or anything linked with it for that matter. She was so young, had barely started to live herself.

Suddenly she found the strength to stand up. Reaching out her hand she gently pressed her fingertips against David's. His hand instinctively responded, searching for more of her skin to touch, but she pulled her fingers back and made a fist, which she used to clench his bed sheet.

Tucking a strand of hair behind her ear she leant over and kissed David's cheek. As she did so one of her tears fell on to it, rolling down David's face as if it belonged to him. Then Kaitlin turned and walked towards the door. She stopped under the frame for a moment, without turning back, before stepping out into the corridor. As she closed the door behind her, David's hospital room suddenly became colder and darker.

29

Evan

EVAN was awakened by the rich scent of coffee. Feeling an ache in his back he stretched his limbs out while still seated in his chair and then rubbed his hands over his face as if to brush away the night.

With sleepy eyes he read the nurse's name badge.

"Angela," he said out loud. "Is this a sign from God?"

"Good morning, Evan," the nurse said, handing him a cup of coffee. "It's a beautiful day and this is the best way to start it."

He followed Angela's gaze over to his son. The morning light was shining on the boy. His head was still bandaged, there were some cuts and bruises on his nose and left cheek, and his right arm was broken and would have to stay in plaster for several more weeks, but the swelling on his brain had gone down and he was on course to make a full recovery. The lovely sight made Evan smile for the first time in days.

"God, thank you for giving him back to me."

"Daddy!" Murray suddenly cried out.

"I'm here, honey," Evan said, his voice trembling.

"I was with Mum…we saw lots of stars. I was holding her hand tightly but she let me loose and told me to go to Daddy and that she'd be back soon. When will she come back?"

Evan's mind raced uncontrollably with the rhythm of his heart. He couldn't hold back his tears any more and put his index finger in his mouth, biting down until he felt the pain right down in his bone.

"Dad, Mum will come back. She promised me."

Evan felt guilty for failing to acknowledge Alison's death

earlier. Now, more than ever, it finally felt real. His breathing was unsteady and his lungs fought for air. How was he going to tell his son that his mum was gone and would never come back? Just thinking of the word 'never' made his stomach heave. He remained silent for a moment trying to swallow his pain and tears.

"Dad?"

Evan was trembling now. The pain was unbearable. He'd lost his other half, his best friend, the mother of his son.

Witnessing the scene, Angela could scarcely hold back her tears. Quietly, she moved towards Evan and gently touched his shoulders.

"Please try to be strong for your boy," she said. "Don't let him see you like this."

Evan nodded, sniffed and wiped his face, inhaling deeply a few times to bring his breathing back to normal. Bending over his son, he kissed his forehead and felt himself coming back to life at the touch of his milky skin.

"The sun will shine for us again," he smiled.

***

Evan stayed at the hospital with Murray for a further week, sleeping in the chair next to his bed and showering in the adjacent en suite. The nurses fetched him food and Irena, his firm's secretary, brought him a case of clothes and post from home. His entire world was now contained within this hospital room and his visitors gave up trying to make him go outside.

Amongst his post were some prints of Alison and Murray that he'd sent off for just before the accident. He flicked through them without focusing on the images; he realised he couldn't bear to.

When Murray was finally discharged, Evan warmly thanked the staff and packed up his belongings along with his son's toys and get well soon cards. He realised as he did so that the room had become his shelter and that now he had to start living the reality of his new life. Murray no longer had a mother and he no longer had a wife. He suddenly felt faint and dropped his case, spilling out its contents in the process. One of the nurses helped him into a chair.

"Are you OK?" she asked. "You look awfully pale."

She waited with him until he felt better, picking up his belongings and putting them back in the case.

★★★

Later on in the day, when Evan and Murray had already left, a cleaner polishing the floor in the corridor picked a photo up off the floor. She took it to the nearest room and, not wanting to disturb the sleeping patient, placed it on the bedside table next to him.

30

David

"Good morning, David," said the nurse, Rebecca, as she walked into his room. "How do you feel today? Soon you'll be out of here and enjoying the sunshine."

She jotted down a quick note in his file before placing it back on his bedside table.

***

That morning David had received his final visit from his doctor, who had deemed him fit enough to return home. Rebecca's gaze turned to the flowers by his bed. They had already wilted.

"Such a shame to see them in this state," she said.

"Yes, they were very beautiful," David muttered in response.

It was Kaitlin who had given them to him, but she hadn't been back to the hospital since he'd informed her of the cancer diagnosis. Seeing the flowers only reminded David of how she had abandoned him. First he'd lost his parents, and with them his childhood, now his love was refusing to hold his hand on the road towards his end. Fate had certainly dealt him some cruel blows.

In the two weeks since Kaitlin had brought the flowers, David had watched them shrink little by little every day. Like him, they were giving up.

"I'll be back with the wheelchair and then I'll get you out of here," Rebecca said. Then, almost as an afterthought, she picked up the flowers and carried them dripping with rancid water to the waste paper basket.

"I'll not be long so you better get yourself ready," she said.

"Yes, but it's going to be weird using wheels now instead of my legs."

David wondered how long he'd be on them before he left the world forever. Then, pulling one of the pillows from his back, he thrust it against his face and sobbed until he heard the sound of the door opening again. Rebecca pushed the wheelchair next to his bed.

"You'll soon get used to it," she said. "This chair will be your friend until your legs heal."

Her gazed move to the disorganised display of cards on David's bedside table. Some of them had fallen down and he hadn't bothered to put them back up again.

"You better take those with you," she said. "They'll remind you of how lucky you were to come out of the accident alive."

"Yes," David replied but inside he was saying, *"if only you knew"*. He may have survived, but even if he hadn't been diagnosed with terminal cancer, his life was never going to be the same again. Every time he closed his eyes he saw the dead woman's eyes. It was as if he could feel her pain, her last breath pressing against his face.

"I'll pack those for you," Rebecca said, grabbing a handful of the cards. She picked up a photo that was among them and smiled at the image.

"Is this your son?" she asked. "Such an adorable face."

"Son? No, I wasn't lucky enough to have a family. What are you looking at?"

"This photo," replied Rebecca, handing it to David. "It was with your cards."

David stared at the image open mouthed. This kid had the same adorable face as the boy from his dream. In fact, it was the very same photo he'd been holding in it.

For a moment he wondered where he was. Had the cancer and the crash really happened or was he stuck somewhere on the junction between dreams and reality? Or was his body and brain already failing him, making him unable to decipher reality from illusion?

He closed his eyes for a few seconds, forcing himself deep inside his dream. He'd never forget the eyes of the woman from it, and he recalled how she'd slipped the photo into his hand. *But why?* It struck him that it was a way of torturing him for what he'd done. "I took a life," he muttered under his breath. Once again, he wondered why he hadn't been the one who was taken. "How can I make amends?" he wondered. He'd have died a thousand times if it meant he could undo the tragedy.

Just then, two more nurses entered the room.

"They'll help you out of bed and into the wheelchair," Rebecca explained. "Are you ready?"

***

David nodded, slipping the photo into his leather wallet. Rebecca noticed and raised one of her eyebrows, but chose not to say anything.

As the nurses helped him into the chair, Fred appeared at the door.

"It seems I'm just in time," he said, forcing a smile.

"He knows," thought David. "Kaitlin must have told him."

He hated to see his friend suffer, wondered again why he was creating such destruction in other people's lives.

Fred dropped his head down as he fought to keep his tears back. He slowly walked towards David, rubbing his hands over his thighs in his nervousness.

"Time to get you out of here, buddy," he said, taking hold of the chair's handles. He seemed so far removed from his usual cheerful self.

"Fred, are you OK?" David asked.

"Yeah, I'm fine," Fred replied, but his voice was breaking and the expression on his face didn't coincide with his words. It was impossible to hide his emotions from his friend.

With Rebecca holding the door for them, Fred promptly wheeled David into the corridor. As they moved towards the exit, David noticed the unmistakable sound of one of the chair's wheels squeaking. It was the same sound that the chair in his dream had made. He closed his eyes and concentrated on just that one noise. It felt as if it was echoing inside his head, then it faded to nothing. A woman's voice took over. It was one that David had heard before.

"Find her. You have to."

"Find who?" David screamed inside his head, but the woman didn't answer. A split second before he opened his eyes again, he saw two green ones sparkling. Shaking his head, he pressed his back harder against the seat, clenching his fingers over the armrest until the pain of the effort the movement required travelled up his arms. The woman's voice and eyes were still inside him.

"Take care, David," said another woman. It was Rebecca, who had crouched down to his level. She put an arm on his shoulder. "I hope I won't see you around here again," she said.

David forced a smile. "You certainly won't," he said. "I can't ride my new wheels more than five miles per hour!"

At the same time he wondered how many tired miles he'd be able to complete before his time was up. "Not many," he reflected.

Outside, the feel of the sunshine on his face and the bright colours of the flowers that had been planted in the hospital grounds made David happy to be alive for a moment, and he breathed in the fresh air hungrily. But after a minute or two his face darkened as he pictured his casket below the ground, how he would exit the earth without leaving any visible trace.

Fred didn't say a word until they reached the parking area. He put the brakes of the wheelchair on and nervously rummaged inside his jeans pocket for his cigarette packet. Pulling one out he tried to light it but his hands were trembling too much. He flicked the lighter with his thumb over and over until eventually a flame jumped out. Taking a long drag from his cigarette, he briefly recalled his phone conversation with Kaitlin that morning. He'd only called to find out what time David was coming out of hospital.

"Hasn't he told you yet?"

"Told me what?"

"About his cancer diagnosis. The doctors have given him a year."

Fred had dropped the phone and made for the door, running out into the street and carrying on aimlessly until his legs were powerless to take him any further. Still he didn't want to believe.

"Tell me it's not true," he said to his friend, dropping the cigarette on the floor and stamping his foot over it after just one drag. He leant against the door of the car, sliding down until his bottom was on the floor. Then he covered his face with his hands, which immediately became bathed in his tears.

David searched his mind for the best words to say, but came up with nothing. The inevitable had to be faced and there was no right way of putting it.

"I can't say that," he said. "I wish I could, but the important thing is that I am alive now."

He paused for a moment, realising for the first time that although Kaitlin had left him, he wasn't alone.

"Now, get off your ass and help me," he added. "I'm starving, so let's find somewhere to eat. I want to have fun today."

Fred slowly raised his head, pulling his hands from his face and smiling through his tears. When his grin was returned it felt like all that was bad had disappeared. None of this was real and the cancer no longer existed. This wasn't true but there was no time to waste; he had to help his friend live out his final days to the full.

31

Present Time
Laura

As Laura stepped out of hotel door she gazed down at her high-heeled shoes, aware that she had no idea where to point them. She didn't bother wave for a taxi and instead walked along 5th Avenue until her feet throbbed with pain.

It was almost nine and the pavement was still wet from the damp morning breeze. Shadows cast by the skyscrapers on the opposite side of the road were preventing the sun from deploying its power just yet. She tilted her head back, slipping a foot out of its shoe for a moment of relief.

"These were a very bad choice," she muttered. "Fancy walking around New York in high heels."

Still a little unsteady on her feet, she crossed the road. The Harlem Meer Lake stretched out in front of her. Surrounded by trees, it was a beautiful, tranquil site. Taking off her shoes, Laura rolled up her jeans and plonked herself on the first bench she found. Gazing up at the vast sky, the buildings reaching towards it reminded her of how alone she was. She was still marvelling over the boldness of her recent actions and what they had led to. And despite feeling like a leaf caught up in the breeze, the sense that she belonged in New York was growing. But she was far from the end of her journey and there was no way she was going to allow herself to give up until she had reached it. She stood up again, noticing that a lump had formed on one of her feet as she stepped into her shoes again. As she walked away she felt the fresh breeze from the lake caressing her back through her thin chiffon shirt.

Laura's feet were hurting so much that she walked into the

first café she came across. The tables were covered in red cloth and only a few of them were occupied. Sighing with relief, she slipped off her shoes again, the strong scent of coffee beans turning her attention to a soothing hot drink. Running her fingers through her hair, she shook her head, tidying up the golden waves that covered her shoulders. She caught the eye of the waiter who made his way over with a smile. Before reaching her table he stumbled slightly over one of the black shoes that Laura had carelessly left in precarious position on the dark wooden floor. He moved it under the table without losing his grin.

"Must have been a tough start to the morning in those, eh?" he said.

"Don't remind me," Laura replied. "It's been torture wearing heels, but a strong espresso will make me feel better."

"Yes of course, right away," the waiter replied, noting down her order and shuffling off.

Laura swiftly slipped her handbag off her shoulder, unzipped it and pulled out the photo from one of the inside pockets. Tracing her finger over the image of the little boy, she pictured holding him in her arms, could almost feel his head resting against her shoulders and his arms curled around her neck. Then she turned the photo over again, just as she had done a hundred times before, and looked at the date that had been written on it.

"Where are you, little boy?" she said under her breath. "How will I find you?"

As the waiter approached the table with her coffee, she put the photo carefully back inside her bag.

The steam from the drink evaporated under her nose and eased her tension. She ran her index finger around the edge of the tiny espresso cup before slowly lifting it to her lips. But before she could take a sip her lips froze; she could sense someone watching her from the other side of the window. Her pulse started to race, for some reason she knew that it was a man, and her entire body flushed with heat. But, as much as she wanted to find out who it was, she didn't move an inch. Instead, she took a deep breath and tried to calm herself. When she eventually did steel a quick glance behind her, she saw that the other side of the window was clear.

"I'm falling in love with a shadow in the air," she said wistfully before turning her attention back to her coffee cup. When she'd finished her drink she checked her watch and saw that it was almost noon.

"Time to move on," she muttered to herself.

It was six days since she'd first landed in the US and it already felt like a lifetime. Each day she had experienced a barrage of emotions that were completely new to her. Uncrossing her legs she pushed her feet out from under the table. The lump had gone down slightly but her foot was still red and sore. Unable to face putting her heels back on she picked them up and walked across the floor towards the counter in her bare feet. After paying for her coffee she caught the waiter's eye and pointed at her sore feet with a pretend grimace that made him smile. Stepping outside, she positioned herself in the best place to hail a taxi.

***

Back in her hotel room, Laura threw her handbag down on the bed and pulled off her shoes once again. Her morning's outing had done little to help her think clearly.

"Where should I start?" she asked herself. "I only have a child's name. It's going to be like finding a needle in a haystack. I just need one little clue, something to at least start with."

She lay down on the bed, feeling her eyelids grow heavy. Turning on her side she pushed her face into a soft pillow and closed her eyes, her thoughts and her body travelling into a beautiful dream in which there was a presence next to her; a masculine body, strong against the softness of her own. Instinctively, she reached out to pull him closer, feeling her lips tingle as she anticipated them making a connection.

Pulling a pillow next to her, she enfolded her legs around it, allowing herself to indulge her deepest desires. Her blood felt as if it was flowing at a heightened temperature as her body contorted and she lost herself in delicious ecstasy…

When she opened her eyes again she felt bewildered and gazed around the room trying to recall her moment of pure pleasure. The fantasy had left her and the room was almost completely silent; all she could her was her own breath, which was heavy on the pillow. Every muscle of her body felt relaxed and she fell into a deep sleep, her dreams taking her to yet more unknown places.

***

When Laura woke up her hair was dishevelled from her afternoon nap. Her gaze drifted to the minibar next to the TV. It was a dark aubergine colour, just like the rest of the furniture in her room. Pulling open its door she examined the contents.

"Lemonade, soda, Sprite, beer, water and juice," she said out loud. She was so thirsty and knew that water was the best thing to quench it. Pulling the top off the bottle she took several long gulps, which only succeeded in whetting her appetite. She was hungry too. Looking at her watch she realised that it was already evening. All she'd had all day was a black coffee. She felt deflated. There had been no regular pattern to her meal times since arriving in New York.

Sliding open the doors of her wardrobe she pulled out a blue floral dress and picked out some white sandals to go with it. She was desperate for something to eat but first she needed to shower. Slipping off her jeans, shirt and underwear, she headed for the bathroom. Standing before the mirror, she gazed at her face.

"I look so tired," she said to herself. Leaning over the sink she scrutinized her skin more closely, examining the dark circles under her eyes as her breath formed a thin veil over the glass. Just then an unfamiliar shape formed in the mirror and a noise buzzed inside her head. Springing back, she clenched her head with both hands. The buzzing sound was still there.

"What's happening to me?" Laura asked herself. "It feels like I'm travelling inside a strange novel."

But rather than filling her with confusion, a plot was unfolding.

"I understand now," Laura said slowly. "It's you, the woman from the accident. You are haunting me and although I don't know why, I do know that I have to find your husband and son. But what will I tell them?"

Laura imagined informing the husband how she could smell his skin, and how she even made love to him in her dreams. She shook her head. No, she couldn't tell him that. It was utterly ridiculous.

"Why me?" she wondered. "Why do I have to do this?"

She didn't even know whether the feelings she was experiencing were really hers. It was something she hadn't been able to fathom. But although she was worried about where her actions would take her, she was unwavering in her intent all the same. Every day that passed she felt even more determined to see the outcome of her fate. Maybe she would find a soothing balm for all the wounds in her heart, or maybe she would uncover acid that would deepen them further.

***

Laura climbed into the shower, luxuriating under the cascade of hot water from the disc-shaped showerhead above her head. Pouring a big dollop of shower gel over her breasts, she started lathering it over her body, which had gone far too long without a man's touch. She was soon covered in white foam, and, closing her eyes, she imagined that she was sharing the steamed filled box with her lover. She could almost feel his hands rubbing the soap into her back, sliding his palms down over her hips, tracing her curves and sending shivers of pleasure pulsating through her body. She felt him gently moving his fingers along her spine and pressing his lips against her neck until she released a moan of desire. Then his hands moved to her full breasts. He cupped each one gently before moving down further to the space between her legs. She parted them slightly to allow him further access while he licked and nibbled one of her earlobes.

Keeping her eyes closed shut amidst the clouds of steam, Laura could see every detail of her lover's face and body. She turned around and curled against him, opening her palms and pressing them flat against his strong chest. His heartbeat, which she could feel beating against her skin, had synchronised with hers. When she eventually opened her eyes again she saw that her palms were flat against the flow of the water. Sighing, she turned off the tap and the figure of the mysterious man drifted away along with the steam from her body. Climbing out of the shower, drops of waters, like diamonds, ran down her soft, clean skin. As she towel dried her hair and body she noticed how good she felt.

"What to do next?" she wondered when she was finished. She turned to the laptop on the table and moved over to it, pulling up the lid and staring at the screen for a moment. It was as if a pulse was contained inside it, waiting to be found amongst the labyrinth of networks. Her laptop was the door that she needed to knock on first, but she knew she had to prepare for any hazards she might meet on the way.

Closing her eyes, she once again pictured the man she'd been imagining making love to. She could feel his touch, his breath on her face, and she knew his scent. Assembling all those elements together, it was as if she had someone real standing next to her, and there was no doubt that she was in love with him.

"I will find you," she said out loud.

But the gurgling noises that her stomach was making were becoming louder and she needed to feed herself before tackling anything else. Heading back into the bathroom she spread her makeup around the marble sink and applied some light foundation and blusher before covering her lips with a glossy pink colour. After styling her hair she examined the results in the mirror. She no longer appeared pale and drawn and instead looked undeniably charming. It had been so long since she'd seen herself this way. Spraying on some perfume, she traced one of her fingers down the gap between her breasts, letting her mind make a turn into the sacred, secret realms of her sexual imagination. Then she pulled herself away from the mirror, slipped on her dress and sandals, and made for the door.

32

Evan

EVAN rummaged in his pocket for his keys. Selecting the right one for his lock, he opened the door of his apartment, hearing the same click he'd heard for a year now. Inside the furniture was sparse and the open-plan space dark; the sun hadn't been welcomed in since Evan had occupied the flat. It was almost always silent, too. No noise from the TV or radio ever troubled the neighbours, the most they overheard was the screaming of the kettle.

He walked slowly through the dark apartment to his sitting area, threw his keys on the coffee table and sunk into the dark leather sofa. The immaculate order of the place left him cold. There was no need to clean much. In the kitchen everything was undisturbed and even the microwave was barely used. It was like an apartment from a furniture catalogue.

Evan rested his head back against the leather and gazed up at the chocolate-coloured blinds that blocked the light from the windows. He hadn't raised them once in his time there. He'd bought the apartment after moving to New York, long before meeting Alison. That had been an exciting time and back then the sunlight was allowed in to brighten every corner. He'd moved back in again following Alison's death. There was no question of him staying in their family home - it would have been far too painful. Murray had gone to live with his mum and stepdad, Evan had thrown himself into his work, escaping everyone and himself.

In the silence of the room, all he could hear were his own anxious breaths.

"Oh Jesus," he muttered. "Why am I so nervous? It's only a date for Christ's sake."

He'd known from Gloria's first day at his firm that she was hoping to become more than a colleague. But with his heart still lost in grief and his mind on his work, any sexual feelings had been put firmly on the back burner. Despite Gloria's obvious charms, which would have proved irresistible to many, until now he had managed to avoid her flirtatious glances, which were laden with expectation.

What did she expect? To screw him out of his mourning?

But now he had agreed to a date and he felt stuck between his unwillingness to contemplate being intimate with anyone else and his erotic desires. He couldn't deny that part of him wanted Gloria, but at the same time those natural feelings filled him with guilt. He didn't know whether he'd ever be able to move on. Would he be able to savour the present again or merely learn to feel comfortable with his grief and carry on living in the past?

He knew he should be feeling excited by a date with a beautiful, intelligent woman, but Evan just felt troubled by it. He felt as if something was holding him back, and it wasn't necessarily Alison's memory.

He'd had the same feeling that morning on the way to meet his friend, Bill, for lunch. Feeling in need for some fresh air he'd asked his driver to drop him a few yards from the restaurant. Stepping out of the cab he'd seen a woman sitting inside a coffee shop with her back to the window. The sight had stopped him in his tracks, and, as he'd watched her run her fingers through her golden hair, his heart had started pounding in his chest. He was overcome with an intense urge to go into the coffee shop and touch this stranger, only he knew that type of behaviour would be liable to get him arrested.

He'd trundled away, his feet feeling heavy. The unfamiliar burst of emotion had knocked the stuffing out of him. He tried to picture the woman's face, but although it felt like he'd taken in every strand of her blonde hair, he couldn't do it. He found himself retracing his steps back to the coffee shop, but when he looked through the glass he saw a waiter gathering an empty cup from the table where the woman had been seated. Her absence left him strangely bereft. Glancing at his watch though, he realised he couldn't hang around. Bill was an old high school friend who was back in New York after a decade in London. He couldn't be late.

***

Now the sun was beginning to set and Evan had another meal out planned. He was meeting Gloria at nine at a restaurant she'd chosen. Pulling off his tie and working on the buttons of his shirt, he pulled his mobile from his trouser pocket and scrolled down his list of contacts for his mum. After a few rings she answered and put Murray straight on.

"Hey, Tiger," Evan said. "What are you doing?"

"Daddy, it's Daddy on the phone," Evan squealed with delight. "When are you coming here?"

"Soon, I'll come and see you soon."

"And can we go for a ride together? I asked grandpa but he can't go. He's walking like a stiff man."

Murray was giggling and struggling to catch his breath in his hurry to get out all his news.

"I learned how to do a turn on my bike," he said. "It's awesome. I can't wait for you to see it."

"I will, Tiger," said Evan. "I'll see it soon."

As Murray talked, Evan wondered how it was possible for him to do this to his only child. It was as if he'd forgotten his role as a father. He'd been so weak, but he'd found it easier to turn his back on his son while he learned to cope with his grief. Even so, he was painfully aware that he risked losing him if they continued living apart.

"Grandma, what's that smell?" Murray cried, before adding: "Daddy, I've got to go. There's a stinky smell here."

He gave the phone to his grandmother, who was waiting ready to pick up where he left off.

"What's going on over there?" Evan asked.

"It's Arthur, he's hurt his back. I've been rubbing some pain relief gel into it."

"Poor Arthur. It will be torture for him if he has to stay indoors. He's the most active man I've ever known."

"He misses you, you know that?"

"Yeah, I know."

"It's been such a long time since you've been here to see us."

"Mum, don't start..."

"I just want it to be like it was before."

"For me it's never going to be like it was before."

"But Murray needs you. Arthur was there for you when you were a little boy and he's there for Murray too, but the boy needs his dad. I've lost count of the times I've caught him looking out of the window to see if you're coming."

"I can't face it, Mum," Evan replied. "I can't cope with seeing his grief. Every time I look into his eyes I see them wanting something more, and I can't give that to him. I am half of what he needs."

"But you have to. You're his dad. He needs you, needs your love. You can't just relinquish him from your life."

"But I'm not, I'm working."

"That's what I'm talking about. Spending every day behind your desk is a form of hiding. You're hiding from your feelings. How about coming to the cabin next weekend? Jason will be there and you'll be able to take Murray for the bike ride he so desperately wants to go on with you."

"Mmmmm, I don't know, there's so many memories tied up with that place, it's hard for me."

"Well, the option is open. If you choose to come I'll make sure that your favourite meal is on the table."

After the call had ended, Evan froze for a moment with the phone still in his hand. He wanted more from life too. His mum was right, he had to start moving on, and at least he was making a start by going on a date, his first since losing Alison.

33

Laura

STILL dressed in her white silk pyjamas, Laura stood in front of the window, stretching out her arms to relieve her muscles, which were stiff from her night's slumber. Inhaling deeply, she filled her lungs with air in the hope that it would give her the energy to begin the new day.

Looking out towards the silent sky all her fears melted. Sunrays were poking through the scattered clouds and she felt their warmth on her face. Gazing down, the cars and people on the street below looked like ants, and Laura realised that part of her had always been down there with the crowds. She felt it deep inside her. Feeling fresh and confident, she opened up her laptop again.

"Good luck," she said to herself, pressing the ON button. But the reality was that she didn't know where to start. All she had was the boy's name. At least his surname wasn't very common. Fingers moving across the keyboard, she brought up the city's White Pages, hoping that it wouldn't lead her on another wild goose chase across the US.

"Topillow," she repeated as she typed the letters of the boy's surname.

A list of names with that surname started appearing on the screen and, to Laura's relief, there weren't that many.

One in particular caught her eye.

Evan Topillow, 44. He was registered at an address with an Alison Topillow, linked to a woman named Judith Topillow. The record had been last updated in 2010.

Rubbing her chin, she thought: "He could be one."

Although it didn't mention anything about a son, there was a logical explanation for this. The record was four years old.

Scrambling in her bag for a pen, she jotted down the details in a purple notepad.

When she'd finished, she turned her attention back to the screen and her eyes widened.

"What am I seeing," she murmured. "Am I dreaming again?"

A little boy's smiling face had appeared clearly on the screen. It was the same boy as the one in her photo. Behind him was a handsome man with strong features. His dad.

Two crystal clear tears ran down Laura's cheek as she became overcome with emotion. Her damp eyes made her blink and when she looked back at the screen again, the images had gone – it was blank. She closed the lid and got up from the table, wiping her face as she did so.

"Maybe this time I will get lucky and find them," she said to herself. While she always tried to prepare for disappointment, something felt different this time. She felt so close to finding them, so close to finding her family.

She still didn't fully understand what was happening, but she felt as if she was about to be reborn again.

She lay down on the bed, and, propping herself up on an elbow, reached inside her handbag and pulled out the photo of the little boy once again. She looked at his lovely face until his features started blurring together. The feeling she had for him could only be described as instant love. Just looking at his photo brought her an overwhelming sense of joy.

"I will find you, little angel," she said. "I love you."

Pressing the photo against her face she felt the warmth of her breath against it.

***

"Hello, curly head."

"Laura, wow," Carla said, her voice shrill with excitement.

"How are you? I was so worried. Did you check your emails? I sent three."

"Oh sorry, I didn't, but I'm fine."

"Where are you?"

"In New York, in a hotel."

"Now tell me. Did you talk to the man who sent you the emails?"

"No, I didn't. When I arrived he wasn't here."

"So, where was he?"

"Dead."

"Oh my, I'm so sorry. How? Are you OK? Your voice tells me that you are."

"Carla, I've never felt better. It's not something I can really explain. I'm being drawn in the direction of my happiness. I can feel it."

"I don't understand. Who was he? What happened to him?"

"He was an artist, a painter. He died from spine cancer."

"But what did he want from *you*?"

"Carla, there are some things that I, as a human, can't explain, but spiritually I am being directed somewhere. It feels like I am in a dream, in another life, a fairy tale book if you will. I just need to find the right page. But anyway, tell me about you. How have you been?"

"Oh, girl, you really sound like you are in a fairy tale! Me? Well, my promotion has meant I've had to put in a few extra hours, but everything else is fine as usual."

"And the boys?"

"Fine. Tom's upstairs studying in his bedroom with his girlfriend. Did we do that in our day? Did our boyfriends join us when we had exams coming up?"

"Ha ha…what study? Can you remember ever doing that with Larry? Have you forgotten what it's like to be a teenager?"

"I guess we did fool around, but not in my parents' house!"

"Oh Carla, you're so funny. I miss you."

"I miss you too, kid. When are you planning on coming back?"

"Oh, I don't know. I'm thinking of cancelling my latest project. I better let them know so they can find another designer."

"Are you serious?"

"Yes, I am. I might even stay here for good."

"You're really scaring me now."

"I'm scared myself. But excited too. I'll keep in touch, tell you how things are going."

After she had bid farewell to her friend, Laura realised that she didn't really know what to do next. She had an address and a phone number, but knew she couldn't just appear at the door or phone out of the blue. She was a stranger to the Topillows.

She paced the room, her feeling of hopelessness growing. Going back to her purple notebook, she stared at the numbers she'd written down before coming to a decision. Sitting on the bed, she started jabbing one of the numbers into her mobile phone. Her heart felt as if it would explode out of her chest. No, she couldn't do it. She terminated the call even before the dialling tone came on, having no idea what she was going to say.

Maybe it was better to see Evan in person, explain everything from the beginning…the email, the images, the voices. She could call and just explain that she needed to see him urgently. But what if he hung up? Laura could imagine him thinking she was a crazy woman.

"Just relax," she told herself. "Whatever you choose to do, you have to see this through before you go back to London, it's the only way you're going to find some serenity."

She picked up her mobile once again and this time didn't end the call before it began to ring. Then, a voice…

"This phone number is not in use anymore."

Laura slumped over, buried her head in her hands.

"Don't give up," her inner voice urged.

Without giving it any more thought, she stripped off her pyjamas and grabbed the first thing she could find from her wardrobe: a black skirt and a black t-shirt, with lace around the shoulders. Then she marched into the bathroom and applied some light makeup before tying up her hair in a golden band.

"Not bad," she said, surprisingly pleased with how put together she looked after getting ready in such haste.

Pulling on her black and white snakeskin shoes, she grabbed her handbag and was out the door in seconds.

34

Evan

HANDSOMELY dressed in a dark grey suit, navy shirt and grey and yellow striped tie, Evan walked behind Gloria as she led him into the restaurant. He couldn't take his eyes off her body; the off-the-shoulder clingy red dress she was wearing left little to the imagination. The skin on her bare shoulders shimmered and her feet, which were encased in killer black heels, followed the rhythm of the tune being played by the restaurant's in-house pianist.

The headwaiter, a tall young man wearing a white jacket with a red collar and buttons and black trousers, took them to their table. The elegant style of his uniform fitted in well with the luxurious ambience of the restaurant. He politely pulled out Gloria's chair, smiled and backed away.

Their table was situated under a cupola ceiling divided into arches that were painted in gold. Two crystal wine glasses stood waiting to be filled on their table, which was covered in a lavish turquoise cloth. The walls were covered in wallpaper depicting a pastoral scene. Evan reflected that it was like being in the private dining quarters of a French dynasty.

As he took his seat, Gloria looked Evan up and down as if he was one of the dishes on the menu. Tonight was the beginning of her dream. Soon, she hoped, he'd be more than just someone she worked with. Seeing him every day had been a form of torture. Her heart had pumped harder from the first moment their eyes had met. His face, his body, his voice were practically irresistible to her. She smiled at him innocuously as she imagined ripping off his clothes and running her fingers over the muscles of his sculptured chest and biceps as he pulled her into his arms.

Feeling her face flush, she bit down on her lower lip and wondered: is the evening going to end and begin with a flurry of fiery kisses?

Taking a deep breath in as if to wake herself from her erotic reverie, Gloria occupied herself with the menu, which was bound in red leather. She ran her elegant fingers over the list of delicacies, all printed in gold. On the other side of the table, Evan opened his own menu and, after flashing his companion a quick, tense smile, tried to decipher the starters, which were all written in French.

When the waiter approached, Gloria gave her order, speaking the language fluently. Evan arched an eyebrow, clearly impressed.

"The same," he said when it was his turn to order.

"Interesting choice!" he said to Gloria when the waiter had departed. "I really have no idea what we are going to be eating, but I hope it's something good."

"It is, trust me," Gloria replied, her voice full of certainty.

Moments later, the waiter was back with the bottle of red wine that Gloria had also chosen. As he poured, the couple focused on the flow of liquid into their glasses.

"Have you even been to Paris?" Gloria asked, breaking the silence.

"No, never," Evan replied.

"What about any other places in Europe?"

"Yes, London, but a long time ago. You seem very knowledgeable about France?"

"Really! You think so?"

"Yes, your French is excellent and you know so much about its food and wine. Is France your second love?"

Gloria chuckled. "Paris was the first place I ran away to," she said. "Me and some friends went there after we graduated from college. We were so young and messed up, but we were hungry to try everything. Paris complemented our spirit back then and I did fall in love with it. I'm still dreaming that I will go back one day with a lover. It's a very romantic place."

Gloria lowered her eyes and then raised them to meet Evan's.

"A toast," she said, seductively raising one of her perfectly shaped eyebrows while lifting her glass from the table. "To our first date."

Evan mimicked her movements but the sound of their glasses clinking sent a shiver through his hand and body. It was as if two hands under his skin were pulling him away.

Gloria's lips touched the glass, and she imprinted the edge of it with red lipstick. Rather than a smear, it resembled a rose petal. Evan forced a smile. The woman in front of him was so impossibly sexy, but his heart was sluggish in accepting her. Something was missing. There was no fire inside to lift his spirit up.

"I remember when my friends and I went to this restaurant in Paris," Gloria recounted. "We took one of the reserved tables by giving false names. We ordered before we saw the prices, which were extortionate. Quietly, one by one, we left. It was so funny to imagine the expression on the waiter's face when he went to our table with a tray full of plates."

While Gloria talked about Paris and her dreams, Evan's mind travelled years back in time, to somewhere in New York. He recalled his first date with Alison. It was such a cold day and she was wrapped up in a red woollen shawl and a white knitted hat. A strain of her wavy hair had escaped from underneath it and was brushing against her cheek. Evan was struck by how beautiful her big, green eyes were.

They had met in front of the cinema but decided to skip the movie they'd planned to see. Instead, they went for a stroll, their steamy breaths mixing together as they walked close to each other. When they stopped for hotdogs, Alison complained that her hands were so cold that she couldn't hold on to hers.

"Open your mouth," Evan had ordered, before proceeding to hand feed her the snack. "Good girl," he'd said, wiping a dribble of ketchup that had smeared the corner of her lip.

After they'd eaten, Alison had laid her head on Evan's chest and snuggled into his arms like a kitten. For the rest of their walk they'd stayed even closer together, gaining warmth from each other's bodies.

Now, in this moment, Evan felt that his mind only had the capacity to look back in time. The memories of his life with Alison were still rooted in him. Their love continued to live on.

***

Although Evan's eyes remained glued on Gloria, his imagination seemed to be working overtime. Slowly, one by one, the features of his date's face were replaced with those of another. But no, it wasn't Alison. It was another version of her: more delicate, more glam.

Gloria stared back at Evan. She couldn't know that her companion was in a different time, a different world, but she was beginning to sense his doubt. She pushed her chair back ready to rise from the table. She had started to feel uncomfortable in her seat, as if her presence at the table wasn't even being noticed, as if it was being eclipsed by the shadow of his dead wife.

She felt the romance she wanted so badly slipping through her fingers. She placed both hands flat over the table, her fingernails pointing at Evan like sharp red arrows ready to poke his heart, and lifted herself up.

"Excuse me," she said, fighting back her tears. "I need to use the restroom."

She was shaky as she walked away, her breaths quick and shallow. She focused her gaze on the floor, as if staring down at her hopes scattered all over it.

Evan watched her walk away. He felt her disappointment but knew he couldn't give her what she wanted. Now, more than ever, he realised that his love remained unbroken between the ground and the infinite skies. This date was just a trickle of a moment. It was not his calling; it was Gloria's.

As their delicious-looking starters were served, Gloria remained in the restroom, and when she returned to their table her face was puffy and almost as red as the dress she was wearing. Planting an emotionless smile on her face, she took her seat.

Evan sipped his wine and scrutinized her disappointment. A sigh escaped from her lips and he realised that she was pretty livid. The date was over. He knew it and now she knew it too. All her hopes of making him fall for her had gone. He was never going to be her man. Her desire for him had vanished in a matter of seconds, like a popped bubble.

She was still baffled though. How could he reject her? They had chemistry and she knew he found her sexy.

As they began eating in awkward silence, the slow piano melody drifted away to be replaced by the beautiful chords of the violin. Evan turned his head to one side in order to listen. It was a welcome distraction that allowed him to avoid Gloria's desperate gaze.

After their meal, Evan drove Gloria home. They spent the entire journey in silence.

"Why has this happened?" Gloria thought to herself. "I've been patient, given him all the time he wanted. Or maybe I didn't. Did I try and move things along too soon?"

One thing was for sure. Gloria had thrown all her cards on the table and Evan hadn't picked even one of them up. In fact, he hadn't even taken a look at them.

Pulling up outside Gloria's house, Evan quickly got out to open her car door for her. Ever the gentleman, he even held out a hand to help her get out. As she did so, he could sense her discomfort, see her watery eyes behind her long lashes. The silence between them was torture for him.

"I'm sorry to disappoint you," he said vaguely, stretching out a finger to wipe away the sheen of a tear from her cheek. "But my heart is taken. It's indelibly marked and there is no room for another."

Gloria lifted her head and stared into Evan's eyes without a word. He leant forwards lightly and kissed her on the cheek before turning on his heel and heading back to the driver's side of his car. He climbed into it and drove away as quickly as he could. But he didn't savour the relief that brought. He hit his head forcefully on the headrest and tensed his hands around the steering wheel until his knuckles turned red.

"Stupid, stupid, stupid," he said to himself. "How foolish was that?" He could detect the sullen tone of his voice. As much as he had tried to pretend that he had developed some feelings for Gloria, he'd hadn't been able to hide from his true self. He would never be able to offer her the love she craved.

***

It was nearly midnight when he arrived home. Moving quickly, he stripped off his clothes and put on a pair of blue floral shorts. Then he slipped his feet into a pair of flip flops, grabbed a dark navy bath robe and took the lift down to his building's outdoor swimming pool. He was in desperate need to clear his head.

For a long time he remained by the edge of the pool, staring into the clear water. He wished he could throw his sadness into it and replace it with something more content.

The moon was full and it shone onto the surface of the pool, making the tiles that lined the bottom and sides oscillate. Evan slipped off his robe feeling the fresh air of the night on his lightly bronzed skin. Anyone who had seen him there would have been in no doubt that he was a beautiful man.

He stretched his hands forward like an arrow before powerfully diving into the pool. As he sliced through the water, the image of Gloria's face was spinning in a blurred, undulating form. He wanted to make the move to be with her, but his heart wouldn't let him. He simply couldn't contemplate starting a new relationship.

The love he'd shared with Alison had seemed continuous, as if it had started even before they knew each other, even before they came into existence. They had simply picked it up when the time was right. And with that came a great sense of belonging. Strangely, he'd almost felt the same thing upon seeing the woman in the café window. The connection he'd felt to her was so mysteriously alluring. He'd felt her under his skin. Since then his mind and body had been haunted by the feeling that someone was out there for him - like a missing part just waiting to be found.

By his third lap, Evan's thoughts were flowing with the water. Then he stopped abruptly mid-stroke and took a deep breath in. He pushed his body down, and, placing his feet flat on the floor, plunged his head under the water. His eyes were tightly shut but he allowed himself to open them for a second. He realised that he wasn't alone.

Alison?

Her face was next to him, her bright green eyes unmistakable.

The sight caused him to lose his balance. Pushing up with his feet he surfaced from the water before ducking down under again. Stretching out his hand he tried to touch his wife's face but she drew away, her image fading as the sound of her voice grew loud in his ear.

"She is coming."

Evan lifted his head out of the water once more, this time gasping for air. He looked around. The water was calm. Only the waves around his body continued to lap against it. The dark sky above his head was embellished with stars.

Making his way to the side of the pool, he pulled himself out of the water and wrapped the robe around his shoulders. Tiny droplets of water gleamed on his naked chest. He shook his head and wished he could shake out his confused thoughts along with the water from his hair.

"Am I losing my mind?" he wondered as he stepped into the lift. His head felt clouded with fatigue, and as he travelled upwards, he pressed it against the stainless steel walls.

35

Laura

LAURA opened the car door, quickly scrambled out of it and glanced nervously around.

"What's this?" she cried out loud.

A 'sold' sign displayed on the house she'd driven to caught her by surprise.

"Why does bad luck follow me everywhere I go?" she asked herself.

But she hadn't come all this way for nothing. She decided to have a look around.

"Would you like me to wait for you, madam?" her cab driver asked. Laura noticed that the material of his t-shirt was digging into his fat neck.

"Please stay where you are," she instructed.

The house was modern and she surveyed it with a designer's eye. The landscaped front garden was spectacular. The grass lawn had that freshly-cut smell and pretty-coloured flowers lined the pebbled path up to the front door.

"Hidden coloured lights placed under the sculptured stones would look magnificent at night time," she found herself thinking. Then her gaze turned back to the sign. The word sold seemed to shout in her ears. She turned to make her way back to the car, but the sound of a door opening behind her stopped her in her tracks. She looked around. The front door of the house was wide open and a Hispanic lady dressed in a blue dress and white apron was standing in its threshold. Her black hair was tied up in a bun and she was clutching a pile of boxes.

"Excuse me," Laura said politely. "Is this the home of Evan Topillow?"

"No, and no one is here," the lady replied in broken English. "I do the cleaning. The people I work for haven't moved in yet. My boss is Mr George."

"Oh, OK," Laura replied, struggling to contain her disappointment.

"Sorry, madam, I hope you find the one you're looking for. Good luck."

"Thank you, I will need that," Laura muttered, lowering her eyes as if wanting to hide some obscene feeling hidden inside her.

"What next?" she wondered as she climbed back into the cab. The driver was busy twiddling the dial of his car radio, pumping his large neck back and forth to the music. She ignored the noise and concentrated on her plan of action, pondering over how one minute the Topillows had felt so close to her, the next so far away.

Then she remembered that she had another address for them, one she'd gathered from the White Pages. It was for Evan's mum. Laura knew she had to go there, otherwise she was just going to get stuck.

"I need you to work for me today," she informed the driver, raising her voice so that it was an octane higher than the music. He turned around, his round stomach almost touching the bottom of the steering wheel.

"Yes, madam," he said and turned down the volume of his radio. Laura reached inside her handbag for her purple notebook and read out the other address she'd scribbled down.

"But that's in New Jersey," the driver moaned.

"Yes, it is," Laura replied curtly. "But do you have anything better to do today than ferrying me around?"

"I am here to follow your instructions," came the reply.

"Good, then drive!" Laura said, wondering how long this

journey would last, and where it would take her. She pressed her head against the seat and closed her eyes. Her nerves were growing and there was little she could do to quell them.

The car pulled out into the road and Laura wound down the window, allowing the wind to blow against her face and send her hair flowing behind her. The temperature was a few degrees lower than it had been previously. Ignoring the streets around her, she threw her gaze up to the sky, letting herself get lost in the clouds. This helped her to relax and she felt the tension in her muscles ease a little.

But, as the car approached the address, she started fidgeting again.

"What will I find now?" She asked herself.

Tight knots twisted in her stomach as the driver pulled up outside Sunshine Clinic, a red brick, two-storey building.

"Let's do this," she mumbled as she forced herself to exit the vehicle.

She came to a stop in front of the building, breathed deeply and then gazed down. The step up to the front door seemed like a mountain to climb, and her feet felt heavy as she tackled them one by one. She was now within touching distance of the bell. She inhaled again, her mind in a daze of fantasy for a moment.

What would Mrs Topillow be like? An old lady dressed in pastel and pearls? In her mind's eye, she saw her as having the familiar features of her grandmother and mum. Maybe they would have tea together.

Then the door swung open in front of her and Laura heard the distinctive sound of a baby gurgling. A young woman, her arms wrapped around her child, brought Laura's imaginary tea with Mrs Topillow to an abrupt halt. Instinctively, she reached out to grab hold of the door. When the woman and her child were safely through it she dashed inside, leaving the door swinging behind her.

As she stood in the foyer, her mind was besieged with questions.

Why do I feel as if she is already part of my family, as if I already knew her? What if she is no longer with us?

She took a quick look around. A few people were in the waiting area. They had their heads up and were watching the TV, which was fixed flat on the wall. Pressing her fingernails into the palm of her hand, she turned her gaze towards the reception area and headed there slowly, with carefully measured movements.

A beautiful young girl was seated behind the counter. She was drinking water from a bottle but put it down as soon as she clocked Laura coming towards her.

"What can I help you with?" she asked with a smile.

"I would like to meet with Mrs Topillow," Laura said. "I was wondering if I could find her here?"

"She used to come in every day," the receptionist replied. "But she retired a year ago. Would you like to leave a message for her? I'll make sure it gets to her."

Laura paused for a moment. What message could she send? Her questions weren't the type you could draft in a note. Sensing her confusion, the receptionist attempted to explain herself further.

"I'll get the message to her through her son," she said. "He's in charge of the clinic."

Laura froze. "What? Her son, Evan?"

"No, the other one. Jason. Do you know Evan, then?"

"No, not really, not directly. Do you know where he is?"

"I think he's some marketing director. I haven't seen him for a while."

The sound of laughter suddenly filled the corridor to the side of the reception desk, causing the receptionist to turn her head.

"There's Jason now," she said. "With Gabriela, his assistant." She leant towards Laura and lowered her voice. "Maybe you could talk to him?"

Laura stood back from the counter. It felt as if the floor beneath her feet was moving. Her knees wobbled.

Jason was tall and elegant. He had a perfectly straight nose that contrasted with his light brown hair, which curled like waves on his head. Even from a distance, Laura could see that his blue eyes were sparkling. He walked with his assistant close by his side, so close that their elbows touched.

Laura felt her throat tighten. He may have felt like a member of her family, but at that moment she just wanted to run away.

"I never imagined that it would feel like this," she thought to herself.

When their eyes met, Jason's mouth gaped open for a moment. It took him a while to process what he was seeing.

"This is impossible," he said to himself. He tried to speak but only one unintelligible word came out of his mouth.

"Mr Topillow, this lady is looking for your mother," the receptionist said.

Jason still couldn't speak, despite noticing the bewilderment on the face of the mysterious visitor. He wanted to pinch himself hard. This wasn't real. Maybe something had happened, some unknown collision that had sent him hurtling back in time. He took a couple of steps forward and blinked his eyes, as if he wasn't able to see properly.

"This is unbelievable," he thought to himself before remembering his manners.

"What brings you here?" he asked Laura, moving closer to her again.

"Me? I am…" Laura was almost choking on her words. Why was she here? Jason's question was completely undemanding yet she couldn't answer it. In fact, it had felt like a slap in the face. Jason's reaction to her was inexplicable and everything was messed up in her mind. She was beginning to lose her grasp on why she had ended up in this New Jersey clinic searching for answers from strangers.

Why was Jason staring at her like that? He looked like he'd seen a ghost.

Laura was floundering, coming out in a cold sweat. She looked back to the receptionist who was now busying herself with paperwork. There was no one there who could save her. She just wanted to disappear.

Instinctively, she searched for somewhere to make a quick exit from. Her heart was racing and she could feel her chest rising and falling beneath her shirt.

"I'm sorry," she said, biting her lip. She turned around and made for the door.

"Wait," Jason said, but his voice was so soft that only he could hear it. In his mind he was running after her but his feet remained glued to the spot.

"Who was she?" he heard Gabriela ask. He felt her hand gripping his elbow.

"I don't know," Jason replied.

"But you looked so shocked," Gabriela pressed. "And she so scared."

"I thought it was someone I know…I mean knew," Jason tried to explain. "She looked so real."

"I don't understand," Gabriela said. "What do you mean by real?"

"I can't fathom it myself."

"What is it? Tell me"

"It doesn't matter," Jason said, trying to put an end to the conversation. He attempted to make his expression appear calm and gave a faint smile, but his look remained peculiar. He was getting scared. This spelled trouble for his family - he could sense it.

***

Laura was completely out of breath by the time she reached the cab. She leant against its side, resting her elbows on the roof and gazing into the distance. The clouds were low in the sky and she felt the beginnings of a drizzle hit her hot face like tiny pinpricks.

"In what kind of mess am I in?" she asked herself before sinking her face into her crossed arms. She contemplated ending this right away. Running to the airport and getting the hell out of there. But she knew she couldn't. She knew she had been directed on to this path and her heart acknowledged that the steps she was taking would lead directly to her happiness and peace of mind. Only right now she had to suffer the indignity of total embarrassment. Why was that? Jason had looked like he'd seen her in another life.

With a sigh, Laura tried hard to recuperate from the shock that was still squeezing her like a clamp. She got into the car and with a broken voice told the driver to take her back to the hotel.

All she could feel was a mounting pressure inside her head. Her chest heaved as she held back a sob. The effort of holding back her tears was exhausting. Soon, the motion of the car lulled her to sleep, yet her dream was as real as anything that had taken place during her waking hours.

She was standing at a crossroads, surrounded by big clumps of sharp branches. The sky was dark, with only one star shining above her head. What little view she had was obstructed by dust, which twirled around her head. She was at the centre of a storm. Shielding her face from the grit, faces swam into view. They were spinning around her like the dust. People she knew or had known.

When the faces disappeared, a desert view spread out before her eyes. A woman appeared, she was just one step away, close enough to touch, but then she started to walk away.

The sky moved downwards, towards earth. The light from the star temporarily blinded Laura. She blinked.

"Please wait…please."

The woman slowly turned her head.

"But she is me!" Laura gasped.

The person before her was smiling and showing her beautiful white teeth.

"It is your turn now," she said. "I have to go. You follow yourself…"

***

The car stopped but Laura didn't move.

"Madam, we are here, at your hotel."

Feeling disorientated, she squeezed her eyes closed before opening them wide. She gazed up. The car roof was above her. In front of her, the cab driver had turned round to check on her. When their gazes met he gave her a shy smile.

"Oh, I was just dreaming," she said, to herself more than the driver.

She rubbed her temple, thinking of the woman and her instructions. She'd told her to follow herself. What did that mean?

She picked up her bag and positioned the straps over her shoulder before paying the driver and exiting the cab. Her head was fuzzy. She inhaled deeply, filling her lungs with fresh air before straightening her shoulders slowly and heading to the hotel entrance.

The porter, who was wearing a black suit trimmed with red, opened the door for her. Stepping inside, she felt a wave of bitterness over the way her day had gone. All in all, it had been far more unpleasant than she had feared.

She walked up to her room feeling empty, at a loss. It was hard to imagine how she could carry on her search. She felt so tired of trying, but deep down she was still hungry for a resolution.

***

The following morning, after a night in which sleep evaded her, Laura found that her thoughts were still weighing heavy on her mind. Releasing a tired yawn, she slid her hand over the soft pillow that had been unable to lull her to sleep, as if attempting to make a silent peace with it.

She decided that she needed to distract herself. Just for one day she was going to be a normal tourist exploring New York. Running to the bathroom she washed her face, combed her hair and got dressed before her wave of enthusiasm deserted her.

Just a few minutes later she was walking along 5th Avenue. After a few yards she hailed a cab on her first attempt and asked the driver to take her to an art gallery.

"Any particular one?" he asked.

"No, just any one that comes to your mind. It's my first time visiting New York and I don't know it very well."

"No problem," the driver replied. "I'll take you to one that I go to myself."

Laura turned her attention to the view out of the window, trying to absorb as much as she could as the driver sped through the busy seats. At this moment the city had possessed her, taking her mind away from the chaos of her life. She wished she could stay like this forever.

***

The gallery was very large and had white brick walls. Laura walked idly though it, holding both hands crossed over her stomach. She could hear the echo of her feet tapping on the dark wooden floor. A couple sauntered by; they were the gallery's only other visitors. Laura could hear their soft whispers to each other, even from a distance. The silence had a hypnotic effect on her. It was the therapy she needed right at that moment.

She stopped before each painting, whether it interested her or not. She'd always found looking at pictures inspiring, would search for every little detail until finally the image came to life.

Just then, the clatter of several feet could be heard echoing off the floor. It was only the second day of the exhibition, which explained the sudden surge of visitors.

A hexagon-shaped glass roof in the centre of the high ceiling was letting in sunlight, which formed a thick diagonal across the floor and up the wall, which Laura was standing before. In fact, it shone directly across the painting she was staring at, illuminating the corner where the artist had left their signature.

David Boyer

Laura gasped and reached her hands up instinctively to cover her open mouth. She realised that it was the same picture she'd seen in London. The same woman's profile, the same naked feet, the same flawless white dress…

She realised with a start that the woman in the picture was the one she'd been talking with in her dreams. And it was as if she could see beyond the flat surface of the painting and into the subject's soul.

She took a step back and felt a strange calmness wash through her body. She was experiencing an indescribable love that transcended time. It was as if she'd somehow tapped into an unstoppable flow of it. And it had given her the strength to continue on her journey. It was time to visit Evan at work.

36

Evan

CLUTCHING a thin black briefcase and a rolled up copy of the *New York Times*, Evan pushed the swing door and entered the café. He headed to his usual table and ordered his usual coffee.

He unbuttoned his jacket with one hand and with the other dumped his briefcase over the table. Then he unfolded his newspaper, but instead of checking out the headlines he turned his head to the side and blindly stared out of the window. He followed people hurriedly going about their business in an attempt to avoid his own thoughts. His evening with Gloria was weighing heavily on his mind. He couldn't enter into a relationship with her, yet at the same time his solitary life brought only frustration and unhappiness.

The waiter came over and placed an espresso and a glass of water on the table. Evan withdrew his gaze from the window to thank him. His fingers clumped around the little coffee cup and he turned his attention to the newspaper in front of him.

Gallery Opening A Huge Success read one of the headlines. Evan was just about to read on when the sound of his mobile ringing pulled him away. He slipped out the phone from his pocket and swiped the screen, which soon lit up with Murray's face. To Evan's delight, it was a video call.

"Good morning, Daddy," Murray said, blowing a kiss. "Are you coming today? Love you, Daddy."

"I love you too," Evan replied, whispering the words.

After he'd bid goodbye to his son, Evan felt a sudden strong desire to get out and do something different from his daily routine. It was an overwhelming urge to dislodge himself from the oppressive emotions inside him. His left hand was flat over the newspaper and his index finger was still on the headline regarding the successful gallery opening.

"That would be a quiet escape," he thought to himself.

Without taking his eyes off the paper, he slurped the last sip of coffee, then, after a big gulp of water, grabbed his briefcase and stood up.

***

Outside, the morning sunshine made him squint. He slipped into the flowing crowd before moving to the edge of the sidewalk to hail a cab.

He felt different today: high-spirited, enchanted even. He was certain that something good was about to happen.

As soon as he stepped into the gallery he started to analyse the paintings, trying to work out by their colours and mood what season the artists had worked on them in. He decided that if he was going to paint something that day he would use pastel colours to express the unusually relaxed mood he was in.

As he walked through the gallery, only one of the paintings caused him to stop for a moment in front of it. It showed a woman, her face in profile.

The same image he'd had in his mind ever since seeing the woman in the café window.

In a flash, a whoosh of air flowing through the gallery pulled his attention away from the painting. That's when he saw a woman heading out of the gallery. She had the same hair and profile as the woman in the painting, *and* in the café.

Evan tried to run after her but he stumbled, dropping his briefcase on the ground. As he crouched down to pick it up, a young woman and a tall man in a black suit cut in front of him.

"Excuse me!" Evan said.

The man turned and smiled, but didn't move out of the way.

"Just move," Evan said under his breath.

But, by the time he got to the door, the woman had gone. Frazzled, he leant against the wide frame of the door.

"Who are you?" he whispered under his shaky breath.

37

Laura

IN front of Evan's tall office building, Laura felt like a mere dot. It reminded her of the day back in London when she'd met John and effectively restarted her design career. She thought of how he'd reassured her, told her not to be nervous, and she took that advice now, as if he was dishing it out for her current situation.

She wondered what corner of the globe John was currently residing in, and hoped that he was having fun.

Pushing the glass door, she entered the building and looked around. She was in a vast hall filled with people dashing in and out, and it took her a moment to work out where the lifts were. Once located, she strode directly over to them and stepped inside one that was already almost full. It was so crowded that she could barely move her shoulders without touching the person next to her. She fixed her attention on the buttons, which lit up at each floor. When she reached the 27th one she stepped out onto a shiny marble surface and headed to the reception desk.

She took her place behind a man who was leaning over the desk while running his index finger over the lines of the letter he was holding.

"Irena, can you make sure this gets out this afternoon, please," he said.

Now it was Laura's turn. She cleared her throat. "Excuse me," she said.

"Yes?" Irena replied without looking up. She was busy jotting down some notes. When she'd finished writing, she turned her gaze to the visitor. The sight of her caused her to spring up and clasp her hand over her mouth. Laura looked behind her, wondering if it was someone else's presence that had startled the woman. But there was no one there.

"I'm looking for Evan Topillow," Laura said. "Is he here?"

Irena sat back down in her seat without taking her eyes off Laura's face.

"He's...he's not here today," she said, a hint of breathlessness in her voice.

"Oh, but he does work here, yes? I am in the right place?"

"Yes, it's just he didn't come in today. He called to say that he's spending the weekend in Woodstock."

"Do you have his address there?"

"Yes," replied Irena, jotting it down on a piece of paper from her notebook and detaching it with one swift movement.

"Thank you," Laura said, taking the address.

Retracing her steps towards the lift, she noticed a woman tactlessly staring at her. She poked the man next to her in the ribs.

"Liam, look," she said.

"What is it, Victoria?" the man replied. He was busy reading some paperwork, didn't welcome the distraction.

"Look at her," the woman pressed.

"Wow!" Liam exclaimed, his task in hand suddenly the last thing on his mind.

Feeling hugely uncomfortable, Laura hurried towards the lift and was relieved when the doors opened and allowed her to slide in.

"What is wrong with these people?" she wondered. "Everywhere I go people stare at me as if they've seen a ghost."

38

Evan

THE closer Evan got to the place where Alison had died, the more disturbed he felt. He felt bile rising up into his throat and his nausea was so bad that he had to stop and get out of the car.

His horror and anger was soon replaced by an overwhelming sense of sadness, and he allowed the tears to roll down his face. After climbing back into his car, it was some time before he was able to continue driving.

It was early evening by the time he reached Woodstock. All the lights inside the wood cabin had been switched on, illuminating the greyness surrounding it. After parking up, Evan allowed himself to look around. The vast beauty of Woodstock was laid out beneath him, and he remembered the many bike rides he'd gone on through the woods. The air felt cleaner here and, despite everything, it felt good to be back.

The door of the garage next to the cabin was wide open and Evan clocked Murray's bike inside, a dozen cans tied to the back of it as a makeshift tail.

"I bet the noise has been driving Judith and Arthur mad," he thought to himself cheerily.

Then his gaze moved to the bikes that were leaning against one of the walls. For a year now he had deprived himself of his favourite hobby and his lovely family cabin. But now he was back. He retreated from the garage and headed to the front door. When he reached for the handle it suddenly swung open from the inside. Judith had sprung to her feet as soon as she'd heard Evan's car pull up outside. And she was overcome with relief to see him standing on her doorstep. To her, his year away had felt like a lifetime.

"Oh, it's so good to see you here," she said softly. She was wearing beige linen trousers and a blue floral shirt. Her grey hair was impeccable as usual.

"You look so good, Mum," Evan beamed. "Such a chic woman!"

"Daddy, Daddy," Murray cried, appearing at Judith's side. He stretched his little arms out, inviting Evan to crouch down for a hug.

Following their embrace, Evan pulled back to get a good look at his son. Then he ran his fingers through the boy's hair and inhaled its sweet scent.

"I was just about to bath him," Judith said. "In fact, the water is still running."

"I'll bath him today," Evan said.

"Yeah, Daddy's going to bath me," Murray cried. Evan picked him up and carried him to the living room, where Arthur and Jason were sitting. By way of a greeting he saluted his stepfather.

"Welcome back to the fun cabin," said Jason, getting up to give his brother a hug.

"It's good to see you," Evan replied. "Bike race tomorrow?"

"You really think you could win? No way, your body must be rusty after all that time behind a desk."

"Well, we'll see about that tomorrow."

"Can I race with you, Daddy?" Murray asked, bouncing up and down in his father's arms.

"Of course you can, son."

"Oh, Daddy, you really are the best."

Evan headed upstairs to the bathroom where he turned off the taps just as the water was about to overflow. He slipped off his jacket, rolled up his sleeves and freed the toys ducks, frogs and ships that had been tidied away in a net bag on the side of the bath. Before long, Murray was sinking and spinning them in the water, soaking his dad's shirt in the process.

Next, Evan poured bath cream into the water and swished his hand around in it until a quilt of white bubbles had formed on the surface. Murray ducked down until only his dark eyes were visible through the foam.

Evan's own eyes filled with tears again, but this time they were ones of joy.

"Thank you, God," he whispered. Being able to enjoy this precious moment with his son meant everything to him. He stood up and unhooked Murray's towel, which was printed with penguins, from the back of the bathroom door.

"Bath time's finished," he said.

"One more minute, Daddy," Murray pleaded. He twirled around in the bath and started splashing his hands and feet as if he was swimming.

When he finally stopped moving he looked at Evan and exploded with laughter. "It looks like you took a shower with your clothes on," he cried.

Evan plunged his hand into the water and pulled out the plug. As he did so he felt a breath on his face, heard a voice laughing. So familiar...

Straightening up, he glanced around the bathroom. The door was half open but he could see that no one was outside it. Was he imagining things?

Meanwhile, Murray continued to splash his legs while the water drained away. He was obviously oblivious to what had just taken place.

Turning his attention back to the task in hand, Evan put his hands under the boy's arms and lifted him out of the bath. Then he wrapped him in the towel, patted him dry and scooped him up in his arms again. Judith had laid out Murray's pyjamas on his bed and Evan helped him to put them on before getting him settled in bed. He lay by his son's side and gently stroked his hair until he drifted off into a deep sleep.

Evan thought again how something had shifted in him. He

was filled with positive energy, seemed to be anticipating good things to come.

"Good night, sweet dreams," he said to his sleeping son before turning off his light. He left the boy's rotating sidelight on, which sent images of planets and stars to the ceiling. Evan stood staring at them for a moment before closing the door behind him. Then he padded downstairs, his face still warm from the sweet kiss of his son.

Judith was busy in the kitchen. In one hand she was holding a pan lid, in the other a wooden spoon containing some steaming sauce ready to try. Arthur was by her side, inhaling the steam coming out of the pot.

"Hmmmm, Bolognese sauce, rich in spice!" he said, trying to imitate an Italian accent. "Bellissimo!"

"And what about me?" Judith teased.

"You're bellissimo, too," Arthur replied, his eyes full of affection for his wife.

"This is done now," said Judith, covering the pot. "It's time to set the table."

She opened the cupboard and pulled out a pile of china plates while Arthur, who was clutching a bottle of red wine, looked around for a corkscrew.

"I had it in my hand just two minutes ago," he said. Now where did I put it? Things are disappearing in front of my eyes."

"I hope you won't lose me like that, my darling," Judith chuckled.

"I don't need eyes to find you," Arthur replied. "Your scent is forever imprinted on my mind."

"You know," Evan interjected. "Even if my dad had lived my mother would still have fallen for you!"

"Evan! That is not a good joke, OK," said Judith, thrusting her index finger in the air and pointing at her son with it.

"My apologies, Mum," Evan replied. Then, running his fingers through his hair, he took a step back and focused his attention on Jason who was being unusually quiet. He was by the window, staring pensively out at the front garden. The steam from his mug of tea was forming irregular patches of condensation on the glass.

Evan went to see what he was looking at. Outside, the leaves of their birch tree were shaking slightly in the evening breeze. Clouds moved across the surface of the full moon.

"What kind of thoughts are you collecting?" Evan asked.

"Oh, it's nothing," Jason said, keeping his gaze fixed outwards.

"Is anything bothering you?" Evan persisted.

Jason turned to look at his brother, who saw the worry contained in his face.

"As I said, it's nothing," Jason repeated, clearing his throat and taking a sip of hot tea.

"I thought you might have brought a guest this time," said Evan, changing the subject.

"Not this time, but in the near future."

"Are you sure?"

"Yes, I think I am."

"Then I will be happy for you," said Evan, clapping a hand gently on his brother's shoulder. He was still marvelling over how much he had missed the cabin. It was the only place now where he felt any sense of belonging.

Jason stayed by the window for a while, still lost in his thoughts. Eventually he spoke out, asking his mum a question as she set out the plates for their dinner.

"Has anyone tried to contact you?" he asked.

"No, why?" Judith replied.

"It's just that a woman was asking for you yesterday at the clinic."

"A woman? When? Why?" Evan interjected.

"She was looking for you, too," said Jason.

"Wait, but no one came to see me. Did you see her, talk to her? Who was she?"

"Yes, but it was just for a moment before she went away again. Her hair was like…" Jason found he couldn't finish the sentence. "Oh, just forget about it," he mumbled.

But Evan couldn't shake the feeling that this was far too important to erase from his memory.

"A lot of women still come and want to see me at the clinic," said Judith. "I don't know what you're making such a fuss about."

Jason signed and turned his attention back to the window. How could he tell his brother that he had seen a ghost? He wanted to protect the others from the potential threat that this mystery woman posed.

Evan opened the door and slowly walked out on to the porch, his hands shoved deep inside his trouser pockets. He tried to analyse every detail of what he had seen over the last few days. The woman by the window, then at the art gallery, his inexplicable desire to see her face.

He remembered what Alison had said to him that night under the water of the swimming pool. "She's coming."

"Who is coming, Alison?" he said under his breath.

"Why am I feeling like this?" Evan wondered. He felt so hungry for a touch, a kiss. It was like being in love, only the woman he was in love with wasn't there. He didn't even know her.

"But I know you're out there somewhere," he whispered into the breeze.

Jason came out to join him. "It feels mysterious out here," he said.

"You're in a very deep mood tonight?" Evan grinned. "Are you writing a novel or something?"

"No, I'm just worried, that's all" he replied honestly. "I sense that something is going to happen to you, and I don't know if it's going to be good or bad."

"I sense something too," Evan replied. "But it's good."

***

Back in the house, Evan and Jason seated themselves at the dinner table. Above their heads, a wooden chandelier spread a warm, yellow glow over their faces.

Arthur poured their wine and pondered over his stepsons' sudden sullen mood. They were both digging into their food, but seemed lost in their own thoughts. He looked over at his wife, who read the question in his gaze and shrugged her shoulders.

After a few more minutes of silence, she straightened her shoulders and made a bid to get their attention.

"So…" she began, only to be swiftly interrupted.

"Dad," Murray called, walking into the dining room in his bare feet.

Evan turned to his son. "Hey there, buddy. Why did you wake up? Did you have trouble sleeping?"

"Daddy, Mum came to me. She sat on my bed," Murray replied, releasing a yawn.

A strange silence enshrouded the table. Evan pushed his chair back and then bent over and scooped Murray up into his arms.

Still no one spoke.

"She said that I must be nice because someone will come," Murray went on, in a slow, sleepy voice. "She said that I should love her very much."

He laid his head against Evan's chest, drifting off into a deep sleep.

The rest of the family couldn't take their eyes off the boy cuddled up in his father's arms. They wished they could dig into his mind and uncover the image he had seen. Evan ran a finger over the boy's pink cheek.

"Sleep, my son," he whispered, as a tear trailed down his cheek. Murray's words had knocked the stuffing out of him. He blinked several times, trying to stop his tears from flowing.

When he was finally able to focus again, he saw that the others were in a similar emotional state.

"Sleep, my son," he said again, pressing his lips into the boy's hair. Then, still with Murray nestled safely in his arms, he stood up slowly and carried him back to his room.

39

Laura

"Woodstock," Laura said to the driver as she scrambled into the back seat, placing her small suitcase on the seat next to her. Packing some extra clothes had been a wise decision. Although she sensed that this could be the last stop on her journey, the first thing she wanted to do was check into a nearby hotel and take time just to breathe.

"Let's hope my premonition is correct," she muttered to herself.

She thought back to her arrival in New York. It felt like a lifetime ago.

As they neared Woodstock, Laura looked out of the window and stared at the beautiful scenery spinning past. The sun had nearly set, casting an orange veil over the vast green forest on either side of the road. The trees surrounding her looked like they were reaching up to the sky.

As they turned a corner, the trees gave way to reveal a blue lake at the bottom of a valley. For a moment, Laura felt at peace. She smiled and closed her eyes, savouring every second. Her mind drifted back in time. Not even the pain and grief she had experienced could bring her down now.

The driver suddenly made a sharp turn to the right. He was going a little too fast, and as he applied the brakes, Laura's back slammed against the seat. In that fraction of a second the broken fragments of a crash came to the forefront of her mind. She had been there once before, felt that pain. It was when she had looked at the newspaper clipping that David had left for her. Her body ached all over.

The driver continued his journey, but it was as if he'd left Laura back in the middle of the road, her face covered in glass, her open eyes pressed against the hard ground.

Soon her dead loved ones appeared before her, one by one. They were looking ahead, towards the end of the road.

"Dad?" Laura said.

Her father stepped forward and was joined by her mother. She was smiling as she grabbed hold of his hand. They moved back to allow someone else to come closer.

"Matt?" Laura said, her voice trembling

Then the man she had loved more than anything in the world took her face in his hands and kissed her forehead. Laura was still relishing the familiar feel of his lips on her face when he withdrew again. The three figures started to walk away, turning their heads so they could continue looking at Laura.

"Mum, Dad, Matt!" she tried to shout, but her voice was breaking. She looked at them walking into the distance until they were mere dots of light.

Bizarrely, Laura didn't feel sad over their absence, she felt strong, powerful. Her pain had left her. She breathed freely again, felt so young, so loved.

"We've reached Woodstock," said the driver, bringing her back to reality.

"Ah, I need a hotel for the night," Laura said. "Can you suggest one?"

"We're already outside one," the driver beamed, pointing towards a beautiful cottage that looked as if it was straight out of a fairy tale.

***

As Laura pushed open the door to the cottage, a soft bell tinkled above her head. The walls of the hallway were painted in white and the floor was covered with a simple Moroccan-style black and terracotta runner. On one of the walls, a large mirror with an antique wooden frame hung over a side table, upon which stood a basket filled with colourful wild flowers. An arch led to the reception area where a boy was standing on a ladder. He appeared to be changing the bulbs in a large chandelier. Next to him, a woman of pension age was gripping the ladder and keeping it steady.

"Give me a minute," she said to Laura, handing the boy a fresh bulb.

A moment later, the boy climbed down a couple of steps and jumped on to the dark wooden floor. "All done," he announced.

"Let's see the lights glow again," the woman said, leaning over and flicking the switch by the side of the archway. Suddenly, the room was illuminated with a soft glow. A huge smile spread across the woman's face and Laura couldn't help but stare at her. Her blonde hair was clipped back, but a few strands had fallen loose around her face. She was a pretty woman whose attractiveness hadn't faded with the years. Laura ruminated what a stunner she must have been in her youth.

The boy bid the woman goodnight and as he left she turned her attention to Laura. Her beautiful smile froze in an instant and she blinked several times, as if mistrustful of what she had just seen. The intensity of her stare made Laura feel uncomfortable. And it wasn't the first time she'd been looked at this way recently.

Eventually, the woman regained her composure and strode over to Laura with her hand held out.

"Welcome, I'm Karolina," she said.

"Pleased to meet you, I'm Laura. Have you got a room for the night?"

"Yes, follow me," Karolina replied, leading the way deeper into the cottage. But instead of showing her the room, she motioned for Laura to take a seat on a sofa in the kitchen.

"Can I make you a tea or something?" she asked.

"A tea please," said Laura and Karolina went to the door and called out for a man named Alberto.

Meanwhile, Laura sank into the floral cushions covering the sofa and rubbed her hands against her knees. Taking a look around the room, she noticed a birdcage hanging from the ceiling on a chain. The bird inside was fast asleep, its head tucked inside its wings.

"She will start singing early in the morning to wake us all up," Karolina smiled.

But when Laura returned the grin, Karolina froze once again and her hand flew up to her mouth.

Laura was flabbergasted. It was as if this woman had seen something deep inside her. It was impossible to understand and she was unsure how to react.

A man with a bald head and a thin face appeared in the doorway. He walked slowly, scrutinizing Laura from a distance.

"Yes, Karolina?" he asked softly.

"Two teas please and some croissants, and before you take this lady's suitcase to room number four, can you check if all the lights are working?"

Albert nodded and came over to where Laura was seated, bending down creakily to pick up the case by her feet.

"Do you plan to stay longer than a night?" Karolina asked.

"It depends," Laura replied. "I'm looking for someone and I don't know how long it will take me to find them."

Karolina was now even more curious. "Have you ever been to Woodstock before?" she asked, in an attempt not to appear too nosey.

"No. Actually, I'd never been to the US before now. I'm from London."

"Yes, I noticed that from your accent. Do you mind if I ask who you are looking for? Maybe I can help."

"The Topillows," Laura replied. "I have their address. Do you know them?"

Karolina swallowed hard, no longer able to hide her emotions.

"That's what I thought," she said, without answering Laura's question.

Then Alberto was back in the room with a tray containing the two mugs of tea and the pastries. He set it down on the coffee table and Karolina thanked him. When he'd gone from the room, Laura turned her full attention back to her host.

"So," she said. "Do you know them?"

There was so much that both women wanted to know, so much that was being left unsaid. Karolina released a sigh and said: "I will take you there tomorrow. They are very good friends of mine."

Laura felt like a heavy burden had been lifted. Finally, this was going to be the last stop.

"Do you know them?" Karolina asked.

"No," replied Laura, shaking her head. "It's a long story, or more like an inexplicable dream."

When Laura looked up at Karolina, she realised that her eyes were wet with tears. Laura didn't know what to say or whether to ask questions. Fortunately, Karolina wanted to talk.

"I've known Evan since he was a little boy," she said. "He was always cycling around on his bike, such a lovely kid."

She paused, before continuing with a trembling voice. "And Alison, oh such a tragedy, and it happened not far from here."

"You mean the accident?"

"Yes, the accident. How do you know? How…" her voice trailed off. She could barely believe who had just walked through her door. She wondered if time had somehow reversed.

"I don't know why, but I feel like I know Alison somehow," Laura said. "On the way here I recognised the place of the accident. I felt the crash, the pain, everything."

"Yes, darling, of course you feel that way. You are her mirror. And you don't just look like her, you have something of her soul, too."

Karolina crouched down before Laura, took her hands in hers, and looked straight into her eyes. "Your heart is bigger than you think," she said. "That's why you are here. And it seems that you've been through a lot, too?"

Laura lowered her eyes before she replied. "You can have no idea how hard it is to lose all your family members one by one," she said. "Even the one you carried inside."

She withdrew her hands from Karolina's grasp and clenched her stomach.

"Everyone leaves something behind, my darling," Karolina replied. "It's up to us to catch it and carry on. All our time is measured and we should accept that death is part of life. I don't know who or what brought you here, but it's a miracle."

Laura nodded, accepting that her fate had someone been written for her.

"I feel very tired," she said, standing up. "I need to get an early night."

"But you haven't touched your tea, or your croissant," Karolina protested.

"I don't feel hungry," Laura replied faintly. She felt exhausted, both mentally and physically.

"OK then," Karolina replied. "I will take you up to your room."

Room number four was at the back of the cottage, facing the forest. It was painted white and the bedspread matched; the only splash of colour came from the fresh flowers arranged in a white porcelain vase. It was enough to make Laura feel that spring had sprung in her room.

★★★

The following morning, the sun burst through the branches of the birch tree outside Laura's window, waking her from a deep slumber. She rolled over on the immaculately crisp sheets before sitting up to stretch out her arms and legs. Walking over to the window, she opened it wide, leaning out to inhale the clear air from the vast green quilt of trees that stretched for miles into the distance. The lyrics of a Nina Simone song popped into her head and Laura couldn't help but sing them.

"It's a new dawn, it's a new day and I'm feeling good," she chanted softly.

Following the line of the trees against the sky, Laura was struck by the peacefulness of her surroundings.

"I feel like I've just popped my head out of the earth's surface," she thought to herself. "Never in a million years did I think I would end up here, following a man and his little boy. They've come into my life in such a mysterious way, but the feelings I have for them are already so powerful."

But today was not the time for thought, it was the time for action. Dashing into the bathroom, she combed her hair and glossed her lips, staring at her image for far longer than was necessary to perform such tasks.

Back in her room, she hauled her suitcase on to the bed and unzipped it, rummaging through her collection of clothes until she found what she'd been looking for: a floaty dress with tiny white, blue and yellow roses sewn onto it. It was close fitting and showed off her delicate body to perfection.

She threw over her shoulders a white silk scarf that made her look and feel like a goddess and then clipped her long hair back, leaving a few strands to hang loose over her forehead and ears. Fastening a watch around her wrist, she saw that the time was 15 minutes past ten. It was time to get moving.

In the dining room downstairs was a table big enough to fit twenty people around it. Karolina was in the middle of serving a middle-aged couple their morning tea when Laura walked in.

"Good morning, dear," she said, putting the teapot down and walking towards her most intriguing guest. "Wow, you look amazing. Now come and sit down and have some breakfast."

"I don't feel like eating."

"Are you nervous?"

Laura shrugged.

"Are you ready to go over?"

Laura shrugged again and looked away, her expression one of pure helplessness.

Karolina reached out and rubbed her forearm. "Don't worry, you will be just fine," she said, looking around the room for her assistant, a girl in a light blue dress.

"Aphrodite, please take over here," she said. "I have to go somewhere."

The girl nodded and Laura followed Karolina to the reception desk where she rummaged in her handbag for her car keys.

On the way to the car, Laura realised that her legs were shaky. She was so nervous, but at the same time somewhat relieved too. Her journey was coming to an end. Only one question remained: *was it going to be the beginning of something?*

As Karolina pulled out of the driveway, the two women remained silent. Laura's mind was focused completely on her first knock on that unknown door. Who would be there? What would the reaction be of the man she'd been searching for?

"It's just a ten minute drive," Karolina said, but the journey felt much longer. By the time they pulled up outside the cabin Laura's mind was blank and her emotions on edge.

Karolina got out first and opened Laura's door, gently resting her hand on her shoulder.

"This is the Topillow's place," she explained. "Everyone should be in."

Laura threw her a hesitant look.

"Go on, this is your moment now. Go, you are home and you will be perfectly fine."

Laura unfastened her seatbelt and slowly swung her legs out of the car. Standing up, she forced her shoulders back and held her head up high.

Back in the car, Karolina leant both elbows on the steering

wheel as she followed Laura's every move and contemplated the scene that was about to play out. She shook her head. She could hardly believe it herself. Maybe what she was seeing was all just a dream.

As she approached the door, it dawned on Laura that she hadn't prepared what she would say to Evan by way of introduction. She searched her mind for the appropriate words, but not a single one came to her.

She stretched her hand out and pushed the bell with her index finger. As soon as she'd done it she thought of running away as fast as she could. The intensity of her emotions was almost too much for her to handle. With her right foot she took one step back, but it was already too late. The door to the Topillow's cabin opened wide.

40

A few minutes earlier
Evan & Laura

THE shock of the previous night had left all of them shaken. They had barely spoken about it with each other and were drifting in their own thoughts.

Evan was on the sofa, his head on the armrest, his gaze directed at the ceiling. Last night, Murray had informed them that someone was coming. And now here Evan was, caught in the margin between two worlds: the past and the future.

Jason was seated on the other side of the sofa. He was holding a newspaper wide open, blocking his view from all directions. Judith was in the kitchen staring out into the back garden and Arthur paced the house, closely followed by Murray who was bombarding him with questions.

"Can anyone help me address the musings of a four-year-old's mind?" he asked, sighing heavily. But no one answered.

Evan noticed the date on the calendar, which was hanging on the wall opposite, and his memory raced backwards. One year ago today he had experienced the most shocking and painful day of his life. His grief had been overwhelming, to the point where he had barely been able to function since.

He felt a cold shiver run down his spine and turned his attention to the grandfather clock in the corner of the room. It was the exact time of Alison's accident.

But before he could dwell on this any further, the sound of the doorbell startled him. He got up out of his seat and Jason put his newspaper down. The sound had pulled them all away from their thoughts.

"I will open the door," Murray cried, running towards it and pulling it open.

"Murray!" Laura cried without thinking. For a moment her legs and arms froze as the little boy scrutinized her. He tilted his head and then his lips, like a red rose, opened to expose his milky white teeth.

"I knew you were coming," he said. "My mum told me last night. She came into my room. You look just like her."

Murray was leaning against the door and Laura moved a step closer towards him. Her knees shuddered and she had to hold the door too, just to regain her balance. Then she bent over, keen to take in every detail of the little boy's face. It was the same face she had dreamt of all her life. Everything seemed so clear to her now. This was the life she had been heading towards all along. She was absolutely certain of it.

"Will you be my mum?" Murray asked, his voice imploring.

A big lump formed in Laura's throat. She extended out a hand and stroked one of Murray's pink cheeks. It was a while before she was able to let her reply out of her mouth.

"Yes!" she said, her eyes full of tears. In an instant she felt the boy's arms wrap around her neck and she folded her own around him. Then, for the first time since arriving at the house, she looked up. The rest of the Topillows were standing before her like statues. Her vision blurred by tears, they were nothing more than silhouettes.

Judith lost her balance and slumped against Arthur, who held onto his wife tightly, clutching both of her arms. Meanwhile, Jason, whose own eyes were wet with tears, looked towards his brother, who was frozen in shock. Stepping closer towards him, he touched his shoulder and gave him a little shove. But Evan didn't move a muscle. So this was the woman he'd been so desperate to see. He felt a new blast of love that managed to eclipse the grief, pain and all the fears he held for the future.

He moved forward one step, laying his palm flat on the wall

to stop himself from falling. Then he felt another gentle push on his shoulder from behind.

"Go Evan, go to her," Jason whispered in his ear.

He took another step forward.

Laura blinked hard and the tears in her eyes cleared. Now the view was clear. She recognised Evan. He was the man she'd been following, the man she'd been feeling and touching in her dreams. And he really was undeniably good looking.

Their eyes met and Laura eased Murray from her arms and stood up.

"I told you she was coming," Murray cried, gazing up at his dad. "She's my new mum."

His gaze zigzagged between his father and Laura, who were both still too overwhelmed to speak.

In the background, Judith whispered to Arthur, "My God, she is an angel on earth."

Laura moved one step closer to Evan until she could hear the sound of his breathing. He gazed at her tenderly before reaching out and gently touching her shoulders. A surge of electricity ran through Laura's body. She closed her eyes for a few seconds and then opened them again - just to make sure she wasn't dreaming. Evan leant in closer and whispered, "I knew you were coming. I've been waiting for you."

"But I'm not her," Laura started to say. Evan stopped her mid-sentence by placing a finger on her lips. He knew what she was thinking but for now that wasn't important. They would have all the time in the world to talk and explain things to each other. For now all that mattered was that they had found each other, and that this was for forever.

"Daddy, will she stay with me?" Murray asked. He was standing by their side, grabbing at their legs.

Laura couldn't wait any longer. She relaxed her body, allowing herself to fall into Evan's arms. With her face pressed against his chest, she could hear his heartbeat.

The tears were flowing freely now from Evan's eyes and they blended with Laura's. Meanwhile, Laura could feel his lips pressing into her hair. She felt so sure of herself, so complete. A part of her soul had always been here in the cabin with the Topillows, she felt it deep inside.

Looking down, she realised that both she and Evan had been stroking Murray's hair. She crouched down to the boy's level.

"I'm so happy that I found you," she smiled through her tears. "My name is Laura."

"Come inside," Murray replied. "I'll ask Grandma to make some chocolate muffins."

Laura looked beyond Evan and his son, to where the rest of the family were standing. They were clearer now, looked so familiar. She read love in their expressions.

Gripping her hand tightly, Murray led Laura inside. Then Evan enclosed her free one in his. She looked up at him, her eyes full of fire. This madness of love had exploded without any notification.

"Welcome home, dear," said Evan's mum, her voice soft and warm.

"Thank you, Judith," Laura replied, pronouncing the name so naturally.

Now it was Jason's turn to introduce himself. His eyes were still red and watery, so Laura decided to make it easier for him.

"Hi Jason," she said, giving him a tender smile.

He raised his head, squeezing his eyes against the tears.

"Hello Laura," he managed to say after a slight pause. "I'm glad you made it. Welcome."

Laura sat on the sofa and took a slow, deep breath. Everyone was standing around her and no one knew what to say. Laura realised that she had to say something. Clearing her throat, she gazed at each of them individually and began.

"It's very difficult for me to know where to start," she said. "I've come from London and I know it will sound strange how

I came to knock on your door, but it's still strange to me. I was in a very dark place for years until I received an email from a person called David. He asked me to come here because my face had been appearing in his dreams for a year – that's why he wrote to me."

Laura stopped and saw the Topillows exchange looks. It was clear to them now. Alison had led Laura here. It was her will, her love.

Evan stepped forward and scooped up Laura's face in his hands.

"It's OK," he said. "We understand everything. You are home now."

Laura nodded.

"It must be time for coffee," Judith announced, attempting to break the tension in the air.

"Yes, it is, and I would love one," Evan replied.

The family dispersed, scratching their heads and resuming what they'd been doing before Laura's surprise visit.

"Do you want to see my bike?" Murray asked, stepping in front of Evan so that he was facing Laura.

"Oh yes, that would make me very happy," Laura replied, gripping Murray's hand while holding Evan's gaze as he followed them out. Evan couldn't keep the smile from his face. What was happening was almost too good to be true. The woman who'd entered his world really was Alison's mirror image, but his feelings for her were based on more than appearances. He felt love for her in every cell and pore of his body.

Reaching out he put his arm around her shoulder, noticing how natural he felt with her.

Murray climbed onto his bike and rode in the direction of the path leading into the woods. Ringing his little bell and beaming from ear to ear, he kept turning to make sure that Evan and Laura were following.

The couple looked back towards the cabin. The small window at the back of the house was crowded. Judith was holding a tray containing steaming cups of coffee, but no one could pull their attention away from the blissful view outside long enough to drink it. They watched until Evan, Laura and Murray disappeared from view and into the woods.

Once they were away from prying eyes, Laura stopped and turned to Evan.

"How did this happen?" she asked.

"I don't know," Evan replied. "Life is a mystery, but we have a lifetime to figure it out."

"Mum, Dad, are you coming?" Murray called out.

Laura and Evan laughed. "Yes!" they cried in unison. Walking arm in arm, they quickened their steps behind him.

Printed in Great Britain
by Amazon